## PERIL

Young Mirrim of Ben... green fighting dragon Pa... Weyrwomen Lessa and Brekke, and ... Robinton . . . but suddenly Mirrim's entire future is put in jeopardy when she's falsely accused of stealing newly discovered Ancients' artifacts from the Southern Wastes! And the dragonrider has no time to solve the mystery, unmask the true thief and clear her name . . .

For the deadly, planet-threatening incendiary Threadfall is mere hours away. Mirrim and Path will need all their skill and concentration to survive and help save Pern—even if they return from the skies to a life of utter disgrace . . .

CROSSROADS™ ADVENTURES are authorized interactive novels highly compatible with the most popular role-playing systems. Constructed by the masters of modern gaming, CROSSROADS™ feature complete rules; *full use* of gaming values—strength, intelligence, wisdom/luck, constitution, dexterity, charisma, and hit points; and multiple pathways for each option; for the most complete experience in gaming books, as fully realized, motivated heroes quest through the most famous worlds of fantasy!

## With an all-new introduction by Anne McCaffrey.

## ENTER THE ADVENTURE!

## TOR'S CROSSROADS™ ADVENTURE SERIES

*Dragonharper*, based on Anne McCaffrey's Pern

*Storm of Dust*, based on David Drake's The Dragon Lord

*Revolt on Majipoor*, based on Robert Silverberg's Majipoor

*The Witchfires of Leth*, based on C.J. Cherryh's Morgaine

*Prospero's Isle*, based on L. Sprague de Camp and Fletcher Pratt's The Incomplete Enchanter

*Dzurlord*, based on Steven Brust's Jhereg

*A Warlock's Blade*, based on Christopher Stasheff's Gramarye

*Encyclopedia of Xanth*, based on Piers Anthony's Xanth

*Warhorn*, based on Lynn Abbey's Rifkind

*Dragonfire*, based on Anne McCaffrey's Pern

# A CROSSROADS ADVENTURE

## in the World of
## ANNE McCAFFREY'S PERN

# DRAGONFIRE

by
Jody Lynn Nye

A TOM DOHERTY ASSOCIATES BOOK

DRAGONFIRE

Crossroads Game/novels are published by TOR Books by arrange-ment with Bill Fawcett and Associates.

First printing: July 1988

A TOR Book

Published by Tom Doherty Associates, Inc.
49 West 24 Street
New York, N.Y. 10010

Cover art by Doug Beekman
Illustrations by Todd Cameron Hamilton

ISBN: 0-812-56423-5
CAN. ED.: 0-812-56424-3

Printed in the United States of America

0 9 8 7 6 5 4 3 2 1

**To Terri Beckett**
—Next time, it's your turn.

Acknowledgments are due to Dr. Daniel Kamen, Todd Johnson, and, of course, Anne McCaffrey, for patiently answering multitudinous questions.

# PROLOGUE
## by Anne McCaffrey

WHEN MANKIND FIRST discovered Pern, third planet of the sun Rukbat in the Sagittarian Sector, they paid little attention to the eccentric orbit of another satellite in the system.

Settling the new planet, adjusting to its differences, the colonists spread out across the southern, and more hospitable, continent. Disaster struck in the form of a rain of mycorrhizoid organisms which voraciously attacked all but stone, metal or water. Fire, too, would destroy the menace of "Thread" as the settlers called the devasting showers.

Using their old-world ingenuity, the settlers bio-genetically altered an indigenous life form which resembled the 'dragons' of legend. Partnered with a human at birth, these creatures grew to a great size and had abilities desperately needed to combat Thread. Able to chew and digest a phosphine bearing rock, the dragons could sear the airborne Thread with their fiery breath. The dragons were not only telepathic but telekinetic, thus able to avoid injury during their battles with Thread.

Being a dragon partner required special talents in humans and complete dedication. Thus the dragonriders became a group apart from those who held the land against the depredations of Thread, or those whose craft skills produced other necessities of life in their crafthalls.

Over the centuries, the settlers forgot their origins in their struggle to survive against Thread which fell across the land whenever the Red Star's eccentric orbit coincided with Pern's.

There were long intervals, too, of four hundred years

1

when no Thread ravaged the land, when the dragonriders in their Weyrs kept faith with their magnificent friends until they would be needed once more to protect the people they were pledged to serve.

During one such interval, twenty five hundred years after the first landing, very few believed that Thread would return again. Few except F'lar, rider of bronze Mnementh, his brother, F'nor, brown Canth's rider, and Lessa, diminutive and fiery Weyrwoman, Ramoth's rider, the leaders of Benden Weyr, Pern's last stronghold of dragons and riders. But F'lar, Lessa and F'nor found unexpected support from Masterharper Robinton and Mastersmith Fandarel whose opinions carried weight across Pern.

When Thread once more began its terrible, destructive rain, Benden Weyr rose to meet the ancient challenge. The Lord Holders had no option but to support Pern's one Weyr and struggle to survive against the depredations of a menace they had thought could no longer threaten them.

In a dramatic adventure, Lessa and Ramoth sought the five missing Weyrs of Pern and brought them forward in time to assist Benden's loyal few. Lessa, F'lar, F'nor and his mate, Brekke, continued to strengthen the Weyrs, and even permitted the white sport, Ruth, to remain alive in the keeping of young Lord Jaxom of Ruatha.

In their turn, Jaxom and Ruth discovered the original landing site of their ancestors, and the Pernese begin to delve into the beginnings of their own origins in the Southern Continent, on the Ship Meadow and the high plateau beneath the inactive volcano, named Two-faced mountain.

It is in the Southern continent that this story begins, at the Cove Hold of Masterharper Robinton, beloved of Pern, where he is tended by Brekke of Benden Weyr and green Path's rider, eighteen turn old Mirrim, the only 'fighting' girl in the Weyrs.

# INTRODUCTION AND RULES TO CROSSROADS™ ADVENTURES
## by Bill Fawcett

FOR THE MANY of us who have enjoyed the stories upon which this adventure is based, it may seem a bit strange to find an introduction this long at the start of a book. What you are holding is both a game and an adventure. Have you ever read a book and then told yourself you would have been able to think more clearly or seen a way out of the hero's dilemma? In a Crossroads™ adventure you have the opportunity to do just that. *You* make the key decisions. By means of a few easily followed steps you are able to see the results of your choices.

A Crossroads™ adventure is as much fun to read as it is to play. It is more than just a game or a book. It is a chance to enjoy once more a familiar and treasured story. The excitement of adventuring in a beloved universe is neatly blended into a story which stands well on its own merit, a story in which you will encounter many familiar characters and places and discover more than a few new ones as well. Each adventure is a thrilling tale, with the extra suspense and satisfaction of knowing that you will succeed or fail by your own endeavors.

3

# THE ADVENTURE

Throughout the story you will have the opportunity to make decisions. Each of these decisions will affect whether the hero succeeds in the quest, or even survives. In some cases you will actually be fighting battles; other times you will use your knowledge and instincts to choose the best path to follow. In many cases there will be clues in the story or illustrations.

A Crossroads™ adventure is divided into sections. The length of a section may be a few lines or many pages. The section numbers are shown at the top of a page to make it easier for you to follow. Each section ends when you must make a decision, or fight. The next section you turn to will show the results of your decision. At least one six-sided die and a pencil are needed to "play" this book.

The words "six-sided dice" are often abbreviated as "D6." If more than one is needed a number will precede the term. "Roll three six-sided dice" will be written as "Roll 3 D6." Virtually all the die rolls in these rules do involve rolling three six-sided dice (or rolling one six-sided die three times) and totaling what is rolled.

If you are an experienced role-play gamer, you may also wish to convert the values given in this novel to those you can use with any fantasy role-playing game you are now playing with. All of the adventures have been constructed so that they also can be easily adapted in this manner. The values for the hero will transfer directly. While fantasy games are much more complicated, doing this will allow you to be the Game Master for other players. Important values for the hero's opponents will be given to aid you in this conversion and to give those playing by the Crossroads™ rules a better idea of what they are facing.

# THE HERO

Seven values are used to describe the hero in gaming terms. These are strength, intelligence, wisdom/luck, constitution, dexterity, charisma, and hit points. These values measure all of a character's abilities. At the end of these rules is a record sheet. On it are given all of the values for the hero of this adventure and any equipment or supplies they begin the adventure with. While you adventure, this record can be used to keep track of damage received and any new equipment or magical items acquired. You may find it advisable to make a photocopy of that page. Permission to do so, for your own use only, is given by the publisher of this game/novel. You may wish to consult this record sheet as we discuss what each of the values represents.

# STRENGTH

This is the measure of how physically powerful your hero is. It compares the hero to others in how much the character can lift, how hard he can punch, and just how brawny he is. The strongest a normal human can be is to have a strength value of 18. The weakest a child would have is a 3. Here is a table giving comparable strengths:

| Strength | Example |
|----------|---------|
| 3 | A 5-year-old child |
| 6 | An elderly man |
| 8 | Out of shape and over 40 |
| 10 | An average 20-year-old man |
| 13 | In good shape and works out |
| 15 | A top athlete or football running back |
| 17 | Changes auto tires without a jack |
| 18 | Arm wrestles Arnold Schwarzenegger and wins |

A Tolkien-style troll, being magical, might have a strength of 19 or 20. A full-grown elephant has a strength of 23. A fifty-foot dragon would have a strength of 30.

# INTELLIGENCE

Being intelligent is not just a measure of native brain power. It is also an indication of the ability to use that intelligence. The value for intelligence also measures how aware the character is, and so how likely they are to notice a subtle clue. Intelligence can be used to measure how resistant a mind is to hypnosis or mental attack. A really sharp baboon would have an intelligence of 3. Most humans (we all know exceptions) begin at about 5. The highest value possible is an 18. Here is a table of relative intelligence:

| Intelligence | Example |
|---|---|
| 3 | My dog |
| 5 | Lassie |
| 6 | Curly (the third Stooge) |
| 8 | Somewhat slow |
| 10 | Average person |
| 13 | College professor/good quarterback |
| 15 | Indiana Jones/Carl Sagan |
| 17 | Doc Savage/Mr. Spock |
| 18 | Leonardo dá Vinci (Isaac Asimov?) |

Brainiac of comic-book fame would have a value of 21.

# WISDOM/LUCK

Wisdom is the ability to make correct judgments, often with less than complete facts. Wisdom is knowing what to do and when to do it. Attacking, when running will earn you a spear in the back, is the best part of wisdom. Being in the right place at the right time can be called luck or wisdom. Not being discovered when hiding can be luck, if it is because you knew enough to not hide in the poison oak, wisdom is also a factor. Activities which are based more on instinct, the intuitive leap, than analysis are decided by wisdom.

· In many ways both wisdom and luck are further connected, especially as wisdom also measures how friendly the ruling powers of the universe (not the author, the fates) are to the hero. A hero may be favored by fate or luck because he is reverent or for no discernible reason at all. This will give him a high wisdom value. Everyone knows those "lucky" individuals who can fall in the mud and find a gold coin. Here is a table measuring relative wisdom/luck:

| Wisdom | Example |
|--------|---------|
| 3 | Cursed or totally unthinking |
| 5 | Never plans, just reacts |
| 7 | Some cunning, "street smarts" |
| 9 | Average thinking person |
| 11 | Skillful planner, good gambler |
| 13 | Successful businessman/Lee Iacocca |
| 15 | Captain Kirk (wisdom)/Conan (luck) |
| 17 | Sherlock Holmes (wisdom)/Luke Skywalker (luck) |
| 18 | Lazarus Long |

# CONSTITUTION

The more you can endure, the higher your constitution. If you have a high constitution you are better able to survive physical damage, emotional stress, and poisons. The higher your value for constitution, the longer you are able to continue functioning in a difficult situation. A character with a high constitution can run farther (though not necessarily faster) or hang by one hand longer than the average person. A high constitution means you also have more stamina, and recover more quickly from injuries. A comparison of values for constitution:

| Constitution | Example |
|---|---|
| 3 | A terminal invalid |
| 6 | A 10-year-old child |
| 8 | Your stereotyped "98-pound weakling" |
| 10 | Average person |
| 14 | Olympic athlete/Sam Spade |
| 16 | Marathon runner/Rocky |
| 18 | Rasputin/Batman |

A whale would have a constitution of 20. Superman's must be about 50.

# DEXTERITY

The value for dexterity measures not only how fast a character can move, but how well-coordinated those movements are. A surgeon, a pianist, and a juggler all need a high value for dexterity. If you have a high value for dexterity you can react quickly (though not necessarily correctly), duck well, and perform sleight-of-hand magic (if you are bright enough to learn how). Conversely, a low dexterity means you react slowly and drop things frequently. All other things being equal, the character with the highest dexterity will have the advantage of the first attack in a combat. Here are some comparative examples of dexterity:

| Dexterity | Example |
|---|---|
| 3 or less | Complete klutz |
| 5 | Inspector Clousseau |
| 6 | Can walk and chew gum, most of the time |
| 8 | Barney Fife |

| 10 | Average person |
| 13 | Good fencer/Walter Payton |
| 15 | Brain surgeon/Houdini |
| 16 | Flying Karamazov Brothers |
| 17 | Movie ninja/Cyrano de Bergerac |
| 18 | Bruce Lee |

Batman, Robin, Daredevil and The Shadow all have a dexterity of 19. At a dexterity of 20 you don't even see the man move before he has taken your wallet and underwear and has left the room (the Waco Kid).

## CHARISMA

Charisma is more than just good looks, though they certainly don't hurt. It is a measure of how persuasive a hero is and how willing others are to do what he wants. You can have average looks yet be very persuasive, and have a high charisma. If your value for charisma is high, you are better able to talk yourself out of trouble or obtain information from a stranger. If your charisma is low, you may be ignored or even mocked, even when you are right. A high charisma value is vital to entertainers of any sort, and leaders. A different type of charisma is just as important to spies. In the final measure a high value for charisma means people will react to you in the way you desire. Here are some comparative values for charisma:

| Charisma | Example |
| --- | --- |
| 3 | Hunchback of Notre Dame |
| 5 | An ugly used-car salesman |
| 7 | Richard Nixon today |
| 10 | Average person |
| 12 | Team coach |
| 14 | Magnum, P.I. |
| 16 | Henry Kissinger/Jim DiGriz |

# HIT POINTS

Hit points represent the total amount of damage a hero can take before he is killed or knocked out. You can receive damage from being wounded in a battle, through starvation, or even through a mental attack. Hit points measure more than just how many times the hero can be battered over the head before he is knocked out. They also represent the ability to keep striving toward a goal. A poorly paid mercenary may have only a few hit points, even though he is a hulking brute of a man, because the first time he receives even a slight wound he will withdraw from the fight. A blacksmith's apprentice who won't accept defeat will have a higher number of hit points.

A character's hit points can be lost through a wound to a specific part of the body or through general damage to the body itself. This general damage can be caused by a poison, a bad fall, or even exhaustion and starvation. Pushing your body too far beyond its limits may result in a successful action at the price of the loss of a few hit points. All these losses are treated in the same manner.

Hit points lost are subtracted from the total on the hero's record sheet. When a hero has lost all of his hit points, then that character has failed. When this happens you will be told to which section to turn. Here you will often find a description of the failure and its consequences for the hero.

The hit points for the opponents the hero meets in combat are given in the adventure. You should keep track of these hit points on a piece of scrap paper. When a monster or opponent has lost all of their hit points, they have lost the fight. If a character is fighting more than one opponent, then you should keep track of each of their hit points. Each will continue to fight until it has

0 hit points. When everyone on one side of the battle has no hit points left, the combat is over.

Even the best played character can lose all of his hit points when you roll too many bad dice during a combat. If the hero loses all of his hit points, the adventure may have ended in failure. You will be told so in the next section you are instructed to turn to. In this case you can turn back to the first section and begin again. This time you will have the advantage of having learned some of the hazards the hero will face.

# TAKING CHANCES

There will be occasions where you will have to decide whether the hero should attempt to perform some action which involves risk. This might be to climb a steep cliff, jump a pit, or juggle three daggers. There will be other cases where it might benefit the hero to notice something subtle or remember an ancient ballad perfectly. In all of these cases you will be asked to roll three six-sided dice (3 D6) and compare the total of all three dice to the hero's value for the appropriate ability.

For example, if the hero is attempting to juggle three balls, then for him to do so successfully you would have to roll a total equal to or less than the hero's value for dexterity. If your total was less than this dexterity value, then you would be directed to a section describing how the balls looked as they were skillfully juggled. If you rolled a higher value than that for dexterity, then you would be told to read a section which describes the embarrassment of dropping the balls, and being laughed at by the audience.

Where the decision is a judgment call, such as whether to take the left or right staircase, it is left entirely to you. Somewhere in the adventure or in the original novels there will be some piece of information which would indicate that the left staircase leads to a trap and the right to your goal. No die roll will be needed for a judgment decision.

In all cases you will be guided at the end of each section as to exactly what you need do. If you have any questions you should refer back to these rules.

# MAGICAL ITEMS AND SPECIAL EQUIPMENT

There are many unusual items which appear in the pages of this adventure. When it is possible for them to be taken by the hero, you will be given the option of doing so. One or more of these items may be necessary to the successful completion of the adventure. You will be given the option of taking these at the end of a section. If you choose to pick up an item and succeed in getting it, you should list that item on the hero's record sheet. There is no guarantee that deciding to take an item means you will actually obtain it. If someone owns it already they are quite likely to resent your efforts to take it. In some cases things may not even be all they appear to be or the item may be trapped or cursed. Having it may prove a detriment rather than a benefit.

All magical items give the hero a bonus (or penalty) on certain die rolls. You will be told when this applies, and often given the option of whether or not to use the item. You will be instructed at the end of the section on how many points to add to or subtract from your die roll. If you choose to use an item which can function only once, such as a magic potion or hand grenade, then you will also be instructed to remove the item from your record sheet. Certain items, such as a magic sword, can be used many times. In this case you will be told when you obtain the item when you can apply the bonus. The bonus for a magic sword could be added every time a character is in hand-to-hand combat.

Other special items may allow a character to fly, walk

through fire, summon magical warriors, or many other things. How and when they affect play will again be told to you in the paragraphs at the end of the sections where you have the choice of using them.

Those things which restore lost hit points are a special case. You may choose to use these at any time during the adventure. If you have a magical healing potion which returns 1 D6 of lost hit points, you may add these points when you think it is best to. This can even be during a combat in the place of a round of attack. No matter how many healing items you use, a character can never have more hit points than he begins the adventure with.

There is a limit to the number of special items any character may carry. In any Crossroads™ adventure the limit is four items. If you already have four special items listed on your record sheet, then one of these must be discarded in order to take the new item. Any time you erase an item off the record sheet, whether because it was used or because you wish to add a new item, whatever is erased is permanently lost. It can never be "found" again, even if you return to the same location later in the adventure.

Except for items which restore hit points, the hero can only use an item in combat or when given the option to do so. The opportunity will be listed in the instructions.

In the case of an item which can be used in every combat, the bonus can be added or subtracted as the description of the item indicates. A +2 sword would add two points to any total rolled in combat. This bonus would be used each and every time the hero attacks. Only one attack bonus can be used at a time. Just because a hero has both a +1 and a +2 sword doesn't mean he knows how to fight with both at once. Only the better bonus would apply.

If a total of 12 is needed to hit an attacking monster and the hero has a +2 sword, then you will only need to roll a total of 10 on the three dice to successfully strike the creature.

You could also find an item, perhaps enchanted armor, which could be worn in all combat and would have the effect of subtracting its bonus from the total of any opponent's attack on its wearer. (Bad guys can wear magic armor, too.) If a monster normally would need a 13 to hit a character who has obtained a set of +2 armor, then the monster would now need a total of 15 to score a hit. An enchanted shield would operate in the same way, but could never be used when the character was using a weapon which needed both hands, such as a pike, longbow, or two-handed sword.

# COMBAT

There will be many situations where the hero will be forced, or you may choose, to meet an opponent in combat. The opponents can vary from a wild beast, to a human thief, or an unearthly monster. In all cases the same steps are followed.

The hero will attack first in most combats unless you are told otherwise. This may happen when there is an ambush, other special situations, or because the opponent simply has a much higher dexterity.

At the beginning of a combat section you will be given the name or type of opponent involved. For each combat five values are given. The first of these is the total on three six-sided dice needed for the attacker to hit the hero. Next to this value is the value the hero needs to hit these opponents. After these two values is listed the hit points of the opponent. If there is more than one opponent, each one will have the same number. (See the Hit Points section included earlier if you are unclear as to what these do.) Under the value needed to be hit by the opponent is the hit points of damage that it will do to the hero when it attacks successfully. Finally, under the total needed for the hero to successfully hit an opponent is the damage he will do with the different weapons he might have. Unlike a check for completing a daring action (where you wish to roll under a value), in a combat you have to roll the value given or higher on three six-sided dice to successfully hit an opponent.

For example:

Here is how a combat between the hero armed with a sword and three brigands armed only with daggers is written:

BRIGANDS
*To hit the hero: 14    To be hit: 12    Hit points: 4*
*Damage with        Damage with*
*daggers: 1 D6      sword: 2 D6*
*(used by the brigands) (used by the hero)*
*There are three brigands. If two are killed (taken to 0 hit points) the third will flee in panic.*

*If the hero wins, turn to section 85.*

*If he is defeated, turn to section 67.*

# RUNNING AWAY

Running rather than fighting, while often desirable, is not always possible. The option to run away is available only when listed in the choices. Even when this option is given, there is no guarantee the hero can get away safely.

# THE COMBAT SEQUENCE

Any combat is divided into alternating rounds. In most cases the hero will attack first. Next, surviving opponents will have the chance to fight back. When both have attacked, one round will have been completed. A combat can have any number of rounds and continues until the hero or his opponents are defeated. Each round is the equivalent of six seconds. During this time all the parties in the combat may actually take more than one swing at each other.

The steps in resolving a combat in which the hero attacks first are as follows:

1. Roll three six-sided dice. Total the numbers showing on all three and add any bonuses from weapons or special circumstances. If this total is the same or greater than the second value given, "to hit the opponent," then the hero has successfully attacked.

2. If the hero attacks successfully, the next step is to determine how many hit points of damage he did to the opponent. The die roll for this will be given below the "to hit opponent" information.

3. Subtract any hit points of damage done from the opponent's total.

4. If any of the enemy have one or more hit points left, then the remaining opponent or opponents now can attack. Roll three six-sided dice for each attacker. Add up each of these sets of three dice. If the total is the same as, or greater than the value listed after "to hit the hero" in the section describing the combat, the attack was successful.

5. For each hit, roll the number of dice listed for damage. Subtract the total from the number of hit points the hero has at that time. Enter the new, lower total on the hero's record sheet.

If both the hero and one or more opponents have hit points left, the combat continues. Start again at step one. The battle ends only when the hero is killed, all the opponents are killed, or all of one side has run away. A hero cannot, except through a healing potion or spells or when specifically told to during the adventure, regain lost hit points. A number of small wounds from several opponents will kill a character as thoroughly as one titanic, unsuccessful combat with a hill giant.

## DAMAGE

The combat continues, following the sequence given below, until either the hero or his opponents have no hit points. In the case of multiple opponents, subtract hit points from one opponent until the total reaches 0 or less. Extra hit points of damage done on the round when each opponent is defeated are lost. They do not carry over to the next enemy in the group. To win the combat, you must eliminate all of an opponent's hit points.

The damage done by a weapon will vary depending on who is using it. A club in the hands of a child will do far less damage than the same club wielded by a hill giant. The maximum damage is given as a number of six-sided dice. In some cases the maximum will be less than a whole die. This is abbreviated by a minus sign followed by a number. For example D6−2, meaning one roll of a six-sided die, minus two. The total damage can never be less than zero, meaning no damage done. 2 D6−1 means that you should roll two six-sided dice and then subtract one from the total of them both.

A combat may, because of the opponent involved, have one or more special circumstances. It may be that the enemy will surrender or flee when its hit point total falls below a certain level, or even that reinforcements will arrive to help the bad guys after so many rounds. You will be told of these special situations in the lines directly under the combat values.

Now you may turn to section 1.

# RECORD SHEET

## Mirrim, rider of green Path

Strength:   14
Intelligence:   13
Wisdom/Luck: 13
Constitution: 15
Dexterity: 14
Charisma: 11

Hit Points: 21

If Path is Threadscored: _____ _____

Items carried by Mirrim
1. Clothes
2. Riding gear (jacket, belt, gloves, hat, scarf, boots)
3. Belt pouch
4. Knife
5.

Items carried by Path:
1. Fighting straps
2. Carry-sacks
3.
4.
5.

# * **1** *

"For the last time, *NO!*" Brekke's normally soothing voice was raised in a tone of command. Mirrim shrugged and went on peeling roots into a pot, tossing the skins over her shoulder. Path snuffled into the sand, decided that peels were not appropriate food for a dragon, and closed her eyelids against the hot tropical sun. Mirrim listened to the footsteps approaching.

*Brekke is annoyed,* Path thought lazily at her.

"Shh," Mirrim hissed. "She's coming."

Brekke emerged from the door of Cove Hold and sat down on the black stone steps, blowing her curly hair out of her face. She wiped moisture from her forehead.

"How's the patient?" Mirrim asked, jerking her head up toward the door to Cove Hold.

"IM-patient," Brekke sighed. "I have told him again and again that it is too hot for him to sit out in the sun, that his heart won't stand another exposure to such fierce heat."

"My very dear Brekke," Master Robinton began, coming up behind them and settling heavily on the topmost step. "Whew! It is hot out here. I am not applying for permission to swim to Nerat. All I asked was that you allow me—quite reasonably, too—to go down to the shore and splash in the waves to abate the heat. Whether or not it is cooler here inside this marvelous Hold with these amazing breezeways to direct the wind does not seem to matter to my poor skin. It craves water!"

# Section 1

"There is no shelter on the shore," Brekke pointed out. "You could roast meat on the sand right now until evening. I could put cool water in the bathing tub."

"Have mercy on me," Robinton pleaded, his blue eyes shockingly light in his narrow, sun-browned face. "I was not meant to live out my whole life in a box, however lovely and in what good company."

Mirrim felt sympathy for the Harper. It was the hottest summer she had ever experienced in her eighteen Turns, even the ones she had lived in Southern Weyr, and they had been hot enough to scorch eggs that hadn't been clutched yet. While living in the High Reaches, and, more recently, Benden Weyr, over the last several Turns, she had lost all her resistance to the incredible heat that the southern sun could produce. The Southern Holders, after an outward show of smugness over the Northern girl's discomfort, admitted, too, that it was the hottest they'd ever known. Thereafter, they'd shared any ideas they came up with to stay cool in the crippling heat. Most of the suggestions were no more than good sense, but they all had to do with frequent swims and cold drinks. And she understood quite well what it felt like to be cooped up like a farmyard bird. "In other words," Mirrim sardonically summed up the Masterharper's thoughts, "you're bored."

Robinton cocked a long forefinger at her approvingly. "You have it exactly. I have nothing to do. I don't mean to criticize, but you two won't let me do a thing! I can't gather fruit for myself, I am not allowed to play or practice as long as I'd like, I can't tidy up—"

"You wouldn't anyway," Brekke pointed out firmly but without rancor. Robinton's incredible memory was the only system of organization in the small workroom, which was nearly full to bursting with record hides, copies of songs, gifts, musical instruments, tools, and wineskins. The sandtable and chairs had been all but buried when Brekke first came in answer to Lytol's plea for a Healer to stay with Robinton through the hottest sevendays of the season.

"Can't even ride on a runnerbeast," the Master Harper grumbled.

"They have the sense to stay undercover out of this heat, too!" Brekke declared. "They haven't so much as put a nose out of their stables this morning. There's no air in this heat. I wish it would rain." She surveyed the skies, squinting at the homogeneous gray haze covering the blue and veiling the sun.

The Master Harper pursed his lips and studied the clouds. "It won't be soon," he predicted, smoothing back his hair, which was sticking to his neck and face. Under his deep tan, there were flushed red spots over his cheekbones. "The humidity is killing. Dry heat doesn't bother me this much. It isn't as overcast inland at the plateau, nor as hot. Can I . . . ?" he began, looking hopefully at Path, whose many-faceted eyes were closed against the glare. As if the dragon could hear his thoughts, she huffed out a great breath of air, sending a cloud of sand tumbling down the beach.

"No, Master Robinton, you know that wouldn't be a good idea," Mirrim scolded him, just exactly as Brekke would have. "The cold of *between* would only aggravate your condition. Lytol flew today, but he is not sick."

Brekke looked a little shocked at Mirrim's forthrightness, but nodded. "I, too, would wait until it was cooler, Master," she said, more gently. "Later . . ."

"Much as though I appreciate your honesty and solicitousness," Robinton told them both, "it doesn't change the present. I won't take any foolish chances with my health, but by the First Shell! I can't just sit here and do nothing! Am I really to stay here in obsolescence until the Lady Doriota's wedding?"

"That's two sevendays away," Brekke said, with another glance at the sky. "You'll be back at the site long before then."

"Then is not now," Robinton said petulantly.

Mirrim stood up and stretched, putting the peeling knife down next to the kettle. "Well, would it help if Path and I went down to the digging site and found out what is going on? If there is anything new Lytol wants you to see, I could bring it to you."

Brekke smiled her approval as Robinton's eyes brightened. "Nearly as good, my dear. Very nearly. Of course, you could tell him to keep it there for me, just for today. Surely I shall be allowed to come a-dragonback tomorrow."

"Not today or for a few days yet," Brekke cautioned him, and held up a hand to still another outburst. "It would take many hours to fly direct. You would have to go *between*. And no dragon will carry you *between* until we're sure you're better. Heat stroke is no joke to anyone, let alone a man who has had heart trouble. Ramoth knew instantly when you'd collapsed the other day, and she told Lessa even before I'd received the message to come to you. Overheating is not cured by dropping your external temperature below freezing."

Robinton cleared his throat, silently acknowledging his gratitude to the dragons for their care. He lifted rueful eyes to Mirrim. "Then I accept your kind offer. I am relying upon you to lift this weight of boredom from my shoulders."

With a brisk, businesslike nod, Mirrim lugged the kettleful of peeled and sliced roots up the black steps and into the kitchen of Cove Hold. "I'll watch these for you, Mirrim," Brekke assured her, following her inside.

"I'll finish the preparations for supper when I return, Brekke," Mirrim assured her, with an anxious thought for the stuffed fish she had wrapped in leaves for baking in the sand. It was just about time to start them. She calculated mentally the amounts of spices already wrapped up in each fish, and decided no more would be needed. They would be very tasty as is.

Brekke peered into the kettle. "My goodness, there's more than plenty. We've only the Weyrleaders, Lytol, and Fandarel coming for supper. You have almost enough here for a Gather." She touched the downcast girl's cheek. "Oh, I'm not criticizing you, Mirrim. It's just that sometimes you are *too* efficient."

"Fandarel's disease," Robinton chuckled from the back step. "He'll eat most of those roots, never fear. The Mastersmith's drive for efficiency will make a good song one day when we have more leisure for writing them."

"Leisure?" Brekke shook her head in mock disbelief. "I thought leisure was what you were complaining of."

Robinton waved a dismissive hand, sweeping away the idea. "I don't need to relax. I need to know what is happening *now* on Pern. I'm too used to being in the heart of activity to enjoy sitting to one side like an old uncle. Fandarel's passion for making the best use of time is already well known. I've no *need* to publicize it. What is important is what is going on right now, here in the South. The discovery of our most ancient ancestors! Make haste, Mirrim! I grow more bored by the moment! . . . My dear Brekke, did I leave that wineskin in my workroom?"

*The Master Harper is well?* Path's gentle thoughts touched Mirrim as she gathered her riding clothes from her sleeping room. The shutters were thrown back from the window and Mirrim smiled at the lithe green creature curled under the trees.

"He's fine," Mirrim assured the dragon, thrusting one leg into her wherryskin trousers. "Have you finished your nap? We have to go to the plateau."

*I know. I heard the Harper.* Path's thought voice was interrupted as she yawned and stretched, extending all her limbs claws out, so that her muscles went taut and then relaxed. As she stood up, dust and sand swirled around her, sparkling in the muted sun. Mirrim admired her beauty, but she also felt a twisting of guilt in her belly.

"I know I promised you an extra good bath this afternoon," she said. "I'm sorry."

*It is all right,* the dragon assured her, love whirling in the jeweled eyes. *There will be time when we return. The sea is always warm here.*

"Ye-es," Mirrim agreed. "In a way, I'll be almost sorry to go back to Benden."

# Section 1

*We do not go yet,* Path reminded her. *Thread falls soon.*

"Not 'til tomorrow," Mirrim corrected Path sharply. "I checked the charts thoroughly this morning. Unless you have a feeling?" She was suddenly worried, since there had been anomalies in plenty since Threadfall began. Mirrim gazed anxiously at her dragon, who first-lidded her eyes thoughtfully.

*No.*

"Good. If we hurry now, we'll get back that much sooner." Mirrim stepped onto Path's forearm and up. As she settled herself between the last two ridges on her dragon's soft neck, four fire lizards appeared out of the woods. Three, two greens and a brown, arrowed toward her, creeling worriedly. The fourth, bronze Zair, circled to Mirrim and flew back into the Hold, berating his master for worrying him.

"I wasn't going to leave you, silly creatures," Mirrim scolded them lovingly. "I'm going to the plateau on an errand for Master Robinton. Do you want to come with us?"

Fire lizard eyes whirled an affirmative, and they hovered nearby as Path launched herself from the ridge. In a few lengths, they all vanished from the sky.

The cold of *between* was almost a relief after the oppressive moist heat in the cove. Mirrim sighed when she saw that Path had brought her accurately to a point high and directly above the cone of the smallest dormant volcano behind the Two-Faced Mountain.

In the diffused sunlight, the strange rows and blocks of silted mounds looked like a field of herdbeasts. In a broad courtyard which had already been cleared of the layered volcanic ash, several dragons raised their heads from digging at the covering on a large mound to answer Path's bugled greeting. Mirrim recognized Ramoth and Mnementh, and realized the Benden Weyrleaders were paying one of their frequent visits to the site. She spotted also Golanth and Heth, blue Trebeth, green Ladrarth, and Betunth, from Southern Weyr. The fire lizards called out glad cries of greeting to fairs of their friends dancing and sailing on the wind that blew in over the sea from the northwest. She shooed hers away, and landed Path near golden Ramoth, who trumpeted happily to them.

*Ramoth asks if I will help her dig. They assist the Smith and the Miner in uncovering that mound.*

"Good. It looks like a lot of people are in the square next over. I think I see Lord Lytol with Fandarel and Masterminer Nicat."

The thick gray and black volcanic dust from the digging dirtied the air as though it were soiled water. Mirrim undid her wherhide riding helmet and waved it on its strap to fan her face. Coughing to clear the ashes from her throat, she came over to join the three men. With their noses all but glued to a folio of joined paper leaves Fandarel was waving before them, they didn't notice her until she spoke.

"Good afternoon, Lord Lytol. Mastersmith. Masterminer."

Lytol jumped, so absorbed that he was surprised to be addressed. "Ah, Mirrim. How does the Master Harper?"

"Much better, sir. Brekke has forbidden him to stay out in the sun until this heat breaks, so he's bored stiff. He sent me here to ask what progress is being made today."

Fandarel let out one of his hearty, booming laughs. "That Harper! Away for two days, and he's sure Pern has stopped on its axis because he cannot oversee its spin! See here!" he commanded, turning the leaves so that she could read them. "This is a new chart of the Ancient Timers' settlement, drawn up to show what manner of fixtures and artifacts have been found in each building as it is unearthed. I shall bring it to Cove Hold this evening to quench my friend Robinton's endless curiosity."

"Oh, even that won't last long," Lytol said, a smile tilting his usually dour mouth.

"Indeed not, but with the work moving as quickly as it is, a day makes a difference," put in Lessa, joining them. "Good afternoon, Mirrim. I see Path is assisting Ramoth and Mnementh to clear that mound. It certainly helps make things move more quickly when the dragons dig."

# Section 1

"I promised her a good bath, and now she'll need it!" Mirrim said, her voice full of exasperation.

Lessa smiled indulgently. "So will Ramoth. They are working as hard as though they were fighting Thread. I trust Master Robinton is well?"

"Bored!" Fandarel roared merrily. His gigantic frame dwarfed the tiny figure of the Weyrwoman, and even Mirrim, who was taller, felt like a child next to him.

"We can't have that!" Lessa cried, grinning. "But it's only hours until we join him for the evening meal. He can hear it all then."

"You know Master Robinton," Mirrim shrugged. "He wants to see for himself. Right now."

Lytol looked thoughtful. "You know, he shouldn't have to go home to the Hold every night. There are shelters here where he could stay. Just in the meantime. Some of my men sleep here every night."

"Nonsense, my Lytol," Lessa insisted. "It'll only be a few days, and he'll be back again, managing us all. You don't need to worry."

"Oh, no, Weyrwoman." The ex-dragonman shuddered. "I would sooner have preparations made just . . . in case. I don't want such a thing to happen again." It was clear he was recalling with perfect clarity the events of two days past. Lytol had been splitting his time between the Two-Faced Mountain's plateau and the Ship Meadow, assiduously supervising the diggers and gatherers. He was very pleased as to how the excavation was progressing. Robinton joined him frequently, but just as frequently stayed at home in Cove Hold with the newly discovered artifacts, writing and copying frantically to keep up with the press of new information and speculation that followed every new discovery.

The weather had been growing oppressively hot as summer came upon them, and Robinton and Lytol had both left more of their tasks to younger hands; Piemur for Robinton, an indefatigable investigator; and for Lytol, a man of the Southern Hold named Breide, a blood son of one of the Northern Lord Holders who had come south. Lord Toric insisted on his presence, just barely keeping back from insinuating that the Northerners would keep things hidden from Southern, and that he wanted a man on site that he could trust. Both the older men ignored his insults, and worked alongside of Breide whom, though dour, was a hard-working, efficient man. It must have been a horrible shock to Lytol, returning from the Ancient Timers' plateau, full of news of new finds, to discover his friend collapsed on the sand like an empty wineskin in the hot sun.

Frantic, he had lured Zair to his hand and launched him with a message on his collar for help, picturing Benden, the Weyr he knew best. Brekke had arrived with Mirrim on Path almost immediately, leaving her recently weaned baby in the hands of Manora. Not that there weren't Southern Healers of skill, but Brekke was most familiar with the Master Harper's case, and Lytol hated to make any of the old dragons in Southern go *between* more often than they needed. Better that they should have the opportunity to lie in the sun when they weren't fighting Thread, and let the young do the harder tasks.

Together, they carried Robinton back inside and treated him for overexposure to the sun. In no time, he was awake again and chiding them for coddling him, but they were not fooled. Thereafter, to Lytol's relief, Brekke elected to stay on, with Mirrim and Path serving as her supply-and-information line back to Benden Weyr and the rest of the Northern Continent. It was sheer oversight that no Headwoman had been chosen to look after Cove Hold and its inhabitants, and Brekke would stay until one could be found and approved by the Master Harper.

"My friend," Lessa said softly, laying her hand on Lytol's arm and drawing him back to the present. "It didn't happen. He is alive and well."

"And dying of curiosity," Mirrim added.

Lytol chuckled. "Can't have that. Well," he sighed, "you can take a look in that building there." He pointed across the courtyard to a long, wide building, a half

cylinder a dragonlength from end to end. "Some very interesting items, indeed. Let Breide show you."

"Thank you." Mirrim smiled and moved off.

She stepped into the coolness of the long building. It was a big place, but so empty that the whisper of her footsteps on the polished floor echoed from wall to wall. Sleepy amber light drifted in through the transparent curved panels set into the roof.

A few people wandered here and there in the room. One was unloading a flat box of little articles onto a table, another checking off each one from a piece of hide. A man with his straight black hair firmly banded out of the way was examining a small round object of metal closely in the browny light. He gave her a brief, piercing look which placed her immediately in his formidable memory. "Mirrim."

"Hello, Breide." She smiled timidly at him. Breide scared her a little. His memory was so good it was a curiosity, a phenomenon. It was said that he could remember everybody he had ever met, and every word that he'd ever seen scribed on a page. "May I take a look around?"

He extended a hand palm up, extended it in a slow arc to indicate the rest of the room. "As you please."

Mirrim nodded her thanks, not trusting her suddenly dry throat to reply. His voice had a curious flat quality that made her more uneasy. Robinton had said it was because the man was completely tone deaf, and he didn't know how he sounded. She felt odd and disoriented, almost ill. Breide's eyes seemed to follow her, even though she knew he had gone back to his study of the bit of metal. Putting her feeling down to the abrupt change in temperature from the outside to the inside, she began to look around at the contents of the room. Other people were walking there, too, some sketching the artifacts and jotting down notes about them, some just browsing in here out of the sun.

Mirrim recognized a few young men from the Harper Hall and others from Wansor's classes in the Smithcraft

# Section 1

Hall, and greeted them. She missed participating in those classes. Jaxom and Sharra always came, in spite of their many other duties as Lord and Lady Holder of Ruatha, and Menolly came from the Harper Hall whenever she was free. Mirrim felt a pang for the old days, before the press of responsibilities grew so heavy on all of them. Another man, a few Turns older than she, practically growled at her when she bent over the table he was working at. She jumped back and moved on to the next one. He looked somewhat familiar to her, but she couldn't place him immediately. In any case, he didn't want to be disturbed by her or by anyone.

Several things caught her eye, including prettily painted shards of unidentifiable material, an intricately carved wooden chairback without a seat or front legs, a handsome disk about three hands across with an intricate but patternless design on it in various colors of metal, a marvelous opaque white bottle with a nozzle on top, which was made of a material as soft as a dragon's skin. There were small household artifacts, like knives and spoons and a tiny flask, all made of the same strange transparent material that made the windows of the Ancient Timers' buildings, and a disk the size of her palm made of a white metal like silver. Each item was painted with a small dot of white paint inscribed with a black number, to indicate in which building it had been found. Nothing was, to her eyes, particularly large or important, but each one told a part of the tale, and was therefore precious.

Mirrim recalled from Fandarel's lecture his speculations that the buildings nearest the lava flow were evacuated the quickest, so the chances were greater that they would find more personal effects of their ancestors there. It would seem that he was right. Picking up the white metal disk, she noticed that it was about a fingertip thick, and the rim was pierced with holes. Above each hole was a symbol. None of them looked like letters, but they were nevertheless familiar. Thinking back, she decided that they were musical notations; she had seen ones like them written on paper leaves in the Master Harper's workroom. The Harper would be thrilled with this little device. It so obviously had to do with his craft. Perhaps she should take it to him. What if it was still functional? He'd love it.

As she pondered the idea, someone walking toward her hit her solidly in the side with his shoulder, throwing her against the curved wall with a bang. She slithered partway down, but bounced up again angrily.

Her assailant was over speaking to Breide, peering very closely at the object Breide had been studying. He was a thick-set, balding man with the badge of a master of the Smithcraft on his tunic. He seemed not to have noticed that he had offended anyone. Mirrim felt her face grow hot. One would think that he would have been able to tell by her wherhide garments that he had just assaulted a dragonrider! She wanted to charge over and demand an apology, but she didn't want the forbidding expression Breide was wearing to be turned on her. Swallowing her indignation, for she could feel Path's questioning thoughts asking if anything was wrong, she put the little metal disk in her belt pouch, and stalked out into the sunlight.

Path was filthy by the time Mirrim found her. Her lovely green hide was coated with an adhesive matte layer of the gritty black dust, and her wings so streaked with ash, she looked like a tunnel snake. The dragon's eyes whirled a hurt color when she caught Mirrim's thought, and the girl leaped to apologize.

"I didn't mean it that way, darling Path. I'll give you a good scrubbing in the cove, and you'll be fresh and beautiful again." She scratched lovingly behind the angle of Path's jaw, and the eyes slowed and changed color to a blue-green shade of contentment.

*Iitch,* Path insisted, lowering her head. Mirrim chuckled. Bless dragons. They never carried anger long. She moved her hand, scratching behind the sensitive eye ridges until the dragon crooned low in her throat like a fire lizard. When Path's itch was thoroughly settled, Mirrim took hold of the fighting straps and began to pull herself up to the great neck.

"Stop! You, Mirrim! Stop!"

She turned to see who was calling her. Across the dusty courtyard, Breide was hurrying toward her, followed by Lessa.

"This girl!" Breide was saying angrily to Lessa, his black eyes flashing. "Does being a dragonrider give you special privileges to wantonly conceal parts of our mutual history? I am appalled! Lord Toric specifically *warned* me . . ."

"It does nothing of the kind," Lessa insisted, her own eyes sparkling with fury. "And Lord Toric knows that dragonriders are as interested as holders and crafters in knowing more about the past. As you say, it is our mutual history. Do you disbelieve? Should I call away all the dragons helping with the excavation?"

Breide's fire was quenched for the moment as he calculated how long it would take to dig using only manpower. "No, Weyrwoman," he said with more respect. "But this is not the first theft I have observed. I know every piece we have taken out of these buildings, and I know to the last one how many have gone missing, taken by the irresponsible and the greedy."

They had reached Mirrim now. She let go of the fighting strap and stood waiting, thinking guiltily of the disk in her pouch.

"Mirrim is neither irresponsible nor greedy," Lessa told him. She turned to the girl, her expression hard and searching. "Mirrim. Breide has missed something from the storage hall. It is a disk about so . . ." She indicated size by her cupped hands. "Do you have such an item?"

Mirrim looked straight at Breide and Lessa. She raised her chin proudly. But what would she say? Should she deny taking the disk?

*If she chooses to lie to Lessa, turn to section 6.*

*If she chooses to tell Lessa the truth, turn to section 4.*

## * 2 *

"And what is that?" F'lar asked, his voice carefully level.

"There are several other things missing from the site," Breide began. "They have been disappearing for almost a sevenday now. In fact, since I have first noticed Mirrim visiting the site."

"That's a coincidence, not evidence."

"I realize that, Lord F'lar, but it is a matter of concern to us. Each contains a bit of our history. So far, the missing pieces have been small, some twelve in number, but the most important, and the most recent, was a bottle about so big"—Breide indicated, holding his hands about a foot apart—"that was discovered early this morning in one of the large halls nearest the lava flow. I noticed that it was missing just after I . . . talked to you, Weyrwoman."

"What makes you think Mirrim took those others as well?" Lessa asked. "And especially that bottle?"

"I have no proof," Breide said frankly. "But it wouldn't be out of line to suppose that whoever the thief was might have stolen more than one artifact."

"I didn't take anything but that," Mirrim said, pointing to the pitch pipe which Master Robinton was holding.

"What about the white bottle?" Breide asked. "That vanished about the same time."

Mirrim squinted, trying to remember. "I think I saw something like that in the hall. But it was still there when I left. I have no idea where it might have gone."

Breide might have said more, but Robinton spoke more quickly.

"Well, I have an easy solution to the first problem," the

# Section 2

Master Harper said. "If Mirrim stays away from the plateau, she can't be blamed for any more disappearances."

"I had already made sure of that," Lessa put in, forcefully. Mirrim sadly nodded acknowledgment.

"And if there are none?"

Robinton spread his hands. "Then we are fortunate that the thief has stopped his depredations, and that we may continue our study of the history of Pern without further worry."

"Well . . ." Breide, aware of the delicacy of his position, was letting himself be persuaded to let the matter drop for the time being.

"Come, come," Lytol said. "Mirrim has confessed to removing the disk, but it was for the Master Harper. Do you need further assurance? Mirrim, would you have any objections to my going through your things to see if there are any other artifacts there?"

"Why, no, Lord Lytol, of course not. But there *aren't* any," Mirrim said adamantly.

Lytol smiled at her, a wintry expression, but Mirrim was grateful for it. "*I* believe you. But for your own sake, I must agree with Lessa. You must not go back until we have solved this mystery."

"There will be no work at the site tomorrow anyway," F'lar said. "Threadfall is due at dawn here and at Nerat. I will send a few dragons to help Mirrim and F'nor clear the skies over the Hold.

"As for your second problem, Breide, I think you will have to look elsewhere for your thief. Perhaps we can ask him to return what he has taken, secretly, with no questions asked."

"Am I the only one here who's hungry?" F'nor asked, from the steps of the Hold.

There was a concerted rush to follow him inside.

The others listened through dinner as D'ram and Fandarel argued the decline of technology since the Ancient Timers. "Well, look at the techniques that have been lost during the four hundred Turns since we came forward," D'ram pointed out.

"Not a loss of inventiveness," Fandarel boomed. "No efficiency in passing techniques along."

"I'd say it was you . . . modern . . . folk who have forgotten more of what our ancestors knew." D'ram looked a little wary of suggesting such a thing, but he set his jaw to show that he meant to say it.

"We've argued the same point before," Robinton said amiably. "But I disagree. Even good methods have fallen into disfavor over time, for one or another reason. There are no secrets to be lost in the Harper Hall, *now*, but our purpose is to remember. I made sure at least my own journeymen knew any developments as soon as I learned them. It is simply that the mere aggregation of hundreds upon hundreds of Turns of forgetting to pass on knowledge has resulted in our being deprived at this late date of techniques that it never occurred to the inventor would ever be forgotten. The hide-preservation process, for example . . ."

"Don't think that all we who were born in the old time are disinterested," D'ram protested.

"Not a bit!" Robinton agreed. "I've greeted quite a few of your fellows at the dig. They've certainly done their part to help out, and supplying us with strong backs from Southern to assist."

"As usual, it's only the few dissenters who refuse to have anything to do with the 'modern' projects," D'ram sighed heavily. "The older men are interested in nothing at all. They fight Thread only reluctantly, and they rarely leave the Weyr. They're tired," he admitted sadly. "So am I, but I'm not dead yet. I'll stop fighting Thread when it stops falling." Robinton patted him on the shoulder.

"We're just a circle of old men poking at the past, guessing and berating one another because we feel we should *know*. But we don't."

"I can't help but think that perhaps the Ancient Timers had other ways of preserving information than by writing it down on hides," Lytol said thoughtfully.

# Section 2

"In spite of the perfect condition of the most ancient hides that have come down to us, there are none so old as the settlement we are now unearthing."

"Well," said F'lar, rising and holding out a hand to Lessa. "This is one old man who is bound for his bed. Thread falls in the morning. Fandarel, may I take you back to Smithcraft Hall?"

"My thanks. I have a few formulae I wish to check before I sleep."

"It is late for us as well," D'ram added. "Breide? To the site or Southern Hold? Though the plateau should be well cleared of all humanity by now. I left instructions with my Wing-seconds to take everyone home, since there aren't adequate shelters for more than the caretakers."

The steward had remained silent through most of the evening. It was clear he felt he was intruding into the private conversation of old friends, and was polite though monosyllabic in his comments. Like his master, Lord Toric, he felt greater trust and respect for the Southern dragonriders. "The Hold, please, Weyrleader. There's no need for me to go back until the all-clear."

"Then, friends, I bid you good night." D'ram bowed to the others, and strode out into the night. In the light of two of Pern's moons, Tiroth rose, a massive black shadow on the sand.

Lessa rose, joined her hand to F'lar's. Robinton stood up and followed them to the door. "A word with you, Weyrleaders, please?" With an arm around each of them, he walked out into the moonlight.

"You must not blame Mirrim for her zeal," Robinton began earnestly. "If anyone, blame me. I'm grateful for your forbearance in not scolding me in front of Breide, too."

"He was rather public in his accusation," Lessa said, pushing his playfulness aside. "By tomorrow it will be all through Southern Weyr and the Hold that a dragonrider was caught stealing. I don't want her coming into contact with the Southerners until the event has faded from memory."

"That could be a long time," Robinton protested. "What about the wedding of Lord Toric's sister? She has kindly offered to fly me there."

"I could send a bronze . . ." F'lar offered.

"Or Canth, of course," Lessa said pointedly, glancing back at the Hold door.

"No, thank you. Mirrim has been helping to take good care of me," Robinton chuckled, "and if it's an honor to haul my old carcass there to officiate at Southern, she should be given the chance to take me. She's rather counting on it."

"Any dragonrider would leap through fire for the privilege," F'lar assured him.

"I don't want her there," Lessa said firmly. "She's disgraced. The Weyr is embarrassed by her action. Breide thinks she stole that bottle, and I can't dissuade him, not in light of the theft she did commit."

"But if she clears her name?" Robinton said persuasively, touching the Weyrwoman on the forearm. "Finds out who took it, or where it has gone?"

Lessa let out an explosive sigh. "Then she may go to the wedding. But not unless!"

Robinton bowed them a good night. "I will tell her what you have said."


"Breide said nothing more about the disappearances," Robinton said, returning to the bright lights of the Hold. "While I agree that we must defend the integrity of the archaeological site because it represents the interests of all Pern, I am sure that something else provoked him to accuse Mirrim. As he said, it was not the first piece to vanish."

"I mistrust this new presence of traders and food sellers at the dig," Lytol complained. "It's likely they have something to do with it. They should be kept away from the site unless they're working there."

"It makes the atmosphere rather like that of a gather," Robinton smiled. "Somewhat relaxed. I find it quite soothing to work in."

"Yes, and no one takes the work seriously when there

are so many distractions. And there are too many Holdless men coming through. The ones that work are welcome, but I am afraid that the idle ones will cause trouble. Lord Toric has demanded their ouster, and I concur. I believe Breide does as well, but he's not forthcoming with opinions to Northerners."

"Why is he so bitter?" F'nor asked. "I don't know the man well, but he doesn't allow even a little camaraderie."

Robinton glanced down sheepishly. "I think I had something to do with that. His Hold harper sponsored him to my craft, but try as I might I couldn't find a way to fit him in. There is no place for a tone-deaf man in the Harper Hall, no matter how extraordinary his memory. He proved it to me: he does know every single Teaching song—the words only—and every Traditional Saga, every line of recorded history. He was bitter when I decided against admitting him. Still, I felt he was best off being the most precious member of a Hold staff. No Lord Holder would want to lose a man who never forgot anything. He'd be invaluable. I gather he had also offered himself as a Candidate at the Weyr, but that isn't unusual. Every young man with ambition has entertained dreams of Impression." The Master Harper grinned. "Even me."

"The dragons always know who would make a rider," F'nor said, yawning. "I know Canth's smarter than I am. He's already asleep."

Mirrim awoke early, feeling a sort of chill in the pre-dawn air. It wasn't a physical sensation; the tropical heat was still baking out of the sand hours after the sun had gone down the night before. It was the feeling that Threadfall was imminent. The dragons knew there was something wrong, and passed on the feeling to their weyrmates. The Red Star would be visible in the sky if she wanted to go and look at it. Most likely it had some influence on the sensitive joined minds of dragons and their riders. She pushed back the light sleeping fur and made her way to the bathing room. She washed quickly, and carried a glow out to see to Path, who was sleeping fitfully in her sandy wallow, eyelids twitching. Laying down the armful of fighting straps, Mirrim stood to admire the sleeping green dragon. The lids parted one by one to reveal the glowing jeweled eyes. Mirrim felt a rush of affection for Path, her beautiful green Path, whom she loved above all others in the world, and who loved her, too.

"Are you hungry, dear one?" she asked the dragon.

*No.* Path thought at her. *But I do itch.* A wingjoint twitched, to tell Mirrim where. Mirrim laughed, and grabbed up a handful of sand to attend to the irritation.

"I won't have time to give you a good sanding and oiling until after Threadfall. This'll have to do as a lick and a promise." She found the small rough place along the gleaming skin of Path's back, and rubbed the sand in until it smoothed out. Path let out a gusty sigh, snorting dust around Mirrim's feet, and settled back into her wallow while Mirrim found the jar of oil and applied it. "There. Will that do?"

*After Threadfall, I want my whole back sanded.*

Mirrim hugged the huge head to her. "Of course. You'll need it anyway to get out the firestone smell." She examined the fighting straps in the light of the glows before holding the double loops up to Path and tested the strength of the seam she had sewn along part of the inner arc of each, joining them. This set was virtually new, made during the long evenings of Mirrim's latest night shift with the weyrlings. Mirrim's fingertips still ached from drawing the needleful of stiff gut through several layers of hide. A rider's fighting gear had to be replaced once or twice a Turn, and each fashioned his own. When the straps rested around her dragon's neck, there was room between the two unjoined edges for Mirrim to sit, and her belt fastened to them by the four narrower straps at her sides, two front and two back. It made as secure a seat as if she had been born part of the dragon. During the diving and swooping of Thread-fighting, her life depended upon it.

Path stuck her nose into the straps, and tossed her

head back, settling the hide gear as far back on her neck as she could. Mirrim stepped up and pulled the loops into place over the neck ridges, tugging at the lengths of hide to see that they were whole and strong. *These fit well,* Path assured her. *They are not at all uncomfortable.*

"Well, you rest. I'll be back." Mirrim patted Path's foreleg and turned back to the Hold.

With Path seen to, she could care for herself. Once she had bathed and dressed, she carried her helmet, scarf, goggles, belt, and gloves into the kitchen to find herself something to eat. Her damp hair was held back from her face with a band tied around her forehead. There was a platter of meatrolls and breadrolls, and a fresh pitcher of klah already sitting out. Mirrim was grateful to Brekke, who must have just taken the rolls out of the cooling bins. She was so kind to fix them a snack, when she obviously had had to rise so early to do it. Mirrim stuffed one breadroll in her mouth, and held two meatrolls between her fingers while she poured out some hot klah. The very thought of fighting Thread made her as hungry as a dragon. Perhaps, Mirrim considered, since Brekke could hear any dragon, she had been as disturbed as they were by the coming of Thread. The flamethrowers and agenothree sprays were already on the back steps of the Hold, though such things were largely unnecessary in the grubbed South. F'nor strode into the kitchen, his boot heels clopping on the stone-flagged floor. He smiled at Mirrim's greedy version of breakfast.

"I hope you left some for me," he teased.

"And me and D'dot," said F'fej, a tall blue rider from Ista, whose sandy curls and deep green eyes had made him a lot of conquests in the Sea Hold. D'dot was a junior brown rider from the same Weyr, and a good friend of F'fej's. He was shorter and stockier than his companion, brown-haired, brown-eyed, and handsome, and was surprisingly strong for his size. They all broke their fast standing around the warming hearth. Mirrim felt uncomfortable in the hot wherhide garments, but she knew she was grateful for them every time Path ducked *between*. She finished eating, and buckled on the fleece-lined belt. It fit snugly halfway up her back, sheltering her kidneys from the cold, and was stiff enough to feel like a backrest between Path's neck ridges. The short straps dangled around her knees.

A bellow from outside made F'nor smile. "Canth says we're slow," he said, gulping his klah and hurrying outside. "Leading edge is in view over the sea."

Mirrim and the two junior riders ran outside, dragging on the rest of their gear, and leaped onto the neck ridges of their dragons. The fire lizards were already high in the air, creeling warnings. Zair was among them, which most likely meant the Master Harper was wakeful, too. Mirrim fastened the four straps of her belt to the neck straps and tugged them to be certain they were secure.

*Canth says we are to fly to the south of him and catch any clumps before they reach the orchard and wherry pen*, Path said. *Elekith will be to the north and Camuth will fly behind and catch any that we miss. But we will not miss any*, Path put in. Mirrim laughed at the smugness of her dragon's boast. But they *were* good fighters. Path was swift and agile.

With a nod from Mirrim, the green spread her wings and was aloft over the Hold. The sun was rising, and with it came the hazy sprinkling of Thread, falling over the sea. Mirrim reached into the sack fastened to the neck strap and offered chunks of firestone to Path until the dragon indicated she had enough in her second stomach to generate the phosphine gas needed to sear Thread from the sky.

"Here it comes," Mirrim said, crouching low into Path's neck ridges.

THREAD
*Does 2 D6 damage.*
*If Mirrim and Path hit any Thread, it burns immediately into cinders and does no further damage.*

## Section 3

*Roll 3 D6.*

*If the total is less than or equal to Mirrim's value for Dexterity, turn to section 8.*

*If the total is greater, turn to section 9.*

* **3** *

The first clump was no problem, and she and F'fej together seared another mass that stretched out between them. Camuth disappeared *between* to avoid colliding with Path, and Mirrim caught a glimpse out of the corner of her eye of the next Threads which she and Path must destroy. It was winking and twisting on the sea breezes, and if it continued on its present course, it would touch Canth, who was angling toward a lower-falling cloud of Threads.

"Warn Canth!" she cried, leaning against her dragon's neck as they swooped toward the Threads falling nearer and nearer the great brown dragon.

*I have. He says F'nor thanks you.* Path inhaled mightily through her nostrils, preparing to burn the Threads to black dust and cinders. In a heartbeat, they reached the perfect position below the cluster, where the Threads would fall right into Path's flame.

"Now!" cried Mirrim.

*Roll 3 D6.*

*If total is less than or equal to Mirrim's value for Dexterity, turn to section 5.*

*If it is greater, turn to section 14.*

## *  4  *

"Yes, Lessa. I have the disk right here in my belt pouch."
She displayed it casually. "Master Robinton asked me to
look for anything new that would interest him. I believe
this is a musical device of some kind, and I think he
would want to see it."

"How would you know that?" Breide demanded angrily, snatching the disk out of her hands. "You are no
scholar of music."

"I know the symbols," Mirrim said haughtily, emulat-
ing Lessa's tone with the holder. "If I am wrong, the
Master Harper will tell me."

"You have no right to remove anything from this site."

"The Master Harper," Mirrim emphasized the title
heavily, "has the right to examine whatever artifact he
needs to, in the interest of recording the history of Pern. I
came here on his behalf."

"That is correct, Breide," Lessa interrupted, stepping
between them, and forcing a note of friendliness into her
voice, though Mirrim could tell she was fuming. *Ramoth
says you will have to explain to Lessa later,* Path told
Mirrim, who schooled her face not to show her dismay.
"Why not allow Robinton to borrow it? At least you can't
consider it stolen, since you know where it has gone. It
will be returned as soon as he has studied it, as Mirrim
says."

It was clear that the sour-faced steward was not happy
with the solution, but he grunted an approval, and
stalked back to his job. Mirrim breathed a sigh of relief
to see him go, and put out a hand to take the fighting
strap as soon as he was out of sight. She felt a hand close

on her wrist, the fingertips pressing sharply into the tendons, and realized she had forgotten about Lessa.

"As for you, Mirrim, how could you take anything from here without permission?" Lessa demanded. The Weyrwoman had lost the smile she had used to charm Breide, and turned the full force of her anger on the dragongirl. "You know the importance of what is going on here. You aren't ignorant of the strictures imposed on everyone. You were about to leave, taking that little disk with you!"

Mirrim couldn't meet Lessa's gaze. She studied the ground between her feet, trying to keep from shaking. "I . . . I'm sorry, Lessa."

"Sorry? Is that what you say? After having disgraced the Weyr, and in such a sensitive place as this? Toric will have a good time when Breide tells him what you have done. He already mistrusts Northerners and dragonriders, believes we'd hide things from him that are found here. Now he might demand to search our carry-sacks before we leave!"

"Forgive me. I didn't think." Mirrim's voice was hardly a whisper. "It was for Master Robinton . . ."

"And I will speak to *him* tonight, for failing to caution you to behave yourself," Lessa promised coldly, "though I would have assumed you had learned responsibility yourself by your age." Her head jerked in a brisk nod of dismissal, and Mirrim scrambled up on Path's shoulder. She called to her fire lizards as they ascended high over the plain, and together they all went *between*.

After Path had been thoroughly bathed and oiled, and she herself had had a refreshing bath in the sea, Mirrim put on a loose robe, which was all she needed in the warmth of the late afternoon. She cleaned her sweaty and dirty wherhide riding clothes, and left them hanging up on a line as she went to take the disk in to the Harper. She found him resting in his study.

"My thanks, Mirrim," Robinton said, turning the

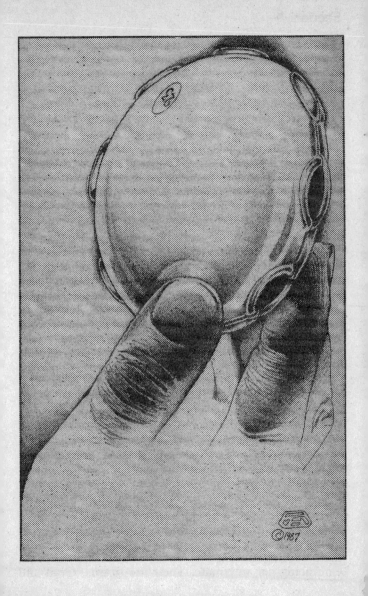

little bit of metal over and over in his hands. He polished it clean with the edge of his tunic and held it up to one eye. Mirrim pulled up a light chair near the footstool of Robinton's own armchair. "What a wonderful find. Probably in the hold of a harper, or another musician. Most likely a singer."

"I thought those were musical symbols," Mirrim breathed with relief. "But what is it?"

"It's a pitch pipe. Here's B flat." Robinton brought it to his lips and blew through one of the little holes. A reedy note sang out. Mirrim giggled as Robinton twitched and wrinkled his nose. "The vibrations tickle," he said. "But it's still in perfect condition after who knows how many Turns? The tone is pure. What a wonder! I am delighted to find that musical notation has not changed in all this time. Our ancestors were not so different in thought than we are today. Thank you, my dear, thank you." Robinton beamed. "Where did you get it?"

"They found it in one of the holds near the lava flow." Mirrim said, then frowned as she remembered that she was in disgrace because of the little disk.

Robinton appeared not to notice her change of expression. "I'll examine this carefully tonight. See if I can't discover how the tone has stayed so perfect all this time." He rose and walked into his workroom. Mirrim could hear him sifting through the little tools, muttering to himself. She smiled, and went back to the kitchen to help Brekke finish preparing the evening meal.

Not long before dusk fell, several dragons appeared in the sky, to be greeted by Path's joyful trumpeting. Mirrim, prodding the baked fish to be sure they were ready, looked up to recognize Mnementh, Ramoth, Tiroth, and Canth. The great brown dragon landed first, backwinging into a huge wallow of sand, and F'nor was off his neck in a moment. Brekke had obviously "heard" them coming, for she was already out across the sand, embracing her weyrmate. Their fire lizards, Grall and

Berd, danced joyfully in the air above their friends' heads. Robinton, too, came down from the Hold to greet the new arrivals, the precious pitch pipe in his hand.

More sedately, Ramoth and Mnementh landed side by side on the beach, and waded into the water to sport in the waves as soon as their riders were aground. Fandarel had flown in behind F'lar, and Lytol with D'ram on Tiroth. Breide all but leaped off Ramoth's neck ridge and was striding toward the Hold, quickly outdistancing the Weyrwoman's shorter paces as she followed behind him.

"Breide!" Lessa called out, in a tone that made the single word a warning. Respectfully, he turned to wait for her, the irritation on his face not one whit abated. "I will not have you making rash accusations. Wait to hear what she has to say before you judge."

Brekke hurried to head off the angry steward, and smiled at all the others in turn. "I know you are hungry. While we eat, you can tell me what you've found today. I'm most interested. Supper is ready."

"Lady Brekke, I must decline," Breide said politely. "There is another more pressing matter I must broach."

*Turn to section 2.*

*Turn to section 2.*

## * 5 *

In the instant it took Mirrim to cry out the word, Path's flaming breath turned a threat into harmless ash. As they whirled by over Canth's head, F'nor cocked them a cheerful salute. Mirrim smiled with satisfaction. She was pleased to have been able to save F'nor from being laced. It was too clear in her memory the condition he and Canth had been in when they tried to go to the Red Star all those Turns ago. They deserved never to be Thread-laced again. From the point of view of an apprentice healer, she would never stop hating Thread for what it did to her friends, human and dragon.

"Come on, Path. Fall isn't over yet! There's another clump!"

*Turn to section 11.*

## * 6 *

"Why, no, Lessa. I haven't got anything from the hall," Mirrim said, swallowing. Breide leaned in toward her, studying her eyes, as if he could see the truth in them. She met his glare.

"There, Steward, you see? Next time, try to be more certain of your facts before you accuse a dragonrider of theft." Lessa was triumphant but no less angry. "Lord Holder Toric would not be pleased that you were bearing false witness."

"My apologies, Weyrwoman," Breide said cautiously, not wanting to anger her more than he already had. "It was agreed in Council with the Lord Holders and the Weyrfolk that nothing was to be removed without permission. I have had a great deal of trouble keeping small items from disappearing."

"I quite understand," Lessa nodded, now prepared to be magnanimous with him. "You have a difficult job to do. Very well, Mirrim, on your way. Tell Robinton we'll see him tonight!"

"Yes, Lessa." Mirrim scrambled up on Path's shoulder.

"Now, why not show me the things that have been

uncovered today." Lessa smiled, laying her fingertips on Breide's arm and turning him back toward the hall. "I am *most* interested in any facet of Pern's past. . . ."

Mirrim called to her fire lizards as they ascended over the plain, and together they all went *between*.

When they got back to Cove Hold Mirrim thoroughly bathed and oiled Path, and then she herself had a bath in the sea. Afterward she put on a loose robe, which was all she needed in the warmth of the late afternoon. She cleaned her sweaty and dirty wherhide riding clothes, and left them hanging up on the line as she went to take the disk in to the Harper. She found him resting in his study.

"My thanks, Mirrim," Robinton said, looking carefully at the little bit of metal and turning it over and over in his hands. He polished it clean with the edge of his tunic and held it up to one eye. Mirrim pulled up a light chair near to the footstool of Robinton's own armchair. "What a wonderful find. Probably in the hold of a harper, or another musician. Most likely a singer."

"I thought those were musical symbols," Mirrim breathed with relief. "But what is it?"

"It's a pitch pipe. Here's B flat." Robinton brought it to his lips and blew through one of the little holes. A reedy note sang out. Mirrim saw Robinton twitch and wrinkle his nose, and she giggled. "B flat. The vibrations tickle," he said. "But it's still in perfect condition after who knows how many Turns? The tone is pure. Magnificent. I am delighted to find that musical notation has not changed in all this time. Thank you, my dear, thank you." Robinton beamed. "I'll examine this carefully." He rose and walked into his workroom. Mirrim could hear him sifting through the little tools, muttering to himself. She smiled, and went back to the kitchen to help Brekke finish preparing the evening meal.

Not long before dusk fell, Path's joyful trumpeting greeted several dragons that appeared in the sky.

Mirrim, putting out the fire under a thoroughly warmed cauldron of stewed meat, roots, and greens, looked up to recognize Mnementh, Ramoth, Tiroth, and Canth. The great brown dragon landed first, backwinging into a huge wallow of sand, and F'nor was off his neck in a moment. Brekke had obviously "heard" them coming, for she was already out across the sand embracing her weyrmate. Their fire lizards, Grall and Berd, danced joyfully in the air above their friends' heads.

More sedately, Ramoth and Mnementh landed side by side on the beach, and waded into the water to sport in the waves as soon as their riders were aground. Fandarel had flown in behind F'lar, and Lytol with D'ram on Tiroth.

Robinton strode out to meet them, waving the pitch pipe in his hand. Mirrim's eyes widened as she saw Breide descend from behind Lessa. She had forgotten to tell Robinton the details of her trip to the plateau and ask him to keep it hidden, especially from the sour-faced steward. She ran toward the Harper, hoping that Breide hadn't seen clearly what Robinton was holding. It was too evident that he had. Breide all but leaped off Ramoth's neck ridge and was striding toward the Hold, quickly outdistancing the Weyrwoman's shorter paces as she followed behind him.

"My thanks, friend Breide, for the loan of this splendid little piece of history," Robinton was saying as she reached them. "I've given it a brief once over, but I'd like to study it further. May I keep it a few more days?"

"It was not loaned," Breide said flatly. He plucked the metal disk out of Robinton's hand, to the flat astonishment of the Master Harper. Breide whirled on Lessa. "It was here! She took it!"

"Mirrim? Without permission?" Robinton asked, trying to make sense of Breide's mood. "Is that what is the difficulty here?"

Lessa matched the steward's ire with her own. Though her eyes were ablaze with anger, she spoke courteously to

Robinton. "That's right. But when we asked Mirrim if she had taken it, she lied."

"Ah." Robinton looked sad and disappointed, and Mirrim slowed her trot, wishing that she could fall *between* rather than face him. The expression on Lessa's face told her she wasn't the only one who wished Mirrim would disappear, preferably *between* times. Robinton put his arm around Breide's shoulders and nodded meaningfully to Lytol. The two of them drew him away nearer the glow-lit Hold, talking intently. "Well, surely, now that it's here, you have no objections to my borrowing it for a few days more. I've some theories that might surprise you. . . ."

Mirrim studied the ground between her feet. For all Lessa's calm exterior, she knew the Weyrwoman was as hot as a piece of Cromcoal. F'lar came up nonchalantly, putting his arm around his weyrmate's waist. "How could you?" Lessa demanded of Mirrim. "With the position between the Weyrs and Southern Hold so delicate? By taking that bauble, you have disgraced *all* dragonriders. How can I argue with Lord Toric when he proposes to search all our carry-sacks before we leave!"

"Forgive me, Lessa. I didn't think." Mirrim's voice was hardly a whisper. She raised her eyes to meet the Weyrwoman's. "It was for Master Robinton. I will apologize to Breide, and to Lord Toric, if you want."

"That will do for a start, but as of now, you are forbidden to go near the excavations except to deliver passengers or supplies."

"Yes, Lessa," Mirrim said, hanging her head.

"I agree," F'lar said evenly, his tone placating. "That would be the best thing to keep from drawing further attention to one errant dragonrider, who might be considered to be thieving, but was only trying to do a good deed."

Lessa exchanged looks with F'lar. Mirrim had no idea what he was talking about, but it didn't seem a reference to her own peccadillo. The Weyrleader glanced briefly but meaningfully over his shoulder at Breide, who was chatting quietly with the others. Lessa smiled a little sheepishly, and squeezed F'lar's waist with her own arm.

Brekke, always sensitive to emotions, hurried to head off more bitter feelings toward her ward, and smiled at all the others in turn. "Yes. I know you all must be hungry. We have stew, bread, roast meat, and cheese. While we eat, you can tell me what you've found today. I'm most interested. Supper is ready."

"Lady Brekke, I must decline just now," Breide said politely, turning away from Lytol. "There is another more pressing matter I must broach."

*Turn to section 2.*

## * 7 *

Pain echoed through both their minds. Path whimpered unhappily as they descended to the beach, favoring her right wing. Mirrim was distraught to see that one main-sail had been Threaded to empty cartilage. Brekke, disregarding the fact that Fall was continuing right over her head, ran out to Path's wallow with a jar of numbweed. Mirrim sobbed, the tears dashed from her face by the wind, frantic to console her dragon.

"I could hear her, dear." Brekke began to slather the soothing ointment all over the injured wing and the place across Path's foot where the edge of a Thread had touched and singed.

Mirrim was torn between worry and embarrassment. Letting her dragon get laced twice was the sort of thing a *new* weyrling would do. Tears welled in her eyes as she pulled off Path's fighting straps and swung the firestone sacks out of her way. "I'm sorry," she wailed. "I'm sorry." Path crooned miserably, pushing her foot closer to Brekke so that numbweed could be spread farther along the score.

"There, there," Brekke said, trying to soothe both of them. She drew out the injured pinion by the fingertip joint and examined it. "It will be all right. It isn't so bad. I've seen much worse. Mirrim, get me splints and bandages for her wing."

The cool tone of command cut through Mirrim's misery, and she ran inside. Robinton and Lytol stood, peering out through a crack in the metal shutters at the remaining dragonriders in the sky. They both turned to offer their sympathies, but Mirrim kept her eyes down toward the floor. She knew that Path would be crippled for several sevendays, and she held herself to blame. It would take all her time and energy to care for Path until she healed. There would be no way that she could ever get back to the plateau to clear herself from having been branded a thief.

*Turn to section 29.*

"There! That one!" The sinuous-looking Threads were falling ominously out of the sky. As Mirrim guided Path toward a clump, the tendrils twisted in the air, forming and re-forming lazy clumps of glowing silver. Mirrim shuddered as they drew closer. An individual Thread unfurled was fully a dragonlength long. Below them, frightened both of the huge swooping dragons and of the skyborne menace of which they, too, were aware, the wing-clipped wherries in the pen were screaming. Path angled in the sky, slightly furling one gigantic pinion, to keep her wingtip away from the deadly silver Threads. She exhaled.

Mirrim felt the heat radiating from the dragon's great neck right through her wherhide trousers. Path opened her mouth, and let out a long orange gush of flame. The Thread crackled and hissed, shrinking and dissolving into harmless black particles which fell on the upturned faces of the penned birds. Mirrim felt as satisfied as if she herself had burned the Threads to a crisp. She glanced around for her next target.

*Turn to section 3.*

## * 9 *

"There! That one!" Mirrim guided Path toward a clump of the sinuous-looking Threads falling ominously out of the sky. As they descended, the tendrils twisted in the air, forming and re-forming lazy clumps of glowing silver. Mirrim shuddered as they drew closer. An individual unfurled Thread was fully a dragonlength long. Below them, the wherries in the pen were screaming, frightened by the huge swooping dragons and the skyborne menace of which they, too, were aware. Path angled in the sky, slightly furling one gigantic pinion, to keep her wingtip away from the deadly silver Threads. She exhaled.

Mirrim felt the heat radiating from the dragon's great neck right through her wherhide trousers. Path opened her mouth, and let out a long orange gush of flame, but it

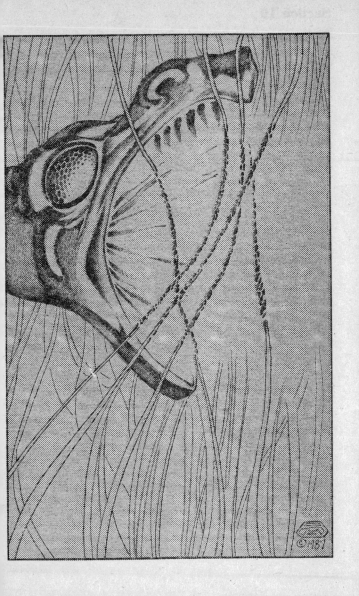

## Section 10

hit nothing. The Thread, caught in a perverse updraft of warm air, swept out of their way, tangling into a compact twist. Mirrim cursed, urging Path to turn away before they were caught by it.

*Roll 3 D6.*

*If the total is less than or equal to Mirrim's value for Dexterity, turn to section 3.*

*If the total is greater, turn to section 12.*

\* **10** \*

Pain, shared pain, lanced through both their minds. Path whimpered unhappily as Mirrim winced. She wasn't hurt so badly, but, oh, Mirrim would be so grateful for numbweed when the Fall ended!

*Turn to section 11.*

## * **11** *

All clear, F'fej signaled to her, angling Camuth away from the puff of smoke which had been their latest target. Black ash was still falling into the sea and on the shore near the little dock. Mirrim signed back a congratulatory thumbs-up. Path murmured deep in her throat, asking for more firestone. Mirrim offered her a few big chunks of rock, and glanced around quickly for more Thread while her friend chewed the firestone to fragments. Mirrim pointed, and Path corrected her downward glide for an upward surge as they flew toward a small clump high overhead.

*Roll 3 D6.*

*If the total is less than or equal to Mirrim's Dexterity value, turn to section 19.*

*If it is greater, turn to section 23.*

## * **12** *

White hot pain roiled through Mirrim's consciousness. Instantly, she and Path went *between*. In the cold, black nothingness, the Thread froze and cracked off, leaving behind only the agony of its touch. They exploded back into the air over Cove Hold. Mirrim swallowed, her eyes filling with tears. To have been laced so early during Fall was humiliating as well as painful.

"Watch out!" F'nor shouted across the expanse of sky as he turned Canth toward their next target of Thread.

*Roll 1 D6.*

*If the roll is 1 to 4, Path has been laced by Thread. Mark it on the record sheet.*

*If 5 or 6, Mirrim has been laced. Roll 2 D6 for damage, subtract the total from her hit points on the record sheet.*

*Turn to section 3.*

## * **13** *

Without waiting for her instructions, Path turned and flew back toward Cove Hold, crooning worriedly deep in her throat. The other dragons acknowledged her departure to their riders, who glanced over at them before resuming Thread-fighting.

"Where are you going?" Mirrim croaked, her voice a mere squeak. "There's more Thread up there!" She tried to pull back on the fighting straps, but Path paid no attention.

*You are hurt,* Path told her, her usually placid "voice" shaken and worried. *I am taking you to Brekke. She is waiting for us. You must be calm.*

Path touched down on the beach lightly as a leaf falling, but Mirrim felt the jar go right up her spine to her head. Her left thigh was on fire, and so was her right arm and shoulder. She must have been caught right in the middle of a clump. It was a wonder that Path wasn't as badly off as she.

"Mirrim? Can you hear me, dear?" It was Brekke's voice, but she couldn't see the woman. There seemed to be a red-black haze swimming through her eyes, impairing her vision. "Don't speak. Just let Path know. Good. We're going to carry you inside now, Mirrim."

Mirrim wanted to tell her that she could walk, that she was perfectly capable of taking care of herself. She hadn't been Threaded that badly. She heard other voices, male voices, and her stomach lurched uncomfortably when she was lifted from Path's neck and brought into the Hold. Path's voice continued right along, telling her she loved her, and she would get well. Robinton's soothing baritone rose and fell through Mirrim's consciousness. He was chatting to her, keeping her from worrying while Brekke salved her wounds with numbweed. She felt a cup at her lips, and drank a few swallows of the fellis-laced fruit juice, and settled in to sleep.

"Now Brekke has two patients to take care of instead of one," Mirrim berated herself, the fellis beginning to take hold. Couldn't she duck better than that?

*Go to sleep,* Path told her gently. *We did very well, but we are finished for now.*

*Turn to section 29.*

* **14** *

In the instant it took Mirrim to cry out the word, the great cluster of Thread fell past Path's flame. She didn't see it hit Canth, but she heard dragon and dragonrider cry out. One second they were there, and the next they were gone *between,* to crack the Thread off. Guiltily, she pulled Path out of the way as F'fej on Camuth zoomed down to burn what she'd missed. She hoped that Canth wasn't hurt too badly. It was too clear in her memory the condition he and Canth had been in when they tried to go to the Red Star all those Turns ago. They deserved never to be Thread-laced again. But she couldn't dwell on that now. She had to concentrate on saving herself and her dragon from Threadscore.

*Roll 3 D6.*

*If the total is less than or equal to Mirrim's Dexterity, turn to section 11.*

*If it is greater, turn to section 15.*

## * 15 *

Screaming with shared pain, Path swept into *between,* letting the frigid darkness crack the Thread into harmless fragments. Mirrim could feel nothing for a moment, only cold. *Between* was terrifying, in its own way. If it were not for the comforting presence of Path's consciousness in her own mind, she would go mad.

They burst out into the sun again. Canth had reappeared, a new Threadscore raw and red on his forked tail. Mirrim was ashamed to have failed her friends, but a cheery wave from F'nor assured her that he didn't consider her at fault. Threadscore was one of the hazards of their lives.

F'nor's pleasant expression turned to one of worry as he realized that they were wounded, too.

"Don't worry," Mirrim called, her voice sounding small on the wind. "It isn't as bad as it looks."

*Roll 1 D6.*

*If the roll is 1 to 4, Path has been laced by Thread. Mark it on the record sheet.*

*If 5 or 6, Mirrim has been Threadscored. Roll 2 D6 for damage and subtract the total from her hit points on the record sheet.*

*If Path has been hit only once, and if Mirrim has enough hit points to continue, turn to section 10.*

*If Path has been hit twice, turn to section 7.*

*If Mirrim is out of hit points, turn to section 13.*

## * 16 *

Mirrim shrieked as the raw Threadscore dripped acid right through the leg of her wherhide trousers. She felt faint, looking down to see the long stripe burned down almost the length of her thigh. If it hadn't been for the firm clasp of the wherhide fighting straps, she might have swayed off. She swallowed, looking down. It was a long way to the ground. She held on tightly with her knees.

Path changed direction suddenly, but not swiftly, easing around in a downward spiral toward the Hold. She spat the rest of her fire in a harmless display, and spread her wings farther to cup the air.

"Where are you going?" Mirrim asked, but her voice was weak in her own ears.

*Brekke is calling to me to land,* Path said. *You are badly hurt, she says. She can see your face pale from where she stands. You need to be taken care of now. I don't like you to be hurt. She will heal you.*

Mirrim resigned herself reluctantly to missing the rest of Threadfall. They were babying her, making her stop so soon. She'd been laced before. She was about to instruct Path to return to her position when Path dropped lightly to the sand and the sharp awareness of pain in her leg made her black out.

*Turn to section 29.*


## \* **17** \*

" 'Ware!" D'dot's voice came from behind her. She and Path twisted and rolled to avoid making contact with the remaining tendrils of Thread. D'dot threw her a high sign, and flew over her head. Path closed her wings slightly and dropped like a stone to avoid Elekith, who crisped the rest of the patch. For a moment she was sorry she had eaten so much breakfast.

*Elekith says hadn't we better be more careful?* Path informed Mirrim.

"Aagh!" Mirrim cried, protesting, as her stomach jumped up into her throat.

Before she could order it done, Path had whisked them both *between*. The lifeless filament of Thread cracked off harmlessly, and then they were back in the sunlit sky.

*Roll 1 D6.*

*If the roll is 1 to 4, Path has been laced by Thread. Mark it on the record sheet.*

*If 5 or 6, Mirrim has been Threadscored. Roll 2 D6 for damage, subtract the total from her hit points on the record sheet.*

*If Path has been hit only once, turn to section 22.*

*If Path has been hit twice, turn to section 24.*

*If Mirrim is now out of hit points, turn to section 16.*

*If not, turn to section 27.*

## * **18** *

The patch of Thread split into two smaller clumps. One of them crisped into nothingness, but the other blew ominously toward them.

"Oh, no!" Mirrim flung herself down on Path's neck, willing her to go *between* to avoid the acid touch of Thread.

*Roll 3 D6.*

*If the total is less than or equal to Mirrim's Dexterity value, turn to section 34.*

*If it is greater, turn to section 30.*

## * **19** *

Path spat a tongue of fire out before her, wiping the third patch of Thread from midair. Mirrim sneezed as they exploded right through the cloud of black dust and out the other side. She wiped ash from her eye with her riding glove. There'd be a round black mark on her face when she took off her goggles later. She couldn't wait until Wansor finished making enough lenses for all the dragonriders' face masks. Apologetically, Path spilled air from between the pinions of her left wing, and they veered away from the puff of cinders.

"That was a good, clever shot, Path," Mirrim praised her. Path turned her muzzle back for another hunk of firestone, eyes whirling blue with contentment and pride. The girl patted her on the shoulder and leaned in close. Fall was about over for them, as the following edge approached. But look! There was more Thread drifting close to the Hold!

*Turn to section 20.*

## \* **20** \*

D'dot and Mirrim moved in toward the Thread falling directly over Cove Hold.

"Tell Elekith we'll take the patch over the orchards," Mirrim told Path. "He can get the other."

*He says he agrees*, Path said. *He is closer to that one.*

It irritated her to let clumps of Thread pass by her to the north and not bother to try to catch it, but there was no need to pursue it over the sea. It would be fish food in minutes, and Southern Weyr was in no danger. The Fall would be over long before it got to them, more than six time zones away. They weren't due for a day or so.

Path circled around and under Elekith, and breathed flame at the greedy filaments which were reaching down toward the mature fruit trees behind the Hold.

*Roll 3 D6.*

*If the total rolled is less than or equal to Mirrim's value for Dexterity, turn to section 25.*

*If it is greater, turn to section 18.*

# * **21** *

"Watch out!" D'dot's voice came from behind her. She and Path had successfully avoided any contact with the remaining tendrils of Thread. Path closed her wings slightly and dropped like a stone to avoid Elekith, who crisped the rest of the patch.

"Uugh!" Mirrim cried, protesting, as her stomach jumped up into her throat. For a moment she was sorry she had eaten so much breakfast. D'dot threw her a high sign, and flew once again into his assigned position as backup.

*Elekith asks hadn't we better be more careful?* Path informed Mirrim.

Mirrim felt hot steam coming out of her ears. The nerve of D'dot! Why, she'd been a dragonrider for *Turns* more than he had. She turned with renewed fervor to destroy the last remaining clumps of Thread over Cove Hold.

*Turn to section 20.*

## * **22** *

Path emerged from *between* with a squeal of pain as the salt-heavy air hit her Threadscored leg.

"Is it too bad?" Mirrim asked her anxiously. "Shall we land?"

*No,* Path said, but her tone wasn't that steady.

"Well, if you're sure you can go on . . ." Mirrim coaxed, trying to see the extent of the damage from her perch. It was impossible. She could see the ground more clearly than she could her mount's legs.

*I can go on,* Path avowed stoutly. Mirrim felt fear twisting in her vitals, but she was unwilling to pull her away if she didn't want to go.

"All right, dear. I'll doctor you properly when we're down."

*Turn to section 20.*

## * **23** *

Partially blinded by the rising yellow-green sun, Path spat a tongue of fire at the Thread. To Mirrim's dismay, only half of it singed away into black dust. She shuddered as they swept right past the half-consumed patch, fearful that it might touch them, almost shuddering as she imagined feeling her skin burn.

*Roll 3 D6.*

*If the total is less than or equal to Mirrim's Dexterity, turn to section 21.*

*If it is greater, turn to section 17.*

* **24** *

Path trumpeted with pain as they emerged into the sun. Mirrim could see the black-edged red scores across one side of the dragon's neck, and Path informed her that her back left leg was badly laced.

"Tell Canth we're setting down," Mirrim said gently.

*F'nor says not to worry,* Path said, turning whirling red eyes to her weyrmate. *They can handle what Thread is left. Fall above the Hold is nearly over.*

Mirrim was grateful. She worried that Path might have trouble landing on the damaged leg, but the soft sand of the beach came up to meet them. Path sat on her tail when the injured leg refused to hold all her weight. Mirrim undid the fighting straps and slid off to guide her weyrmate to the wallow, where Brekke was waiting with a pot of numbweed. She dipped her hand in the jar and began to slather it on the leg score while Brekke treated the wound in Path's neck. To her dismay, she found she was weeping. Carefully, she wiped the tears away with the edge of her sleeve, trying to keep from getting numbweed in them. Path crooned in sympathy to Mirrim's distress in spite of her pain.

"There, there," Brekke said, trying to soothe both of them. "It will be all right. It isn't so bad. I've seen much worse. Mirrim, get me bandages for her neck and leg."

The cool tone of command cut through to Mirrim, and she ran inside, her mind clearing. Robinton and Lytol stood, peering out through a crack in the metal shutters at the remaining dragonriders in the sky. They both turned to offer their sympathies, but Mirrim avoided them by keeping her eyes down toward the floor. She knew that Path would be forbidden to fly for several sevendays. It would take all Mirrim's time and energy to care for her. There would be no way that she could ever get back to the plateau to clear herself from having been branded a thief. She knew in an instant when the numbweed stopped Path's pain, but all the worry and dismay stayed within her.

*Turn to section 29.*

## * **25** *

The patch of Thread crisped from bottom to top like a torch, shivered into nothingness and blew away. Path blew out the rest of her flame, and indulged in a little victory flight over the Hold, bugling triumphantly. Mirrim just let her have her head. She pulled off her flying helmet and let the breeze's tousle her sweat-matted hair. When they flew together, they were as one—the living wind. Since Path's first mating flight, she and Mirrim had been closer and more entwined mentally than she would ever have believed two beings could be. She loved flying with Path, simply soaring upward on the warm thermals, gliding down on a whim, and sharing the sensation of a freedom that dragonless men would never know.

*That's the last,* F'nor said through Canth, and Mirrim could tell he was smiling indulgently at their joyful flight. *Come down whenever you're ready.*

*Turn to section 31.*

## * **26** *

Path whimpered in her throat, and Mirrim felt pangs of grief as she saw that one of the dragon's spar mainsails had been threaded bare by the last clump of Thread. She stroked Path on the neck, willing the pain out of her friend's wing.

"Tell F'nor we're going back," she instructed, her voice soothing, as if with that alone she could heal Path. "It's all right, dear one. You've done a wonderful job, and we can make you better. It's all right. Can you make it?"

*I think so,* Path said, but her voice was shaky.

As they descended to the beach, Mirrim was already preparing to jump off to find bandages. Below her, she could see Brekke waiting for them. She had anticipated their needs, and had a big jar of numbweed in her arms.

Mirrim was depressed, and not only about her weyrmate's injury. With Path's wing hurt as badly as it was, she would be forbidden to fly against Thread, or anywhere else, for several sevendays. It would take all Mirrim's time and energy to care for Path until that sail grew back. She fretted that the dragon would never get better, and the pain Path suffered made her crazy with worry. They would have to stay in Cove Hold whether or not Master Robinton needed or even wanted them there. There was no way that she could ever get back to the Ancient Timers' plateau to clear herself from having been branded a thief.

*Turn to section 29.*

## * **27** *

Mirrim shrieked as the raw Threadscore dripped acid right through the leg of her wherhide trousers. She felt faint, looking down to see the stripe burned across her thigh. If it hadn't been for the firm clasp of the wherhide fighting straps, she might have swayed off. She swallowed, looking down. It was a long way to the ground. She held on tightly with her knees.

Path changed direction suddenly, but not swiftly, easing around in a downward spiral toward the Hold. She spread her wings farther to cup the air, dumping velocity.

"Where are you going?" Mirrim asked.

*You have been Threadscored. Brekke has numbweed to put on your leg.*

"I've been scored before, silly thing," Mirrim chided her. "It hurts, but it's no worse than other times."

*I do not remember other times very well,* Path said. *I do not want to.*

"Well, it takes more than this to stop me. Come on, Fall is almost over. Let's burn some more Thread!"

*Turn to section 20.*

## * 28 *

Mirrim hissed through her teeth. Her arm was scored right through the thick hide of the jacket. "It hurts like wherspawn, but I'll be fine," she sent back through Path, her eyes stinging with tears. "I can't wait to get some numbweed!"

Path expended the last of her flame on a brief aerial fireworks before they glided in toward land. *Canth has already told Brekke. She'll be waiting.*

D'dot shot past them on Elekith. "Last one down is a wherry!" he shouted.

*Turn to section 31.*

## * 29 *

Back again at Benden Weyr, Mirrim mooched around the weyr that she shared with Path. Her fire lizards sunned themselves on the ledge, staying clear of Mirrim's uncertain temper. The green dragon was down in the Bowl, bathing and sunning herself, but Mirrim had no taste for lying around in the sunshine. She was too depressed.

She'd been unable to attend the wedding ceremony at Southern. The lucky dragonriders who'd been privileged to see it had talked of nothing else for the past sevenday. Mirrim thought disconsolately of her new duties— drudgeries, *she'd* called them. Baby-sitting new weyrlings, mixing medicines for the Healers, stewing numbweed salve, fetching and carrying for the women of the lower caverns. All of those chores were usually only assigned as penance to dragonriders, but since it would take time before she was expected to fight Thread again, Mirrim had many sevendays of onerous tasks to which she could look forward. In the meantime, except for her daily care of Path, she was confined to quarters. Mirrim had nothing else to do but lick her wounds and feel sorry for herself.

*This time Mirrim has failed in her efforts. If you wish to join her in another attempt, turn to section 1 and begin again.*

* **30** *

The cold blackness chilled the skin of her face and scalp to wax, and she sensed, rather than heard, Thread cracking off from burnt skin.

Emerging into the same airspace over the dock, they saw a shower of little black particles being swept away by the salt wind, and Canth swooping low enough to catch fish in his claws, his fire spent.

"Are you all right?" F'nor sent through Canth.

*Roll 1 D6.*

*If the roll is 1 to 4, Path has been laced by Thread. Mark it on the record sheet.*

*If 5 or 6, Mirrim has been Threadscored. Roll 2 D6 for damage and subtract the total from her hit points on the record sheet.*

*If Path has been hit only once, turn to section 33.*

*If Path has been hit twice, turn to section 26.*

*If Mirrim is now out of hit points, turn to section 32.*

*If not, turn to section 28.*

## \* **31** \*

"Well flown," F'nor said, nodding to the three junior dragonriders over Canth's neck. "Very well flown. Especially you, Mirrim. I saw you chasing those tricky clumps. Many dragonriders get laced by thread that get caught in a fast-moving air current like that."

Mirrim glowed with pride, but she knew better than to assume the credit for herself. "What would I do without you, my green darling?" Mirrim said, scratching Path behind the eye ridge. The first lids closed over the huge eyes, making them look like milky jewels.

*You could not fight Thread so well,* was the smug reply.

Brekke bandaged and slathered numbweed until she was satisfied that all riders and dragons who needed it were properly treated, and would heal without complications. "I don't need more patients," she said, looking meaningfully at F'nor.

"We were all careful," he assured her. "With only four riders, we'd scant backup in case of injuries."

"You could have brought more riders."

F'nor's reply made the three junior dragonriders puff
up with pride. "I have faith in the ones I have."

The four dragons waddled contentedly into the shal-
lows as soon as their riders loosened fighting straps and
firestone sacks. The riders stripped off their heavy fighting gear and piled it out of reach of the waves on the
beach.

"We'd best see if there is any Thread left," F'nor said,
looking longingly at Canth, who had just surfaced with
an explosive puff of air. He turned back to the Hold.

"As soon as everything is cleaned up, I'll give you your
bath," Mirrim called back to Path.

Not much assistance was needed to wipe away all
traces of Thread. Using the hand-held flamethrower,
Lytol burned out a hissing infestation just beyond the
edge of the wherry pen that was scaring the silly birds
halfway *between*. The grubs were efficiently taking care
of the rest. As fast as Thread sank into the fertile soil, the
little gray insects covered and consumed it. But no
clumps had fallen into the immediate area of the Hold.

Still stinking of firestone, Mirrim helped scout around
to make sure no Thread remained where any living thing
would touch it. The tidal pools on the beach were filled
with drowned Thread, and the tiny fingertails which
inhabited the strand were feasting on it. Her stomach
turned when she realized she had almost stepped into
that stream to get across the beach. It didn't matter that
Thread went inert as soon as it hit water. Stepping back,
she took a running jump across.

Mirrim's fire lizards returned to her, sending images of
their adventures while fighting Thread. "Shoo, you sillies!" Mirrim said, scattering them with a wave of her
hand. "I was there, too. Now, if you're not helping me,
go away! Hunt! The water's full of fish."

Creeling, Lok and Reppa zoomed away and swooped
over the salt strand, dipping out easy prey from among

the busy schools of fingertail. They joined Path, who was splashing energetically in the waves with Canth and Elekith, and dove in to help bathe her. Tolly draped himself langorously around her shoulders and went to sleep with his tail wound around her neck. She stroked his soft hide with a forefinger, and went on with her search.

"Astonishing," Master Robinton said excitedly, sitting with the others on the wide porch. "I was scared bone dry. My mouth could have been used as Hatching sands." As if reminded of his deprivation, his hand extended toward the wineskin sprawled next to his chair. He poured himself a gobletful and sipped. "Now I have enjoyed firsthand the experience which inspired Menolly to write her Running Song. Although I was safe and secure, and her situation was much more terrifying, I can imagine the rest."

Mirrim and Brekke sat side by side against the outer wall of the Hold with a pot of oil between them, oiling their fire lizards' hides. The little ones hummed with pleasure as the rough patches on their skins were soothed. Grall flitted, shimmering gold in the hot air, watching Brekke daub oil on her mate's belly. Berd's eyes were half-lidded, whirling green with sleepy contentment. Zair saw that others were receiving caresses, and flitted onto his master's shoulder, creeling for attention. Laughing indulgently at his little friend's transparent jealousy, Robinton scratched Zair's head and neck ridges with a gentle hand.

"Another Tradition altered," Lytol said, shaking his head. If he noticed the fire lizards, he never mentioned them. It was enough that he rode dragons now almost daily without falling into the despair that had affected him since the death of his brown dragon Larth many Turns ago. "If it got out that the Master Harper of Pern was watching Threadfall through slitted windows and not sealed safely behind shutters, there would be an outcry."

"Or they'd want a song," F'nor smiled, plumping an armful of ripe fruit onto the table next to the wineskin.

Robinton grinned, and wrapped his long fingers around a redfruit. "Well, it will be our secret, then. As if anyone could do without a breezeway in this weather! But I felt perfectly safe with our skillful protectors here. I wouldn't have missed my chance to see it for anything. As Turns go by, more and more folk have seen Threadfall from out of doors: Menolly by accident, yes, but Piemur . . . possibly design, possibly not. I'm never sure with that particular young man. Once the North is grubbed, it will be much more common than even now, as people see that Thread can be beaten. . . . It enhances greatly my respect for those brave souls who have to go out to fight Thread, so such as I can cower within metal doors and stone walls. When the clumps came into my view, I trembled, I frankly admit, until a green rider—it was you, my dear"—he turned to Mirrim with a half bow— "appeared from nowhere and burned the threat to ash. My heart started beating again." He glanced back at the window of his workroom, and Mirrim could tell that his mind was already making a song out of today's events, just like Menolly would do. She smiled to herself. Harpers were all alike. The wonder was that he hadn't already gotten up to get his gitar.

"We should be without Thread for another two days," Brekke said.

"Well"—Lytol put his cup aside and got to his feet— "there is more work to do. If Thread will stay away, I should go out to the plateau and look into what my assistants have left me. I'm sure Breide has already gone back to work. The cataloguing is not yet finished for this sevenday's discoveries."

"I will take you there," F'nor said, beating Mirrim's offer by half a breath. The tall rider rose to his feet, dusting sand from his trousers. He met her eyes, and Mirrim's fell. She had forgotten about her disgrace. Somehow she had to clear herself of suspicion and find the real thief! But how could she do that when she wasn't permitted to go back to the site? Reppa crooned sympathy from her ridiculous position upside down in Mirrim's lap.

"My thanks, F'nor." Lytol glanced at Robinton, who was gazing out over the sea and humming to himself. "Just a few more days, my old friend."

"What? Oh, I was just thinking," Robinton said, coming back from *between* and taking a juicy bite of redfruit. "Just don't discover *everything* before I can come back."

*Restore all of Mirrim's hit points. If Path has been laced, use numbweed, and remove the Threadscore mark from the record sheet.*

Mirrim sunned herself on the hot beach for a few hours. It had been nearly a sevenday since she and Brekke came to Cove Hold. She was baked brown, and bored. Master Robinton had taken her aside and told her that Lessa had said she was not to go to the wedding at Southern Hold ten days hence. After a stormy cry curled up in Path's wallow, she had attacked her duties with a fierce hand. Every pot in the Hold gleamed; every floor had been sanded, scrubbed, and polished; and the evening meal was laid out and prepared for cooking when it should be wanted. Each day she had worked herself into exhaustion and lay bored and indolent in the sun next to Path. There was nothing more for her to do, unless she wanted to sweep the beach clear of sand.

Master Oldive had visited the day after that Threadfall and pronounced that Master Robinton would be able to stand the extremes of heat and *between* within a couple of days, if he took it easy. Robinton promised him faithfully that he would, protesting that there was nothing wrong with him. Oldive had left, shaking his head with an understanding smile for his friend. Since then, the Hold had been nearly deserted, except on Threadfall days, from sunup to sundown. The heat was not nearly so oppressive as it had been. The next day on which

Threadfall was due, there had been a violent tropical storm so bad they'd put the animals under cover and closed the heavy metal shutters on every window. Mirrim chased the few patches of Thread that endangered the Hold and the wherry pen, but they were heavy with water and already deteriorating before Path's flame took them. She returned to the Hold, feeling battered by the waves of rain, but cool at last. When Brekke and Lytol went out after the storm had passed, there was sticky drowned Thread everywhere. The grubs, fish, and lizards made short work of whatever was left.

And the day after that—today—Robinton had pinned Brekke down to let him go out to the excavations. "I can wait no longer," he declared. "I'm Turning old in ignorance." Throwing her hands up in resignation, she let him go with F'nor on Canth.

Mirrim was forbidden the plateau, as Lessa had insisted, and F'lar had tipped her the hint that she might be best off staying away from Benden and out of Lessa's way for the time being. She felt as though she had been exiled to Cove Hold. It was an attractive place, when you didn't *have* to stay there, Mirrim thought. The Weyrwoman was still fuming about the insult to dragonriders, and blamed Mirrim and Breide equally. She had forgiven the pitch pipe, but there were still the other twelve small items and that bottle! How, Mirrim wondered, could she clear herself from being branded a thief when she couldn't visit the scene of the crime?

Path was asleep in the sun, with Mirrim's three fire lizards curled up behind her eye ridges and in the crevice between her crossed forelimbs. None of them would move until evening. Though the extreme heat had broken, it was still too warm for vigorous activity. Mirrim ran a dry tongue around the inside of her mouth and remembered there was cold fruit juice inside.

Until her eyes adjusted to the cool, dim kitchen, Mirrim had to feel her way around, gathering up a cup and the sought-after jug of juice. The blackness was beginning to sport stars of yellow light behind her sun-dazed eyes, and she could soon see normally again.

"Hello? Master Robinton?" There was a tap at the kitchen door, and a man's voice called out. Mirrim heard feet on the steps, and turned around. "Well, hello." Standing in the doorway was a tall young man, with dark blue eyes in a long face. He had on a broad-brimmed hat woven out of stiff marsh grasses, which he swept off when he saw Mirrim. His hair was fine, ice-pale blond, and swept nearly to his shoulders. He smiled at her, and his gaze was so frankly interested that she blushed.

"Good afternoon," she greeted him politely. "I'm sorry, Master Robinton isn't here. He's up at the plateau."

"Oh. Well, I just stopped by . . ."

"Dannen!" Brekke appeared from the hall. The young man looked up and Brekke rushed over to take his hand. "It *is* you! Oh, Dannen, it's been Turns!"

"Brekke!" He was obviously as pleased and astonished to see her. "Well, I guess I was just a little smaller when you saw me last."

"Indeed you were," Brekke smiled. "It's been more than ten Turns. Welcome! What brings you to Cove Hold?"

Dannen pulled a satchel from his shoulder. "Herbs, new kinds, for Master Oldive. Klah bark from a stand of trees I found. Very potent, Master Robinton'll like it. Feather herb, golddust fern, feverwort, and a few others to fill out the medicine supply here. I stop by here occasionally to get a square meal, talk to people instead of plants, and to sleep under a roof. My runnerbeast's in your stable. But who is this young lady? One of the Harper's students?"

"This is Mirrim, my fosterling. Except she doesn't really need my fostering anymore."

"Indeed not," Dannen said, looking her over with admiration. "Which dragonrider is here? I saw a green dragon on the beach."

"That's Path," Mirrim said, a little irked. "She's mine."

"Yours? A fighting dragon? But I thought that women only Impressed queens?"

Brekke said quietly but firmly, "Path wanted her. And the dragon is always right." She turned to Mirrim. "Dannen was *my* foster mother's blood son, back in the Farmcrafthold. He was a genius with plants."

"Thank you." Dannen swept her a bow with his wide hat. "I still am, I hope." He told them how he had come to the Southern Continent with other young, adventurous men and women, who'd been promised land to hold by Lord Holder Toric. "My father is a Farmcraftmaster in Telgar. He's let us know, blood and foster children alike, that he has no thoughts of dying early, so all of us have to find places of our own, and stop casting greedy eyes at his. One of my sisters went into the Weavercraft Hall, one was found on Search by Ista Weyr. She hasn't Impressed yet, but she likes it in the lower caverns; and my brother, Roak, the heir, lives with Father, a ruddy stern taskmaster he is, bless him. Here I am, as you see me. When I made journeyman, I came south, to a farmcraftsman in Southern Hold. When we worked out what best I could do for the craft, I elected to search in the wild for botanical specimens."

"You gather plants?" Mirrim asked.

"Not exactly." Dannen wrinkled his nose as if Mirrim had suggested that he ate seaweed. "I look for new plants, or new strains of ones we use in the North. Sometimes I gather seeds, sometimes take cuttings of plants. Sometimes I just leave 'em alone, marking where they grow for future need. What I want are hardier strains, better tasting, stronger juices, to breed with the Northern plants. It's all for the sake of my craft—I'm a Southerner, now. I've lived outside through Threadfalls you couldn't possibly imagine—" Dannen broke off, ashamed of bragging. "So sorry. I'd forgotten you were dragonfolk. My doings are probably sour wine compared to yours."

Brekke smiled sadly and turned away. Mirrim was a little cross that this young oaf had so offhandedly hurt Brekke's feelings. Hadn't everyone on Pern heard about the battle and death of the two queen dragons? She changed the subject, hoping to distract Brekke. "It's a hot day. Would you like some cold fruit juice?" She reached for a couple of earthen cups.

Dannen's face broke into a wide, white smile. He realized he had made a mistake, and was grateful for any escape from his folly. There *had* been some bad news concerning Brekke Turns back, but as it hadn't to do with any of his interests, he'd forgotten the details. "Oh, I'd love some. My tongue is dry as a log. I've been dreaming about a cool drink for days. Even the water in the streams is warm. This heat'd kill you, wouldn't it? I was glad for the rain yesterday." He accepted a cupful and drained it, held it out for more. "By the way, what are *you* doing down here, Brekke?"

"Attending Master Robinton, of course." Brekke shooed them out into the sun. "Let Mirrim tell you all about it."

Leaving Brekke to organize the herbs, replenishing the Cove's and her own store of healing supplies, Mirrim took Dannen down to the beach. "Come and meet Path," she offered, dragging him away from Brekke, whose mind was already seeking to occupy itself in activity.

Dannen accepted with pleasure. "I don't get to meet too many dragons up close," he admitted regretfully. "I'm so seldom in the Hold. Did I miss something back there with Brekke?"

Mirrim stared at him for a moment, then decided he wasn't feigning ignorance. In a few sentences, she summed up the tragedy of the queen dragons' deaths. Dannen whistled through his teeth.

"Put my foot in it, didn't I? I remember now. How stupid I was not to remember it. I'd heard about it at the time. Well," he said, changing the topic, "this is Path, eh? What a magnificent shade of green she is. She's quite a beauty, isn't she?"

Mirrim smiled fondly at Path, who roused slightly when she heard them coming down toward her but opened only the outermost lids of her eyes. "Yes she is, my lazy one."

Two fire lizards, a blue and a gold, flew creeling out of the trees when Dannen appeared. He waved them over to him, smiling. "There are my little friends." Mirrim guessed by their size that they were no more than a Turn in age.

"I found the clutch at the end of last summer," he continued, fondling the two little creatures who landed on his shoulders and were whistling in each of his ears. "These were the only two I could save when they began Hatching. It was a terrible sight, with them half starving and the others killing each other for meat." Mirrim nodded, remembering the chaotic fire lizard Hatchings she'd witnessed. "I had very little food to offer, and these got it all. This is Somi and this blue fellow's Kern. They're good company, and they look after each other when I don't want to be bothered with 'em. I nursed a few for folk at Southern Hold who didn't know what to do when the little beasts got hurt. Fire lizards seem to trust me."

His certainly did. They looked perfectly content, even with the gigantic form of Path nearby, who raised a sleepy head to look at them. Mirrim called Reppa, Lok, and Tolly to her, and they started an aerial dance of greeting for Somi and Kern, who bounded from the farmcrafter's shoulders to join them. Dannen looked at them in amazement. They hovered in the air before them for a moment, and then swooped away, chirping and calling. "Are all three yours?"

"Oh, yes," she said. "But I haven't the greatest handful. You ought to meet my friend Menolly. She has ten."

"I've heard of her. She's as unique as yourself, being the first female journeyman in the Harper Hall in hundreds of Turns. I've often wanted to meet her and ask how she gets so many to behave. I've got my hands full with two." They were interrupted by a stream of raucous chittering from Somi, as she tried to muster the gathering fair of fire lizards into some kind of order. Dannen grinned. "She's a bossy little brute, but I love her. I've tried playing a pipe to get them to sing, but they're too lazy. They peep along, then they quit."

"Just keep playing," Mirrim advised him. "Yours are still very young. They have a mighty short attention span. Besides, Menolly just *lives* music. Hers picked it up early because that's all they ever heard." She rubbed an ear vigorously, remembering several impromptu early morning concertos while she and Menolly and the others had been down here last Turn.

Dannen chuckled. He had a warm tenor voice that made a song out of his merriment. "I will," he promised, his deep blue eyes smiling at her. She felt her heart leap. He was very handsome, except for the near-white hair, which made him look many Turns older than he was. She decided that he must be as old as she was or a turn or two older at most. Not that she wanted to seem eager, but he was so nice, she thought she would like to get to know him. If he could only stay for a while!

Path responded favorably to Dannen. He knew, without prompting, where dragons liked to be caressed. She moved her great head slightly so that his scratching fingers would be in just exactly the right spot on the top of her sensitive eye ridges. Soon, her eyes were half lidded. Mirrim was a little jealous of Path's unquestioning approval of this stranger.

"So," Mirrim asked, with forced casualness, "when will you be leaving here?" She turned red instantly. That was discourteous. It wasn't exactly what she meant to say. "I mean—I don't . . ."

He was amused, but even his chuckle was kindly. "I'll stay around as long as you'll let me, but I do have work to do. I took a turning in the jungle about four days back that brought me here. I decided I needed to socialize more than I needed to collect tuft grasses. It's just about time for the tuft grass to be at its best. When powdered, the roots are good for aching joints. You have to catch them when they're full of sap, but in this heat they'll have all dried up and died off long before I can get to them." Dannen sighed, squinting up at the greeny-yellow sun whose rays were beating down heavily on their heads. "And sweet onions, too. They're about to go to seed, and I cross-pollinated some wild ones this spring southeast of here with pollen from onions from Telgar. The mix should grow big, round roots with a sort of sweet taste instead of the bitter kind that makes your eyes tear. I'd never come to Cove Hold this way before, and now I guess I'll have to wait 'til next Turn to find out how my experiment turned out. It'll be too late by the time I get there. It's about a quarter of the way between here and the big mountain. Foolish of me, when I *knew* how much time I had left."

"Is there a field or a flat place large enough for a dragon to land near your picking ground?" Mirrim asked speculatively.

"I think so. I marked a big open hilltop about an hour's walk away." Dannen eyed her. "Why?"

"Well . . . we've nothing to do until next Threadfall. If I were back in Benden, I'd have tasks in plenty. When I think of all the cleaning up I'll have to do when we get back . . . ! We can go as far as you need," Mirrim let her implied offer sink in, "because Brekke can always be-speak Path if she wants us."

Dannen's smile flashed again, and Mirrim again was struck by how attractive he was. She patted at her hair a little self-consciously.

"I'd truly appreciate that, Mirrim. Only, I'm used to working alone. I wouldn't want to put you off by my ways."

"If you're in as much of a hurry as you say, you should welcome an extra pair of hands. Not to mention a faster way to travel."

"Oh, but I'm accustomed to having my runner with

me, and he'd pine being left behind." He looked sheep-ish. "There isn't any way Path could carry him, is there?"

"Not that he would enjoy," Mirrim said tartly. "Except for riders, Path only carries animals she eats. Most runners are afraid of dragons."

"Oh, not this one. He was raised near the Southern Weyr. The beastcrafthold is careful to get their runner herds used to seeing dragons, so they won't go mad when the wings pass overhead." Mirrim couldn't understand why anyone would prefer a wherry-necked, spindly-legged, coarse-furred runner to a lithe, shimmering, soft-skinned dragon, but she didn't want to question her guest's choice. "I could ride him, and you could fly on ahead, if you want."

"I'm not sure you could ride him that way if you wanted to. The area south of here is full of fissures and ravines," Mirrim said promptly. "If you want to come with me, we can pass over all that. Do you want to fly a little over the jungle, Path?"

*Certainly. It is a nice day.*

"And it would take us only a couple of hours to fly the distance it would take you days to walk there," Mirrim said temptingly. She wasn't sure why she was pushing as hard as she was to go plant gathering, which could be grueling work, and with a complete stranger, too. But, she reasoned, Brekke knew him, and if she, Mirrim, didn't get out of Cove Hold for at least a while, she would explode with frustration. Hunting for herbs with Dannen would keep her mind off her dilemma.

"Well . . ." Dannen looked half-persuaded, but still undecided. Mirrim dashed back to the Hold, and found her flying gear and took down fighting straps for two.

"I've let Brekke know where we're going," she said briskly when she returned, dumping her burdens on the sand. Path got to her feet and stretched lazily as Mirrim tested the straps for strength and slipped them about her neck. "I have three pots of numbweed, some bandages, rope, a jug of cold klah, and some meatrolls. Brekke says if you walked that way, you'll need to take a detour that's twice as long to the flat hill. She will look after your runner. He's got plenty of fodder. What else do you need?"

Dannen laughed heartily. "Only my collecting sacks," he smiled. "You sure are efficient."

Mirrim beamed. He couldn't have complimented her more than if he'd said she was beautiful. Although she wouldn't have objected to that.

While Path flew direct, there was plenty of time to get to know one another better. Although, as Dannen confessed, he had never ridden on a dragon before, he was relaxed, and enjoyed pointing out from above landmarks which he recognized.

"Doesn't look so hard to get around from up here," he said, leaning his chin into Mirrim's shoulder. "But it's a long way down." Claiming it was for his security, he tightened his arms around her waist.

Not that Mirrim objected to the closeness. He was a polite and entertaining companion, and he knew all the gossip and changes going on at Southern Hold and Southern Weyr. He seemed also to be immune to her famous acerbity. After a while, she relaxed in his company, and her bitter comments grew fewer and less vitriolic. After all, she wasn't mad at *him*. Mirrim simply felt that she was unimportant and very far away from things at Cove Hold. Living at the most important Weyr, she was in the center of all things. Whatever happened on Pern was reported to Benden. She needed to clear her name, and have the freedom once again to range Pern as she chose.

Dannen coaxed her to tell him the whole story, promising against her concerns that he would keep it all to himself. He was sympathetic. "The Weyr wouldn't like it noised about that riders were being considered thieves. If I hear anything that might help, I'll come forward with it for you. You can trust me."

In gratitude, she squeezed his hand where it rested on

her belt buckle. "My thanks, Dannen," she said. "I'm sure I can."

The lush vegetation below them rarely broke, except to reveal shining bands of rivers, the deeper green of marshlands, or the bare, dry tan of a precipice. "I'm glad we didn't take my runner," Dannen confessed. "There's no way he'd ever get across that one," he pointed to a deep, sharp-edged chasm. "My stomping ground's just ahead. It's a popular place because it's easy for foot travelers to find. The trails are well marked, though the way things grow down here, they don't stay open very well. You have to burn them through."

"With firestone?" Mirrim inquired. "Do you have dragons blaze your trails?"

Dannen chuckled at her pun. "No, but I wish we did. It's back-wrenching work. It's possible we may meet some of my beastcraft or farmcraft friends out here in the jungle, too. This season's the one when you get the most plants maturing. It's too hot for most stinging insects."

"I'm certainly glad of that!" Mirrim agreed.

As Path circled around toward a flat hill which protruded between groves of huge trees and fern bogs, Mirrim heard a sound, a roaring whine, begin from far away to the west, and move toward them at a tremendous speed, gaining in volume. Following the sound, the very trees and rocks danced a staccato tattoo.

"Up, Path!" The green dragon turned her nose upward and soared farther into the sky.

"What's wrong?" Dannen shouted, hanging on tightly.

"Earth-shake!" Mirrim yelled back, for now the sound was rumbling deafeningly around them.

Dannen was impressed. "I'd never seen one from the air before. That was amazing! But it's just a tremor," he said. "I've been in hundreds of these. The land here is fissured clean down to the core. This is a small shake. It will be over in a moment."

Dannen's prediction was correct. As they watched, the shaking passed under them and ran toward the east. Path flew along its line, and then doubled back as soon as it had moved far enough away so that the hill was no longer moving.

"Well, we can't stay up here all day."

"No, indeed," agreed Mirrim, and requested Path to land.

Path set them down on the plain. Dannen leaped off her neck and offered to help Mirrim down. She nearly slapped his hand away, but realized it was only courtesy, not a suggestion that she was inept. She put her hand in his and stepped down from her dragon's shoulder with dignity. Mirrim's and Dannen's fire lizards had peeled away from them as soon as they had landed, and, from what Mirrim could see, were dancing gaily in the air with their wild cousins. Not too many strange fire lizards appeared, and they all stayed well away from Path.

Path tasted a few shoots, but decided that she didn't want grasses or herbs. She told Mirrim she would rather take a nap. She stretched out on the dry hilltop with her back turned to the sun. "Well," Dannen said, letting out a deep breath and rasping his hands together in anticipation of his task, "are you going back to the Hold? I'm grateful you brought me. Is there any reason why you should hurry away?" He glanced at her hopefully.

"I don't know," Mirrim admitted. "I'm not really sure why I came."

"You were in a rut, and you need to figure out what you want to do about your problem. Now, I've found that the best thing for coping with troubles is to do some hard work."

Mirrim made a face. "I tried that. I scrubbed the floors so hard I made them thinner."

"This'll be different for you," Dannen insisted. "Botany's an interesting experience, being a botanist. Once you get the knack of choosing the best plants and using your analytical faculties, you often get a clearer perspective on your own concerns. I often take a walk to put my mind in order. Here." He handed her a folded carry-sack. "Place any specimens you gather carefully in here, and we'll go over them tonight. And if you find anything unique, mark where it came from, and the crafthold will bless your name. But watch where you go. There are dangerous plants as well as animals down here in Southern."

"I know!" Mirrim replied acidly. "I've lived in Southern."

"So you have," Dannen assented cheerfully.

"Are you coming with me, Path?" Mirrim asked, though she could see the green dragon was already making herself comfortable in the long grass.

*If you do not mind, I will stay here. That was a long flight.* Path let out a huge breath and began to close the triple lids over her eyes one at a time.

"Of course not, dear one. Rest well. We will be back by dark." She signed to Dannen that she was ready to start out. He immediately set out walking down the south face of the hill.

"If we're lucky and there aren't any more aftershocks, shall we try down that slope out by the river? I'm looking for goldvine. It's good as an eye remedy."

Mirrim nodded, and refrained from mentioning that she knew all about the medicinals, and that she'd gathered goldvine before. And pink root. And feather herb. And red wort. And numbweed. Especially numbweed.

They stumped down the slope. Mirrim found a well-grown clump of young feather herb, which Dannen exclaimed over happily. "I want to try culturing these in Northern soil. Probably they won't grow as large . . ."

"They're already far larger than most Northern plants." Mirrim turned the plants in her hands while Dannen bound the roots in a broad leaf with a tie plaited of grass. "I want some of these for the herb garden in Benden Weyr. It's colder there, but I bet I can nurture them properly. The slope is protected from the prevailing winds." Manora would be so grateful for such healthy herbs.

"Of course! Take what you want. We're searching

together," Dannen said, putting a companionable arm around her, "so we share the spoils." Reassured, Mirrim looked up at him. From the look in his eyes, she decided that he was about to kiss her. She wasn't prepared to allow him any intimacy yet, if ever. In panic, she twisted out of his grasp and pointed ahead, ignoring the hurt expression on his face. "Look! Goldvines!"

At the bottom of the hill, several mature vines visible wound around the boles of tall fern-top trees. Dannen pronounced them just right for his purposes, and began carefully to unwind one from its tree. Tucking the coil into his bag, Dannen moved off eastward into the undergrowth without a word.

Mirrim looked around, and decided that Dannen was right about his solitary habits. She would be better off making her own explorations and not bothering him. That is, if he even remembered she existed. She noticed that there were two fairly wide openings in the undergrowth opposite where Dannen had disappeared. To her surprise, when she peered into them, she found they did not open out onto a clearing, but instead led to paths going off in diverging directions, one going due west and the other angling southwest. The thick greenery prevented her from seeing too far. She drew her knife to cut through any stubborn vine or branch that might bar her way.

The smell of brackish water assailed her nose from the path to the southwest, warning her that the land might be boggy in that direction. The other path was far more overgrown, though she caught tempting glances of herb clumps between the waving shrubs. In the burgeoning garden of Southern Continent, either held promise. Mirrim judged which path would yield more. Perhaps she'd find a ripe redfruit along the way.

*If she wants to try the path to the southwest, turn to section 61.*

*If she wants to try the path to the west, turn to section 53.*

# * 32 *

Mirrim moaned. She had ducked, but not quickly enough. Thread had sunk in at the back of her flying helmet, cutting right through the thick wherhide into her scalp. They had flashed *between,* so the Thread was no longer there, but the agony of its bite made her head spin. "No," she muttered over the flying straps, which were the only things she could see clearly through the haze of pain. "My head aches. Path . . . ?"

But Path was already wheeling, and tilting her wings to let air spill out to make the landing as gentle as possible. Mirrim was hardly aware of the hands which helped her from her dragon's neck ridge. Threadfall was over for now, and Brekke was there on the beach with numbweed and fellis juice. F'fej had been laced across the wrist, and D'dot's Elekith had his tail-fork singed, but Mirrim was by far the worst off. Robinton helped Lytol and F'nor carry her inside the Hold to her room.

"You sleep as long as you need to," Brekke said sternly, taking the cup of fellis-laced fruit juice away from Mirrim's lips. "Most of the time healers make the worst patients. You'll be good for me, won't you?"

Mirrim could hardly open her jaw to reply. The bandages covering her scalp wound and passing around her forehead and chin were too tight. Robinton sat down beside her and patted her hand. His baritone chuckle was friendly, though his eyes were worried.

"We'll be company for each other for a while," he said in a warm tone. "Until we're both ready to fly again."

*Turn to section 29.*

## * 33 *

Path crooned deep in her throat, fretting about the pain, but protested that it was only a scratch. Mirrim patted her gently on the neck ridge. "Tell F'nor we're all right," she said. "We're going back to the Hold now, and I'll bathe you in numbweed."

They turned a gentle circle in the air, and Path set them down on the beach. Mirrim scrambled down off the neck ridge to examine Path's outstretched leg. It wasn't as serious as she had feared, and she sighed with relief. "Now you soak that well," Mirrim instructed her. "As soon as it's good and clean I'll coat it in numbweed. It won't even need a bandage." Ignoring the firestone stench, she hugged the dragon's big head to her. "You're the best, most skillful fighter in all the Weyrs."

Path's eyes whirled.

*Turn to section 31.*

## * 34 *

The cold blackness chilled the skin of her face and scalp to wax, but there was no feeling of Thread cracking off from burnt skin. They had eluded it.

Emerging into the same airspace over the dock, they

saw a shower of little black particles being swept away by the salt wind, and Canth swooping low enough to catch fish in his claws, his fire spent.

"Are you all right?" F'nor sent through Canth.

"Yes!" Mirrim sent back.

"Fall's over," D'dot yelled, following Canth down. "Last one back is a wherry!"

*Turn to section 31.*

## * **35** *

Mirrim moved closer and stretched her hand out to touch the needlethorn's surface.

*Roll 3 D6.*

*If the total is less than or equal to Mirrim's value for Wisdom/Luck, turn to section 39.*

*If the total is greater than Mirrim's value for Wisdom/Luck, turn to section 37.*

## * **36** *

The wherry flew at her, claws poised to tear at her face. Mirrim ducked, swiping with her spear at the creature as it went by. It caught no more than a few strands of her hair. Her fire lizards exploded from behind her, arrowing after the creature as it wheeled and dodged, trying to evade them. The wherry's mighty wings looked stronger than the fire lizards' delicate pinions, but they matched it without trouble. Reppa and Lok tormented it by clawing and biting at its back and scalp, forcing it to twist away from its human target.

Screaming, the huge bird turned and flew higher. When it reached the treetops, it stooped, bearing down on Mirrim with all its talons outstretched. The greens shrieked frantically.

Mirrim stood fast. She didn't have a chance if she turned to run. The wherry would sink all four sets of claws into her back. She braced the spear on her hip, extending the point well above her head. Reppa and Lok followed it down, trying to distract it, but it was blood mad. Mirrim wondered what had happened to Tolly, and worried that the wherry had wounded him when she wasn't looking.

Suddenly the little brown fire lizard appeared out of *between* right under Mirrim's nose. He surged upward, moving straight for the wherry's eyes, shrilling a cry that went clear out of the range of human hearing. Distracted, the wherry flapped its wings to recover momentum, and batted Tolly to one side. He had managed to draw blood, but the wherry wasn't completely blinded. It turned and dove for the glinting metal blade of Mirrim's knife.

# Section 36

Unable to see clearly what it was attacking, the wherry grabbed for the knife blade. As the claws of one of its forelimbs closed on the point, it realized it had made a serious mistake. Furious, it battered at the spear shaft with its wings until it had been knocked out of Mirrim's hands. She reached out to retrieve it, and the full weight of an angry wherry hit her full in the chest. With a cry, she overbalanced, dragging the wherry with her. Together, they fell into the pool.

Sharp claws raked her side and belly, drawing blood. The cold water stung in the gashes. Mirrim gasped and kicked furiously, shoving away from the wherry. It was lucky she had taken her boots off. The pool was deep enough to drown her if she had been weighted down. She paddled to the side of the pond and began to pull herself out. The wherry flapped stupidly, and made as if to run up her back over the pool's edge. Mirrim rolled out of its way as it floundered up the bank. Evidently it felt overmatched, and was trying to flee. Mirrim was happy to let it go.

She lay on the bank, clutching her tunic to her wounded side, mopping at the blood that stained its fabric. The claw marks were not as deep as she had feared, but she still felt faint. The wherry hauled itself up onto the stones, shook water out of its wings and tail, and flung itself ungracefully into the sky. Mirrim sighed with relief as it flew out of sight. She closed her eyes and rested her head on the spongy cress.

*If Mirrim still has some hit points, turn to section 43.*

*If her hit points are down to 0, turn to section 29.*

# * **37** *

The plant looked soft and squashy, its pale blue-green surface thickly speckled with the spine pores. Like many plants, it seemed to have three distinct faces, almost triangular when seen from the top. In fact, it looked almost like a head. The resemblance was carried further because one side of its "face" was bare of needles. Mirrim avoided touching any of the long spines and stroked the skin of the plant. It had tickly little hairs that were invisible from any distance. She wondered if it would be difficult to extract the needles from its face. There were so many, she'd surely get scratched.

Without warning, the plant sprayed her with hundreds of needlelike thorns, denuding the side facing her. In astonishment, she looked down at herself. Long brown spines hung quivering in her flesh. She was too shocked to let out more than a small cry. The pain made her catch her breath. The needles were so sharp and thin that the ache was more of an amplified itch than anything else, radiating through her arm, shoulder, and chest and making her twitch in reaction. "Poison. They must be unripe." Her other hand, which had been curled in her lap, mercifully escaped the barrage, guarded as it was by her wherhide-covered knees. The injured hand was shaking, but she didn't dare take hold of it with her other hand. Very slowly, she plucked the needles out of her skin one by one.

*Roll 2 D6 for damage, and subtract the total from Mirrim's hit points.*

*If her hit points are reduced to 0, turn to section 44.*

*If she still has hit points left, turn to section 42.*

## \* **38** \*

Beyond a stand of redfruit trees, Mirrim stopped to listen. There were only jungle sounds, birds and animals, and the sounds of trees swaying in the wind. Dannen must be pretty far away by now. Well, he had to come back this way eventually, so if she stayed around here, they'd find each other.

There were no roads or regular paths, but there did seem to be routes blazed in the bark of the largest trees. This was a much-used trail. It was wide enough for a wheeled cart to pass, or three men walking abreast. Though not quite wide enough for a dragon, Mirrim smiled. The branches had been hacked off along the path at two man-heights, so possibly gather-wagons, or the moving homes of the Holdless, made their way along here occasionally.

At the first turning, Mirrim found a large rock to sit on. Her bag, with her findings and the meat for the evening meal, was getting heavy. She plopped it down next to her and rubbed the muscles in her thighs.

Reppa and Tolly swooped in on her at once for a caress, and Mirrim gathered them both to her before they started a squabble for precedence. "Foolish creatures," she said fondly. Lok, jealous, settled onto the carry-sack and began to paw through it to get to the meat.

"No!" Mirrim commanded, handing away the green fire lizard. Tolly and Reppa started arguing with their fair-mate, and in the resultant spat, they knocked into the sack, which disappeared behind the rock. "Now see what you've done," she reproved them, and jumped off the rock. She stepped around behind and retrieved the sack from the brambles. Where the sack had rested, something shone out at her from its hiding place. Carefully, she picked it up.

It was a small cylinder made of metal. Mirrim turned it over in her hands. She didn't recognize the shape or size as anything specific. It was made of bronze or brass, since there was no sign of corrosion, or in fact any clue to how long it had lain there. She shook it. The cylinder was hollow, and there was something inside. When she twisted the two ends, a thread-thin line around the middle pulled apart, and it separated into hollow halves. Inside, Mirrim discovered five mark pieces and a piece of hide. "It's someone's hoard," she said. Each of the marks were different: a Smithcraft two-marker; two halves, one from the Weavercraft and one from the Minecraft; and two one-markers, Baker- and Harpercrafts. She unfolded the slip of hide, which was an old piece, much scraped and overwritten. Most distinguishable was the word "more." The rest of the writing was unintelligible. "I wonder what it means," Mirrim said curiously. She folded the hide away and tucked the marks back into place. "I can't take someone's property, but what a curious place to leave it. I wish I knew whom it belonged to."

She replaced the cylinder where she had found it, and pulled the bracken over it again.

Mirrim left the rock and followed the blazings the easy way around a stand of klah bark trees. To her amazement, she found a runnerbeast tethered to a low bush. There was no one else in sight. That the beast had been here for some hours, she could tell by how far the runner had pulled its tether, trying to get closer to fresh fodder. The foliage around it had been nibbled to roots. Mirrim wondered who would be this far away from civilization.

# Section 38

Dannen said some of his fellow farmcrafters and beastcrafters came out here from Southern. Perhaps the marks belonged to one of them.

The runner let out a conversational cry that surprised her. They eyed each other, but the runner gave way first. Snuffing the air, it backed suspiciously away from Mirrim, its ears laid back to its skull. It must smell Path, Mirrim decided. She plucked up a handful of shoots and offered them at arm's length to the beast.

At first it stood well back, then gradually the broken blades of tender greenery wafted their scent to its nostrils. Gradually, carefully, it stepped toward her, muzzle out, and began to munch her offering hungrily. She stroked its rough forelock and tall ears, making her way softly back to the saddle ring where a bag was fastened. Perhaps the contents would give her a clue as to who had abandoned the poor thing.

The runner finished her handful, and nudged her legs with its nose, pushing her out of the way so it could eat more. She undid the rope and led the beast to another tree, where it began to eat with gusto. By the quantity of weeds and grasses it could tuck away with each mouthful, Mirrim judged that it had been there long enough to miss a meal or two. She undid the bag and peered inside. A long, multicolored, wingless lizard sprang up at her face. "Aaaahhh!" she cried, dropping the sack in shock. Before the bag fell to the ground, the lizard clambered out, up over her arms, scrambled over her shoulder and up the nearest tree. Mirrim felt her heart racing, feeling the scratches the creature left on her hands and shoulders. Who would keep a lizard in a bag? Suddenly she heard a rustling close by.

"Hello? I say, is there anyone here?" she called.

Dannen's voice responded with a distant-faint query. "Mirrim? Anything wrong?" but there was someone closer than he was.

"Hello?" A man's voice, behind and below ear level. She spun, trying to see through the thick brush who could be addressing her.

"Hello?" the voice called again, weakly.

Mirrim crashed forward, pushing branches out of her way, until she all but stepped on a man, who was lying in a horribly contorted position on the forest floor. His light brown hair was plastered to his face with sweat, and his brows over dark brown eyes were drawn together on a concentrated forehead.

"Young lady, help me!"

Mirrim dropped to her knees beside him. "What happened to you?" she asked, feeling his ruddy forehead and cheeks for fever. There were snake venoms that affected the victim by twisting his spine into a spiral or a hoop. He wasn't warm, so it was probably not disease.

"Fell out of a tree onto my back. Earth-shake caught me while I was capturing a lizard. Vicious monster, just like a miniature wher. I collect odd species. Ooh!"

Mirrim ran experienced fingers down his spine, finding the swellings just above his right hip. "Well, you're bruising here but the nerves are still intact, which is good. If there was no feeling, you'd be in worse trouble."

"There's too much feeling," the man complained. "When I feel it, it starts to jerk and twitch all by itself. I can't stop it!"

"That's bad. It could make your back worse."

"Help me. There it goes!"

And, indeed, his leg began to twitch and jump. Under Mirrim's concerned gaze, the convulsion became stronger, and it was apparent by his grimaces that he was in considerable pain. For just a moment she hesitated, worrying that she could hurt him, but his back would get worse if she didn't. With all of her weight, she sat down on his leg at the thigh, and pressed the palms of her hands to force the knee down. In a few minutes, the jerking ceased, and then Mirrim knelt by the man's head.

"By heaven, that's better, young lady. When I—"

At that moment, Dannen came crashing through the undergrowth. In his right hand was his collecting bag, but in the left was a rough club made of a tree branch.

# Section 38

"Mirrim, what's the matter? You didn't answer. I heard you call out—why, Joras!"

"Dannen?" the man asked. "What are you doing here? And who is this most capable young lady?"

"My name is Mirrim, green rider of Path from Benden Weyr," she said, accepting the compliment. At least she could pride herself for her nursing, if not her plant-gathering skills. "I've worked closely with healers. Dannen, Joras has seriously injured his back. I don't think it's broken, but it would be risky to move him. He needs a healer."

"I'm woefully far away from one," the man said wryly. "I tried pulling myself back to my beast to send a message back to Southern. By the First Shell, I'm glad you appeared."

Mirrim chewed on a fingertip. "If Brekke was here, she could do something."

"But Brekke isn't here. What can we do?" Dannen pleaded.

Mirrim looked speculatively at the man and Dannen and considered what would be best.

*If she should try to fix the man's back herself, turn to section 48.*

*If she sends Dannen back for Brekke and stays with Joras, turn to section 51.*

*If she leaves Dannen there with him and goes for Brekke, turn to section 55.*

# * **39** *

"Of course, it might be poisonous," she continued thoughtfully, and let her hand drop. As Mirrim moved closer to the plant to get a better look at its peculiar surface, a squat shape exploded out of the brush and scooted past her. Mirrim jumped back, her eyes wide with surprise. It was a whersport, lying almost invisible in the grass, probably frightened by her shadow passing over it. The little beast, terrified by the big human, dashed right in front of her feet. To its ill fortune, it touched the spines of the needler.

Instantly hundreds of spines shot out and embedded themselves into the unlucky creature's side, some even penetrating right through its neck. A few of the thorns flew over its back and hissed into the leather of Mirrim's trousers. She stared down at them in amazement. The whersport carried on running for a short distance on pure momentum, but it was finished. It collapsed in a heap before it got all the way out of the clearing.

"So that's what they meant," Mirrim said in a small voice. "By the Egg, I almost touched it myself." She plucked out the few thorns in her pants legs and looked at them closely. The Healers at Southern prized them, because the thorns were hollow right through, and could be used for intravenous injections. She had given injections herself, but she had never seen the thorn in its native state. Northern needlethorns were not as big or as well developed as this monstrosity. She looked around for the *ging* tree, which always grew nearby where needlethorn bushes appeared. The huge green tree sported thousands of dark-tipped buds. "Well," Mirrim said, recovering her wits and assuming a businesslike tone. "If those flowers aren't open yet, the bush is still dangerous." Needlethorns could suck the juices out of a creature. They were omnivorous, and somewhat toxic. Mirrim shuddered as she realized how near she had come to being its victim. She saw how the whersport died, and she treated the needler with considerable respect.

*Turn to section 41.*

## * **40** *

The wherry flew at her, claws poised to tear at her face. Mirrim ducked, swiping with her spear at the creature as it went by. The wherry caught no more than a few strands of her hair, but her spear only grazed along its side. The fire lizards exploded from behind her, arrowing after the creature as it wheeled and dodged in the air a few feet from the dragonrider, trying to evade them. The wherry's mighty wings looked stronger than the fire lizards' delicate pinions, but they could keep up with it without trouble. Reppa and Lok tormented it by clawing and biting at its back and scalp, forcing it to twist away from its human target.

Screaming, the huge bird turned and flew higher. When it reached the treetops, it stooped, bearing down on Mirrim with all its talons outstretched. The greens shrieked frantically.

Mirrim stood fast. She didn't have a chance if she turned to run. The wherry would sink all four sets of claws into her back. She crouched and braced the spear on the ground, extending the point well above her head.

Reppa and Lok followed it down, trying to distract it, but the wherry was blood mad. Mirrim wondered what had happened to Tolly, and worried that the wherry had wounded him when she wasn't looking.

Suddenly, the little brown fire lizard appeared out of *between* right under Mirrim's nose. He surged upwards, making straight for the wherry's eyes, shrilling a cry that went clear out of the range of human hearing. Distracted, the wherry flapped its wings to recover momentum, and grabbed for Tolly with its front claws. Tolly cheekily swooped in close to the wherry's breast, and sweeping upwards, scratched at its eyes. The wherry reached for him, but ended up battering its own beak. Tolly flashed *between,* and reappeared over the wherry's head, be-laboring the back of its skull with all four of his paws. Mirrim watched Tolly twist and soar like a miniature brown dragon battling Thread. She was afraid to thrust her spear for fear of hitting him. Still crouching, the dragonrider cheered him on, shouting encouragement. Never had she believed Lessa's com-plaints about 'useless' fire lizards, and she never would!

Half blinded, the wherry flew in circles, pursuing Tolly around and around to the left with its good eye. Down stained with blood drifted on the breeze as the fire lizards pecked and gouged at their enemy. The fight moved down gradually near to where Mirrim stood on the bank, trying to figure out where she could strike without hurting any of her friends. If anyone she knew had been with her, she would have put on a stoic face and tried to pretend she was unconcerned with the battle going on above her head, but as she was alone, she could let her fear show. The bird was trying to escape, now, but the fire lizards harried it from all sides. It was on the defensive now, pushing away its enemies with feet and wings.

Suddenly, the wherry smacked into the stand of reeds which loomed up on its blind side, and fell out of the sky practically on top of Mirrim. She sprang back and

# Section 40

shortened her grip on the spear and put her weight behind it. The crude weapon plunged into the wherry's heart and the bird convulsed in agony. The wherry surged upwards along the shaft of her improvised spear, too mean and stupid to know it should die. It pushed up Mirrim's spear until they were nearly face to face. Upright, the wherry stood as tall as the dragonrider. Mirrim goggled and tried to throw away the spear. It clawed at her before she could drop the shaft. She ducked, but its talons tore right through the shoulder of her thin blouse and into the flesh below. Mirrim screamed.

In fury, she found the strength to pick up the spear again. She stuck a boot against its breast for leverage and tore the blade out of the wherry's body. The creature collapsed backwards. Above her, the fire lizards shrieked as Mirrim sank the blade in again and again until the wherry stopped moving.

Mirrim let the spear fall and stood panting. Her fire lizards settled on the rock near her, emitting inquisitive cheeps.

"I'm all right," she assured them tartly. "I've just got to rest."

After a few breaths, she cleaned the blood off with a strip torn from her shirt dipped in pondwater. Prying her knife out of her makeshift spear, Mirrim went to work gutting the wherry. She dumped the entrails on the ground for her friends. Her shoulder hurt, but the wound had bled clean and had already clotted.

"I can't carry this whole bird back with me," Mirrim explained, as she cut free the breast meat and wings, and wrapped them in leaves. "It's too big. The rest'll make nice gleanings for some other scavengers. Wherries are so stupid, they even eat each other."

Before she headed back to the hill, she bent over the pond to take a long drink and wash her hot face. "You," she pointed at her reflection, "were nearly wherry bait."

*Turn to section 38.*

## * **41** *

She passed through stands of trees, following a familiar sweet scent. Unless she was very mistaken, there were redfruit trees growing nearby. A snack after her midday labors would be welcome. To her delight, the fruit trees were easily found, only steps down the excuse for a trail into which Dannen had disappeared. She pulled down a few of the ripe fruits and bit into one. The tangy juice refreshed her mouth and throat. It smelled of sweetness and sunshine and gave her a new sense of well-being.

"Well, I'm ready to go on," she declared, looking around for her fire lizards. They swirled around her head in a colorful pattern, creeling. She smiled up at them. "Come on, then."

*Turn to section 38.*

## * **42** *

To her great relief, Mirrim found that the needles were barbless, so the skin didn't tear when she pulled each thorn out. They left no more than single dots of blood, but the wounds itched. Her eyes filled with tears as she worked, teeth gritted in frustration and irritation, since the pain was more of an undercurrent than a life-threatening concern. The thorns had not penetrated deeply anywhere but in her hand and wrist. Evidently, the needler had a limited range. Those she could not remove easily she left until she could get to the numbweed she had with her gear on the hilltop. More than anything else, she was afraid of breaking a needle off below the surface of the skin. As a trained Healer, she had used these very thorns again and again, but Mirrim was never required to give herself an injection, or sew up her own wounds. It was easier when someone else did it to her. Then she didn't know when each pinch would come, and she could just concentrate on staying calm. This time, she was on both sides of the operation, and it was all she could do not to cry.

She felt as though someone was watching her. When she looked around, there was nobody there but a *ging* tree, its blossoms wide open, the black edges giving the creamy flowers definition, like a thousand white eyes staring at her. Ignoring it, Mirrim went back to her task.

"Come on. Manora always says there's nothing so awful as an unfinished job," Mirrim told herself sternly. She kept her jaws pressed tightly together until they ached. One by one she dropped the needles onto the ground. Pretty soon, there was none left in her shoulder or chest, and only a few that she didn't dare touch. They had all been shallow, but the little heap of needles on the big leaf before her was fairly impressive. She became aware of Path's repeated question. *Mirrim? Are you hurt? Where are you?*

"I'm all right, Path. I'm coming back to you now," Mirrim assured her. "You just sit tight. I need some numbweed."

She hurried down the trail, clutching at her sore side, which ached anew at each step. Every time she winced, she could feel an answering twinge of anxiety from Path. She strove to conceal her discomfort, but the very soul-to-soul meld she shared with the green dragon prevented her from sparing Path worry. Mirrim met Path's anxious eyes as she mounted the crest of the hill and made her businesslike way to the sacks huddled among the gear.

"Good heavens, you would think I was going to collapse on the spot!" Mirrim exclaimed, rummaging through the sacks among Path's fighting straps. She found a small pot of numbweed and opened the lid. Pulling off her tunic, she smoothed the creamy yellow salve over the network of tiny red dots on her skin. She was relieved to see that none of them was bleeding any more profusely, but there would be bruise marks all over her. She had been very, very lucky that none of the needles had punctured any major blood vessels. Instantly the numbweed deadened the pain in her shoulder. Mirrim sighed with relief as it hardened swiftly into a shell to protect her skin while it healed. "See," she assured Path heartily. "Nothing to worry about."

Path's eyes slowed their revolution and changed from worried yellow to a blue-green hue of contentment. She knew Mirrim wasn't telling her all the truth, but she was relieved that her rider was well. *I am unhappy when you hurt.*

Mirrim hugged the huge neck. "I know. I am unhappy when you hurt, too. But I'm fine. It was just scratches. I'm going to go find Dannen now. I'll be back before evening."

*Roll 1 D6 and add this to Mirrim's total hit points for each pot of numbweed used. She may use up to two. At no time may she ever have more hit points than she started with. Remove one pot of numbweed from the character sheet per use.*

On her way down the hill, she all but tripped over a softish, lumpy mass in the path. Springing backward in surprise, she realized that it was a body of some kind of animal.

She retreated and used her walking stick to turn the body over. Half expecting it to jump up and run, Mirrim held herself ready to flee. It was quite dead.

## Section 43

"Why, it's a whersport," she exclaimed. Whersports were small relatives of whers, but they were much easier to catch and kill. This one had had an accident of some kind. It had been pierced all along one side with thorns. She recognized them immediately. "It must have run into the needler, too, before the *ging* flowers were open." That meant the whersport had been poisoned. Mirrim shuddered. Her luck must have been in to have avoided the same fate.

"The needler would have sucked this beast dry if it had fallen within range. I guess it was dying even when it shot the whersport. I don't blame it. Whersports are good to eat."

Enthusiastic creeling above her head added the fire lizards' assent. Mirrim made a face at them as she hefted the sack over her uninjured shoulder. "Oh, you agree, do you? Well, dinner's not for hours yet. Let's go find Dannen."

*Turn to section 41.*

* **43** *

Mirrim sensed that someone was pulling on her hair, and she could hear Path's voice frantic in her mind. *Are you hurt? Mirrim? Where are you?*

Mirrim struggled to sit up, and batted away the fire lizards. They had been trying to pull her the rest of the way out of the pond. "I'm all right," she hastened to assure them and Path. "I'm all right, dear one. I'm coming up to you to get some numbweed. Stay where you are. There's no place for you to land."

She hurried down the trail, clutching at her sore side, which ached with each jarring step. Every time she winced, she could feel an answering twinge of anxiety from Path. She strove to conceal her discomfort, but the very soul-to-soul meld she shared with the green dragon prevented her from sparing Path worry. Mirrim was relieved when she reached the hill, and caught a glimpse of Path peering down at her, the glowing eyes whirling yellow with fear.

"Good heavens, you would think I was going to collapse on the spot!" Mirrim exclaimed, rummaging through the sacks among Path's fighting straps. She found a small pot of numbweed and opened the lid. As soon as she smoothed it on, the creamy yellow salve deadened the pain in her shoulder. It hardened swiftly into a shell over the wherry scratches, to protect her skin while it healed. "See," she assured Path heartily. "Nothing to worry about."

Path's eyes slowed their revolution and changed to a blue-green hue of contentment. *I am unhappy when you hurt.*

Mirrim hugged the huge neck. "I know. I am unhappy when you hurt, too. But I'm fine. It was just scratches. I'm going to go find Dannen now. I'll be back before evening."

*Roll 1 D6 and add this to Mirrim's total hit points for each pot of numbweed used. She may use up to two. At no time may she ever have more hit points than she started with. Remove one pot of numbweed from the character sheet per use.*

On her way down the hill, she all but tripped over a softish, lumpy mass in the path. Springing backward in surprise, she realized that it was a body of some kind of animal.

She retreated a man-length from the body and used her walking stick to turn it over. Half expecting it to jump up and run, Mirrim held herself ready to flee. It was quite dead, but still warm. It must just have been killed.

"Why, it's a whersport," she exclaimed. Whersports

were small relatives of whers, but they were much easier to catch and kill. This one had had an accident of some kind. It had been pierced all along one side with thorns. She pulled one of the thorns out of its flesh and peered closely at it. Scrutinizing it closely, she identified it as a needlethorn, from the plant of the same name. Swiftly, she looked around the clearing for *ging* trees. With relief, she saw that the dark-rimmed creamy flowers were wide open. It was one of those useful natural signs she'd been taught to look for. Until the *ging* flowers opened, a needlethorn was deadly. That meant the whersport would probably be safe to eat. Probably the poor beast had stumbled against a needler that was nearly inert and stabbed itself to death.

"And they're good, too," Mirrim declared to herself as she stowed it in her carry-sack. With her knife, she cut a wide *ging* frond for removing and storing what undamaged needles she could find later on.

Enthusiastic creeling above her head added the fire lizards' assent. Mirrim made a face at them as she hefted the sack over her uninjured shoulder. "Oh, you agree, do you? Well, dinner's not for hours yet. Let's go find Dannen."

*Turn to section 38.*

## * 44 *

To her great relief, Mirrim found that the needles were barbless, so the skin didn't tear when she pulled each thorn out. But nonetheless her eyes filled with tears as she worked. Teeth gritted in frustration and irritation. The pain was more of an undercurrent than a chief concern. But she was tense, fearing that the needles would break off below the surface of the skin, and she would have to cut into her flesh to get them out. As a trained Healer, she had used these very thorns again and again, but Mirrim was never required to give herself an injection, or sew up her own wounds. It was easier when someone else did it for her. Then she didn't know when each pinch would come, and she could just concentrate on staying calm. This time, she was on both sides of the operation, and it was all she could do not to cry.

She felt as though someone was watching her. When she looked around, there was nobody there but a *ging* tree, its blossoms still tightly furled, the black tips looking like the pupils of a thousand eyes. Swallowing, she went back to her task.

"Come on. Manora always says there's nothing so awful as an unfinished job," Mirrim told herself sternly, fighting to stay conscious. She kept feeling as if she were about to black out. At last, the only needles left were embedded in her hand, between her fingers and in the fleshy part of her palm. Mirrim's stomach flip-flopped unhappily as she took hold of each needle with thumb and forefinger. She experienced a sensation of sluggishness in her pulse. Had those thorns pierced far enough to poke holes in her lungs and heart sac? It was becoming hard to breathe, and there was a singing in her head, competing with Path's voice. *Mirrim? Are you hurt? Where are you, Mirrim?*

"I'm all right," Mirrim told her adamantly, steeling herself. She got to her feet and moved toward the opening to the glade. She must get back and calm her dragon. She must—

Five steps along the trail, the blackness filled her field of vision, and she fainted.

*Turn to section 29.*

## \* **45** \*

The wherry screeched as the blade pierced its breast, a long drawn-out scream of anger and pain. Mirrim pushed the spear with all her strength, keeping the bird at bay as it pecked and clawed at the shaft. Its struggles nearly took the spear out of her hands, but she could tell it was done for. The wherry's movements were slowing as she watched, and its eyes grew glassy. Its legs splayed and slipped crazily on the boulder. As the wherry staggered, Mirrim twisted the spear, and the bird toppled off the boulder to the bank, where it lay with its long legs trailing in the water. Mirrim pulled loose the blade, and a gush of blood followed it, flowing down the wherry's side. In a moment, it stopped moving. The fire lizards chattered jubilantly and settled on its wings and side to drink the still-hot blood.

"Greedyguts, *wait* a minute!" Mirrim exclaimed, jumping forward. The fire lizards fluttered off the carcass. Mirrim circled cautiously around it, holding the spear ready to plunge it into the wherry's neck if the bird showed any sign of life. "Very well, go ahead. I'm cutting some meat out of it for later."

Prying her knife out of her makeshift spear, Mirrim whetted it sharp and went to work gutting the wherry. She dumped the entrails on the ground for her friends who fell to on them happily. Her shoulder hurt, but it was only bruised.

"I can't carry this whole bird back with me," Mirrim explained as she cut free the breast meat and wings, and wrapped them in leaves. "It's too big. The rest'll make nice gleanings for some other scavengers. Wherries are so stupid, they even eat each other." She stood up, shouldering her carry-sack. "Come, let's find Dannen and show him what we've got."

*Turn to section 38.*

## * **46** *

The fish was not a large one, and Mirrim had to move very slowly. She moved less than a span at a time, keeping her face close to the cress on the bank. If she'd been standing up, she could have retreated instantly into the grove. Since she could not, it was necessary to sidle like a spider-claw up the bank to a break in the foliage wide enough to admit her shoulders without rustling too much and giving her away. On top of the rock, she could see the wherry's wings baiting. It must be nearly finished with the fish.

An almost inaudible cheep came from behind her. Mirrim risked a look over her shoulder. Her fire lizards stayed where they were, but they were watching her carefully. With a flick of her free hand, she gestured to the other side of the clearing. "Go there," she whispered.

The two greens stared at her, puzzled, but her little brown launched himself from his perch. Tolly went *between,* and reappeared far across the shallow stream. The two greens caught on, and in an instant, they joined him. All three let out piercing whistles that went far above the range of human hearing with what must have been unspeakable insults about wherries. The big bird sprang into the air and set off in pursuit. They were gone from sight in a moment, but Mirrim had no fear that her little friends would lose the wherry in no time at all.

# Section 46

Picking herself up, Mirrim gathered her boots and jammed her feet into them as she hopped and then ran back up the streambed to the narrow path. She could hear her fire lizards' mocking voices floating back to her and smiled. That big bird would be so confused when they finished with it!

On her way back to the hill, she all but tripped over a softish, lumpy mass in the path. Springing backward in surprise, she realized that it was a body of some kind of animal.

She retreated and used her makeshift spear to turn the body over. Half expecting it to jump up and run, Mirrim held herself ready to flee. It was quite dead, but still warm. It must have just been killed.

"Why, it's a whersport," she exclaimed. Whersports were small relatives of whers, but they were much easier to catch and kill. This one had had an accident of some kind. It was too young to have died of old age. She examined it. The creature had been pierced all along one side with thorns. She pulled one of the thorns out of its flesh and peered closely at it. With relief, she identified it as a nonpoisonous needlethorn, from the plant of the same name. She herself had never seen one, but the Healers at Southern prized them, because the thorns were hollow right through and could be used for subcutaneous or intravenous injections. She didn't want to hunt up the plant, because it was reputed to be a dangerous beastie to handle, but there were enough undamaged thorns in this poor thing's body to take back.

"And the whersport is a find, too," Mirrim declared to herself as she stowed it and the thorns in her carry-sack. "They're good to eat."

Enthusiastic creeling above her head added the fire lizards' assent. "Oh, you agree, do you? Well, let's go find Dannen and show him what we've found."

*Turn to section 38.*

## * **47** *

The wherry peered around, its tiny eyes puzzled. Where had the fire lizards gone? Mirrim watched as it flew in a circle over the pond. It made a hopeful dive at the dead fish lying on the stones. As soon as the wherry set down and picked the fish up, Mirrim took her chance. Keeping as low as she could, she crept on her knees and elbows, making for the thick stand of reeds behind the boulder.

*Roll 3 D6.*

*If the total is less than or equal to Mirrim's value for Dexterity, turn to section 46.*

*If greater, turn to section 60.*

## * **48** *

She took one of Dannen's empty sample bags and spread it out on the ground. With Dannen's help, she rolled the man onto his stomach. They eased his tunic up far enough for Mirrim to look at his spine.

"I think it's only sprained," Mirrim said, after a moment. "I might be able to fix it myself."

"Then, do something quickly," Joras begged. "I'm in terrible pain."

At a word from Mirrim, Dannen dashed up the slope,

and returned in a moment with the bag of numbweed pots and bandages. Mirrim opened one of the small clay pots and spread the healing salve all over the small of the man's back, and up and down his spine.

"Now, I've no fellis juice," Mirrim said, cautioning Joras, "so you will have to lie as relaxed as you can, no matter what it feels like."

"All right," Joras said, screwing his eyes tightly shut.

Reaching deep inside herself for all her courage and confidence, Mirrim signaled to Dannen. "Now, here's what I want you to do."

*Roll 3 D6.*

*If the total rolled is less than or equal to Mirrim's value for Wisdom/Luck, turn to section 49.*

*If the value is greater, turn to section 54.*

## * **49** *

Mirrim picked up Joras's arms and held his wrists in either hand. "Take his hands like this, and when I say 'pull,' you pull, slowly but firmly."

Dannen nodded, setting himself at his friend's head, and looking anxiously at Mirrim. She approved his stance, and went to sit down across Joras's legs and placed her palms one on top of the other in the middle of his back. The beastmaster looked up fearfully at Dannen, but the farmcrafter only winked down at him. "All right, *pull!*" Mirrim shouted.

Dannen ground his heels into the dirt, and hauled up and back on Joras's arms. Mirrim put all her weight behind her hands and thrust down. There was an audible *pop!*

Mirrim nodded, and Dannen let go and settled his friend's upper body gently onto the sacking. Joras lay for a moment panting, then he turned his head to smile at the curly-haired woman. "The pain is gone! You cured me!"

"It was only dislocated," Mirrim admitted. "Those muscles would have kept the bones out of place indefinitely. They won't relax when they're pushed to one side like that. You must take it easy for a while, a sevenday at least. We can take you back to Southern, or we can come back to check on you every day."

"Oh, I'll be all right now," Joras waved them away. "I'm most grateful, lady. I thought I'd be stuck here until that passel of nosy Telgar traders came back through."

"Traders?" Mirrim asked, remembering Lytol's complaint of a sevenday before.

"Oh, aye. They were traveling through to the Two-Faced Mountain. Heard tell that Ancient Timers' possessions were for sale. Ever heard such a thing? Knowledge is to be shared, like the discovery of my lizard." He noticed the embarrassed look on Mirrim's face. "Oh, I see. Let him go, didn't you? Well, it's never to mind. They're all over this place. I'll be catching them again in a sevenday. Just help me make up a shelter I can live in, and you can be on your way."

*Turn to section 52.*

## * **50** *

"It happened just after you left," Dannen said, trying to ease the suffering beastcrafter into a comfortable position. Brekke ran to Joras and examined his spine. The man's face was contorted into a pained mask. "His leg started kicking out all by itself. I tried to hold it down the way I saw you doing it. He practically flung me off, but I managed to keep him from moving until the spasm passed."

"Good," Brekke said, running her hands up and down the man's spine. "The pain is greatest here?" she asked, touching a place between two of his vertebrae.

"Yes," gasped Joras. Brekke took the pot of numbweed which Mirrim handed to her and liberally daubed the man's back. "Take his arms, Dannen," she said, sitting down on Joras's legs. She gestured to Mirrim to join her. "Mirrim, behind me. We must straighten his spine out, and these bones will pop back into place. Ready?" They nodded. Brekke leaned forward, and planted her palms down, one on top of the other, onto the two misaligned vertebrae. "Pull!"

Dannen ground his heels into the dirt, and hauled up and back on Joras's arms. Brekke put all her weight behind her hands and thrust down. There was an audible *pop!*

Brekke signed for the farmcraft boy to let go. Dannen settled his friend's upper body gently onto the sacking. Joras lay for a moment panting, then he turned his head to smile at the curly-haired woman. "The pain is gone! You cured me!"

"Not entirely yet," she said, laying a hand on his back. "You must lie very still for a while, and let the muscles relax. They would have held the dislocated bones in the wrong position indefinitely. You must rest for a time. Then it would be best if you kept away from strenuous activity for at least a sevenday."

"Well, now I *can* rest," Joras said cheerfully, the deepest lines already beginning to smooth out of his face. "You have no idea what a relief that is!"

Brekke stood up, smiling, and drew Mirrim with her. "Can you look after him while Mirrim takes me back to Cove Hold, Dannen?"

"Certainly." Dannen flashed his brilliant smile at her.

"Oh, I'll be all right now," Joras waved them away. "I

thought I'd be stuck here until that passel of nosy Telgar traders came back through."

"Traders?" Mirrim asked, remembering Lytol's complaint of a sevenday before.

"Oh, aye. They were traveling through to the Two-Faced Mountain. Heard tell that Ancient Timers' possessions were for sale. Ever heard such a thing? Knowledge is to be shared, like my lizard." He noticed the embarrassed look on Mirrim's face. "Oh, I see. Let him go, didn't you? Well, it's never to mind. They're all over this place. I'll be catching them again in a sevenday."

"You could have realigned his back by yourself, Mirrim," Brekke told her gently on the way back to Cove Hold. "It was an easy procedure. But I'm glad that you aren't ashamed to call for help for the sake of a patient. That's the mark of a sound Healer."

Mirrim glowed, but she swallowed her jubilation. "Cove Hold, please, Path."

*Turn to section 52.*

## * 51 *

"I can't fix his back without help," Mirrim said in a rush. "I want you to go back for Brekke."

Dannen stared curiously at her. "How?"

Mirrim swallowed. She wasn't sure if her idea would work, but she remembered how Brekke flew Ruth once without Jaxom. It might work. "On Path. I can't leave Joras. If he gets another convulsion in his leg, it could permanently damage his back. Brekke can hear any dragon. I'll have Path bespeak her at Cove Hold, and you can help her find her way back here. I don't dare try to transmit the coordinates for a jump *between* from there. She'll need to have someone with her who knows this area."

"I don't know if I can do that," Dannen said, nervously wiping his palm on the front of his pants leg.

"Why not? Are you afraid?" Mirrim couldn't keep the frustration out of her voice, and it came out as anger.

"Yes!" Dannen cried: "Why can't you send one of your fire lizards?"

"Because one of them can't carry a Healer back to me, and Brekke has no other way to get here. I need your help."

"All right," Dannen said, his face nearly as white as his hair. "I'll go." He still didn't look convinced. "You said you have Healer training . . ."

"Not enough. If it wasn't a desperate situation, I would never ask you," Mirrim told Dannen seriously. "I'm taking a risk, too."

They made Joras as comfortable as they could, and hurried up the hill to Path. "You heard what I asked him, darling. Are you willing to carry him to Brekke?"

*If you want me to, I will.* Path's eyes glowed with love and trust.

Mirrim untied the carry-sack from the ring under the fighting straps. "Please bespeak Brekke and tell her what happened, and that we need her."

Path's eyelids closed as she sought Brekke's mind in Cove Hold. *Brekke will come. She waits for us, and sends me strong pictures to visualize my landing point. I know Cove Hold well.*

"You'll have to fly back to me direct," Mirrim said, helping Dannen strap himself firmly between the last two ridges of Path's long neck. "I can take care of Joras until you return."

Path gathered herself, and bounded into the sky, her wings beating strongly. In a moment, she winked out. Mirrim felt a wrench as Path disappeared into *between*, as if half her soul had been torn away. Mirrim swallowed. If anything happened to Path, she'd live the rest of her life as half a person, or suicide. She was taking an enormous risk, and she knew it. As her mind reached out for the reassuring touch of Path's, she counted, one, two, three, the time it would take to cough three times, and the strength of their bond flooded back to her as Path hovered over Cove Hold. In her mind she could see the dragon's eye image of Brekke, bags in hand, racing up the stony ridge and disappearing out of Path's line of sight.

*We are coming back now,* Path's distant voice said. Mirrim sank to her knees in sheer relief.

She ran down the hill with the carry-sack draped over her shoulder. She had left Joras alone as long as she dared. A sort of sixth sense told her she must get back to him right away.

Underneath the tree, Joras was suffering another convulsion. He had both hands planted flat on the ground, and was trying to hold himself still. Mirrim snatched the rope and a pot of numbweed out of the carry-sack and flung it aside as she ran. She plumped herself down on the man's leg and planted both hands firmly on his knee, keeping it to the ground. In a moment the tremor passed.

Joras's face was twisted into a mask of pain. With a sympathetic twinge every time he groaned, she flipped up the back of his tunic and spread numbweed the length of his spine and across the back where she had felt swelling.

As the numbweed took effect, and Joras paid less attention to his wound and more to his surroundings, he chatted with her, forcing his voice into more cheerful tones. "Ah, that's better! At this rate, I'll be up and chasing lizards in no time."

"I can see why you and Dannen are friends," Mirrim chided him. "He's a man of one thought, too." She tied one end of her rope around the wide-boled tree and drew the length out to where Joras lay on his back. Bracing him up against her chest, she tied the rope around his chest just under his arms. Then she set his feet flat on the ground so his knees were tented up.

"What's all this for?" Joras wanted to know.

"It's in case you get another spasm before the Healer arrives," Mirrim said, slipping on her wherhide jacket. "I can hold your back immobilized by myself this way."

She had not long to wait to try out her apparatus. She gave him a sip of cold klah from the jug, and they chatted quietly for a time. In the middle of telling Mirrim a joke, Joras got an expression on his face of mild discomfort.

"What's wrong?"

"I think it's my leg again," Joras said. "Please, do something, dragonrider!"

In a few moments, the spasm began. With determination between her brows, Mirrim turned her back to Joras, picked up his legs and slung one over each shoulder. She braced her hands on his thighs and leaned well forward, trying to ignore the heels battering her. Fortunately, the thickness of the lined hide jacket absorbed some of the force of Joras's involuntary kicks.

"I'm sorry!" he wailed, swinging uncomfortably in midair. His arms were stuck straight out, pressed against his ears. "I can't control it, you know."

"I know," Mirrim grunted. "It should be over in a moment." She gritted her teeth and took a half step forward, her patient shaking, twitching, and swearing behind her. She let her hands slide down and embraced his lower legs, seeking to get a better grip.

Suddenly there was a loud pop, and Joras's leg stopped kicking. "The pain!" he cried. "It's gone! You've cured me!"

"It was only dislocated," Mirrim said with relief, setting him down. "Those muscles would have kept the bones out of place indefinitely. They won't relax when they're pushed to one side like that. You must take it easy for a while, a sevenday at least. I can fly you to Southern, or come back to check on you every day."

"Oh, I'll be all right now," Joras waved her away. "I'm happy on my own. I'm most grateful, lady. I thought I'd be stuck here until that passel of nosy Telgar traders came back through from Southern."

"Traders?" Mirrim asked, remembering Lytol's complaint of a sevenday before.

"Oh, aye. They were traveling through to the Two-Faced Mountain. Heard tell that Ancient Timers' possessions were for sale. Ever heard such a thing? Knowledge is to be shared, like my discovery of that lizard." He noticed the embarrassed look on Mirrim's face. "Oh, I see. Let him go, didn't you? Well, it's never to mind. They're all over this place. I'll be catching another again in a sevenday. Just help me make up a shelter I can live in, and you can be on your way."

"Oh, my!" Mirrim said. "I'd better bespeak Brekke that the emergency is over."

When Path returned, Dannen escorted Brekke down the hill. By that time, Joras was sitting up, propped against a cushion of brush, padded with enormous leaves.

Mirrim hung her head when Brekke appeared. "I'm sorry to make you waste your time coming here."

"Not at all," Brekke assured her, examining Joras. "You did it all properly. I'm proud of you, being so responsible."

Even though Mirrim was no longer the small child that Brekke had taken to foster, her praise caused Mirrim to glow with pride. In contrast, Dannen was pale and nervous.

"It's from going *between*," Dannen confessed. "I've never done it before, and with less than half an idea of how it would feel. I was terrified. I'll never get over it."

"I never have," Brekke said, patting him. "No dragonrider ever does, either. Well, I'm not needed here. Mirrim had everything well in hand. But I'm glad that you aren't ashamed to call for help for the sake of a patient. That's the mark of a sound Healer."

"I'll take you back to Cove Hold now," Mirrim offered.

*Turn to section 52.*

# * **52** *

Dannen began to dig young herb plants and tie up their rootlets in leaf coverings stuffed with earth. As he finished a handful, he placed them in the carry-sack as gently as he could. Mirrim knelt beside him and started to help wrap his selections, but he soon waved her away. "I'm sorry," he said apologetically. "I always do them all myself."

Mirrim was irritated for a few moments, but shrugged and went away to see to Path. *Why should you be angry?* Path's gentle thoughts interrupted her cross ones. *You have never let anyone else look after me.*

"That's right," Mirrim laughed and stroked Path, her mood forgotten. "You're too important to me. I suppose those silly seedlings mean that much to Dannen."

"They do," Dannen said, coming up near them. "I couldn't hear Path's half of the conversation, but I can guess what she must have said. I'm sorry to be beast-headed. I know I'm overprotective where my plants are concerned."

"What's the difference between a farmcrafter and a Holder?" Mirrim asked as they resumed their hunt for plant samples.

"Not much, in some cases," Dannen admitted cheerfully. "But the craft also comprises people like myself and my master, who work to improve the strains, and increase quality and yield of crops. I like plants, but I hate to stay in one place. My foster mother said I was born with the road under my feet. My master likes to experiment with biological combinations and hybrids. No Holder could afford to do that; he's got to bring in the crops Turn after Turn. You should meet Master Urlet; he talks a good yarn. His son is a Holder, beholden to Southern." Dannen eyed a hanging trailer hopefully and then shook his head. "Sindain wanted to go for a farmcrafter, but he prefers to have someone else test his seed strains for him. No talent for botany, that one; no experimental bent. So, instead, he's what you might call an enlightened Holder. Tries our seed crosses when we tell him what they'll do. The rest of us are too inquisitive. We want to know for ourselves. Sindain, he's marrying young Lord Toric's sister Doriota pretty soon."

"I'd heard," Mirrim said expressionlessly.

"Well, his son and me are mates from way back. He's asked me to stand with him as best friend. Will you be there in Southern Hold for the wedding?"

Mirrim thought of Lessa, who would certainly be there as Weyrwoman of the most important Weyr on Pern, and wondered if Lessa was still angry with her. Mirrim remembered that she still hadn't solved her problem. "I hope I will."

"Good! I'll introduce you. You'll like him."

"Menolly should certainly be at a wedding that important. I'll introduce *you,* and you can ask her about fire lizards." Mirrim smiled, but she was worried all over again. She accidentally mutilated several young plants before Dannen firmly took them out of her hands.

An hour's walk from the hill, Dannen found his plot of experimental onions. Some had already gone to seed, but others were on the edge, the flowers heavy with tiny black pips. Still others hadn't flowered, and he dug up one of these to admire the solid, round root. "Look how big they are," Dannen crowed. "And so healthy!" With a forefinger, he gently tapped the flowers, causing them to drop their seeds into a big leaf folded into an envelope. He put the fold into his belt pouch, but several samples of the young roots went into his bag.

"It takes two Turns for these to grow from seed to flower," he explained. "These mature roots are this

Turn's growth. Grubs actually stir the soil, so these are bigger than any sweet roots I'd ever grown in Telgar. And they're sweet as fruit. You can eat them raw."

"Eyahh." Mirrim made a face. Dannen chuckled at her and went on working.

The tuft grass was close by. When he was through digging roots, Dannen followed the sound of a stream to an expanse of flat wetland that adjoined the huge marshes north of them, halfway between Cove Hold and the Ancient Timers' plateau. They picked their way down to the extreme edge of the marsh, where Dannen insisted the best grasses grew.

Mirrim held on to a thick vine and stumbled down into the muddy tract. Her heavy riding boots were sucked into the mire as she struggled to catch up with Dannen.

"Wait up!" Mirrim called. The heavy sack caught on saw-edged grasses, and she had to yank it free. Dannen's attention was obviously on plant-gathering, to the exclusion of all other subjects.

"Farmcrafting is close to Holding in many ways," Dannen explained while uprooting several clumps of grass. "We provide Holders with innovations and discoveries that will make life on Pern better. Take these tuft grasses, for example. See this shaft? It's stronger and thicker than an equivalent plant up north. It looks almost like a tube within a tube."

"It looks like it has white fur inside," Mirrim said, peering into the stem.

Dannen stripped seeds off the tall stems which waved high over the rest of the plant and poured them gently into another leaf envelope. "Northern tuft grass has long filaments that run the length of each blade which probably are vestigial hairs. I've wanted to borrow the device that the Smithcraft discovered which makes small things seem large. Then I'd be able to see for sure. The funny thing is, that in spite of the fact it's warmer down here, and always is, this variety of grass is better suited for surviving cold weather than the kind that grows up north." He pulled the patch of vegetation apart and slit the root ball open with his belt knife. "Beautiful. I wish my father in Telgar Hold could see these. He'd enjoy experimenting with them; probably try crossing some hybrids." He gave Mirrim a speculative look. "Could we take some of them to him, on Path, say in the morning? I know it's too late today. By the time we get back to Path it will be full dark. I'm sure my parents would love to meet you and your green dragon." When she didn't answer right away, he smiled, abashed, and stripped more stems of their seeds. "I'm sorry. Just because I have an obsession doesn't mean anyone has to humor me. I know it's a lot to ask."

"No, don't apologize." Mirrim held out a hand. "I was just wondering if it would be a good idea."

"Of course it's a good idea," Dannen said playfully. "I always have good ideas."

Mirrim made a face at him. "Well, you think that these grasses will live through cold weather, but would they survive *between?* That's far colder than any snow-time I've ever known. And flying direct would take us a very long time."

Dannen frowned, pinching his chin between thumb and forefinger. "I think they should be all right. They're pretty hardy." He started to pack plants into the already-bulging sack. "You can sleep on it, okay?"

The walk back to the hill was not at all as easy or as soothing as the walk out had been. The trees, bigger than any Mirrim had ever seen up close, threw long, threatening shadows over her as the sun went down. Beasts deep in the forest broke through the undergrowth unexpectedly and shot across their path. "They're more scared of us than we are scared of them," Dannen said cheerily, but she noticed that he looked worried when they saw a full-grown wher scamper by them, staying deep in the dim undergrowth. Wild whers were afraid of the light, but they'd charge anything that moved at twilight or night. Their two-clawed forepaws and sharp teeth were dangerous weapons.

## Section 53

Mirrim spent the night curled thankfully close to Path. No wher would attack a full-sized dragon.

When she woke the next morning on the hilltop, Mirrim noticed the Red Star pulsing menacingly at her from the eastern sky, lit by the still-hidden sun. Shuddering, she cuddled against Path for a moment, and then resolutely arose and began to poke at their fire. In spite of the daily heat of summer, the nights were cool. Mirrim heated what was left of the jug of klah in the embers and thankfully sipped the hot, fragrant drink from one of the earthen cups stowed in the carry-sacks. The smell reached Dannen's nose, where he was buried under a handful of empty gathering bags. He emerged stretching and yawning, to empty the jug into his own cup.

"Good morning," he said sleepily. "Have you thought about my request?"

*If Mirrim agrees to take the plants and Dannen to his father's home in Telgar, turn to section 57.*

*If she has misgivings about it, turn to section 73.*

## * 53 *

"What do you think?" Mirrim asked Tolly, who rode coiled around her neck. The brown fire lizard cheeped drowsily. "You don't care, do you, unless you get fed. Is that it?" She scratched his little head with a careful hand. He flattened his head on her shoulder, surrendering to her caress, and making happy crooning noises. "Well, you aren't much help. I think I'll try this way. It looks drier."

The two green fire lizards angled up above Mirrim's head, and floated lazily, their fragile-looking wings stretched to near transparency on the breeze. Mirrim smiled as they disappeared over the treetops. They were beautiful, almost as beautiful as Path, whom a quick listen told Mirrim was still sound asleep. It was a hot, dry day, so there was no need to hurry back to get Path under cover in case of inclement weather. "Silly," she chided herself for an overprotective mother, for so she felt herself to be sometimes. "Dragons won't melt. And Thread doesn't fall again until tomorrow."

There was little room to do more than squeeze through. Mirrim decided that this couldn't be a path, but more of a trail forded by jungle beasts. It was less than a man-height high, and if Mirrim had been any taller, she would have had to walk stooped over. She was worried that she might run into something, a wher or a tunnel snake, and have no room to maneuver or defend herself. The trail sloped upward and the earth changed in color, becoming sandier under her feet. To her relief, the way opened out quickly into a small glen, where a tall tree with thick fronds prevented much other plant life from growing beneath its shadow. Twisted burrows in the grass told Mirrim that beasts frequented this area. Her suspicion was borne out by the nibbled tree bark and well-cropped plants and grasses. Long twists of hair were caught here and there. Mirrim examined one with interest. Wild runners, or bearded herdbeasts? The latter would eat anything, and was well suited to living wild.

Ferns grew thick on the ground near the landing hill, but the land was much drier here. Green succulents were spaced throughout the grass. Mirrim's fire lizards chased flying insects, and Mirrim herself stopped to watch a chain of trundle bugs making its slow way across the glade.

If dragons did blaze the trails for wanderers, they'd be wider than these little passages through the brush, but most likely a lot of useful plants would be lost, crisped to ash by the flames, or damaged beyond saving. Dannen would object to waste like that. These pretty *ging* trees would have all their creamy white blossoms burned off.

At the far end of the clearing, Mirrim discovered an interesting succulent plant, one she had never seen before, though she thought she recognized it from drawings in the Healers' texts. It was a squat, round plant with sharp, thin protruding spines all over.

"Why, it's a needlethorn," she exclaimed, pleased, hunkering down to look at it. "But I've never seen one like this. Won't Brekke be happy if I bring some fresh thorns for her medical supplies." She peered at the plant and raised an inquisitive hand. "I've been told these were dangerous, but they don't *look* dangerous."

*If Mirrim chooses to touch the needlethorn, turn to section 35.*

*If she decides not to take any needles, turn to section 39.*

## \* **54** \*

She sat down to take off her boots and then motioned to Dannen to stand by Joras's shoulder. "I'm going to step gently on his back, and I need you to brace me so I don't slip and hurt him. My weight will push the vertebrae back into place. It takes a fair amount of force to get the bones back where they belong once they've been dislocated like this."

Dannen nodded. "It happens to my runner's hip once in a while. But it will usually pop right back."

"It will rarely do that with a human spine," Mirrim told him tartly. "The muscles will build up almost a protective splint around the misplaced bones. It can stay that way for Turns!"

She put one hand on Dannen's shoulder, and stepped gingerly onto Joras's broad back. Dannen put both of his hands about her waist to further steady her. "I can feel the skewed bones with my toe. One more step . . ."

Suddenly Joras's left leg began to twitch. "Shouldn't you stop the spasm?" Dannen asked, cocking his head toward the leg, which began to kick uncontrollably.

"Do something, dragonrider!" Joras pleaded. "I'm in agony."

She looked up and frowned. "I'd better hold it down," Mirrim said, starting to set her foot back on the ground. Joras gave a tremendous kick. In spite of the double hold she had on Dannen, Mirrim slipped out of the lad's grasp and fell, landing half on and half off her patient. Joras screamed, his limbs jerking him on the forest floor like a pinned insect. Mirrim rolled off, and twisted around, grabbing for the leg. With all her strength, she held it down until the convulsion stopped.

"I'm sorry," Mirrim gasped, her face ashen. Joras's was red, and his eyes were tightly shut against the pain. "I couldn't help it. I was thrown off balance."

"What can we do now?" Dannen asked.

"We'll have to take him to the Healers at Southern," Mirrim said. "I'm sure they've dealt with accidents like this one before."

Together, they built a travois and gently set Joras down and strapped him to it with the length of rope from Mirrim's carry-sack. They slung the stretcher on one side of Path's back behind her wings and balanced it with a sack of rocks on the other side. Mirrim climbed up between the neck ridges with a guilty look at Joras. The beastmaster had fallen into a kind of entranced stupor from which he didn't stir, even on the takeoff or the passage into *between*. Mirrim wished that she had been able to cure the man. Instead, she was sure she had made matters worse.

*Turn to section 52.*

## \* **55** \*

"I can't fix his back without help," Mirrim said in a rush. "I want you to go back for Brekke."

Dannen stared curiously at her. "How?"

Mirrim swallowed. She wasn't sure if her idea would work, but she remembered how Brekke flew Ruth once without Jaxom. It might work. "On Path. I can't leave Joras. If he gets another convulsion in his leg, it could permanently damage his back. Brekke can hear any dragon. I'll have Path bespeak her at Cove Hold, and you can help her find her way back here. I don't dare try to transmit the coordinates for a jump *between* from there. She'll need to have someone with her who knows this area."

"I don't know if I can do that," Dannen said, nervously wiping his palm on the front of his pants leg.

"Why not? Are you afraid?" Mirrim couldn't keep the frustration out of her voice, and it came out as anger.

"Yes!" Dannen cried.

"Then I'll go myself!" Mirrim replied, a cutting edge in her voice. "But you had better watch those nerve tremors. It could permanently damage his back if he had another."

"It'll be all right," Dannen said firmly. "I've done some nursing, too. I know what to do."

Mirrim was by no means sure of his boast, but she said no more. Backs were tricky to work with. It was with great misgivings that she climbed the hill back to Path.

"Speak to Brekke, please, Path," Mirrim asked as they hurtled aloft. "We have to hurry back to them."

\* \* \*

It took only the time to visualize the coordinate points over Cove Hold, and to fly down to the rocky ridge over the dock, but Brekke was already running toward them with a case of medicines.

"It's lucky for Joras you found him," Brekke said as she climbed onto Path's neck, using Mirrim's arm to pull herself up. "Have you given him numbweed or fellis?"

"No," Mirrim said, ordering Path off the ridge and into the air. "I didn't want sensation to be lost before you diagnosed what was wrong."

"Very good, Mirrim," Brekke said approvingly. "I'm proud of you. Now, let's see if there's anything I can do for the poor man."

*Roll 3 D6.*

*If the total rolled is less than or equal to Mirrim's value for Wisdom/Luck, turn to section 50.*

*If the total is greater than Mirrim's value for Wisdom/ Luck, turn to section 59.*

\* **56** \*

With a cautious hand, she reached around the side of the rock and picked up most of a small yellowtail which one of her fire lizards had dropped. The fish dribbled blood and entrails over her hand. It would serve as bait. The fish was small. Would it be enough to entice a big wherry like that? She had to try.

On her knees, the dragonrider crept backward, forcing her way between the stands of sturdy reeds. They would afford some protection from the wherry's beak and talons. If the fish lured the creature close, she could stab

through the reeds with her lance. There wasn't much room for her to stand among the reeds, so it would take all her strength and skill to wield her spear, but it would be impossible to miss her strike. The bird would be in easy range.

Keeping one hand steady on the shaft of her lance, she flung the fish so that it landed on the rock on which she had been sunning herself earlier. It fell with a plop. At the same time she urged her fair to fly high enough to be beyond the wherry's further concern.

The wild wherry, deprived of its fire lizard targets, was quickly attracted by the dripping fish whose blood glistened on the hot stone. As Mirrim hoped, it settled on the rock, and its greedy foreclaws closed on the fish. As it raised her bait to its beak, Mirrim raised her lance to thrust it into the wherry's breast.

*Wherry skin is notoriously tough, which is why dragon-riders use it in their flying gear. Mirrim has to thrust hard enough to penetrate the thick hide on the wherry's breast with her improvised spear.*

*Roll 3 D6.*

*If the total is equal to or less than Mirrim's value for Strength, turn to section 45.*

*If the total is greater, turn to section 60.*

* **57** *

"I'll have to take us directly *between* to Telgar Weyr," Mirrim said the next morning after she had bathed and oiled Path, "but it's only a few minutes flight from there to the Hold. I'll bespeak the watchdragon to let Path stay

on the fire ridge until we've finished our visit. Thread
falls later today after Cove Hold, so I may not stay too
long."

Together they loaded Dannen's bags onto Path, and
fastened themselves firmly to her neck with the fighting
straps. Mirrim decided not to give her gear the whole
checkover because they were only taking a simple flight
*between*, nothing so complicated or daring as Thread-
fighting. Path moved to the edge of the hilltop and
sprang upward, using the extra depth of the slope to give
herself wingspace on the narrow earthen crown. Dannen
clutched Mirrim nervously as they flew high and slipped
into *between*.

Mirrim gasped as they came out of *between*. It was full
spring here in the north, but the temperature was far
below that of the hot tropical morning they had just left.

The blue watchdragon on the fire ridge of Telgar Hold
warbled a challenge, and Path answered with her name
and Weyr affiliation. *Berelth says welcome, and S'tarl
sends his greetings.*

"Good," Mirrim said as they circled down into the
Hold courtyard. "Give him mine, please, and tell him
we're visiting Farmcraftmaster Folidor in the Hold."

*He says I may stay up on the fire ridge with Berelth, and
he will tell Lord Larad we are here.*

Mirrim stripped the flying straps from Path's neck and
put them on a hook on the wall of the stable. As soon as
her riders had dismounted, Path spread her wings and
bounded upward. Berelth, on the heights, trumpeted
cheerfully to her. The fire lizards soared off in a colorful
explosion to join the fairs of local fire lizards already
coming to greet them.

"Come on," Dannen said. "I'll take you to meet my
parents."

Telgar Hold was one of the handsomer habitations on
Pern. The prow-shaped cliff face out of which the central
Hold was hewn had a sheer, smooth facade marked along
five levels with broad bronze-shuttered windows. Brightly
painted designs decorated the colored eaves of each

stone cothold, and the people wore clothing dyed in the vivid hues imported from Southern Boll and Igen. Mirrim, in her wherhide, felt quite drab by comparison.

They stood back to let by a train of small wheeled carts pulled by canines. Each cart was piled high with a different sort of vegetable, all familiar to Mirrim—redroot, tubers, greens, orange finger-roots, river grains in sacks, and the like—food for the Hold. A plump, berobed steward stood at the door with a slate and stylus, checking the produce in. He barely noticed them as they went by him after the last cart.

Master Folidor was not to be found in the family's sleeping quarters. Instead, a drudge directed them to a small building outside the main Hold, where they came upon the Masterfarmer doling out quantities of seeds to his journeymen. He was a round-bellied, heavy-jowled man with gray hair and thick black eyebrows sketching surprised arcs on his forehead. Mirrim decided Dannen must look like his mother.

"Those are to be monitored, mind you," Folidor insisted. "Have the Holders *count* every seed they put in the ground, and count every one that comes up. Or doesn't come up. We will see to calculating the yield. Well, hello, boy!" the Masterfarmer said, turning away from his work, a pleased expression warming his face. "This is a pleasant surprise. Have you seen your mother?"

"Not yet, sir," Dannen said, embracing his father. "May I introduce Mirrim?"

"Charmed, dragonrider. M'rim, is it?" He put out his hand palm up, and she covered it with one gloved hand. Folidor looked down at her glove quizzically, one eyebrow up.

"Forgive me," Mirrim said, and pulled off gloves and flying helmet.

"Well met, indeed," Folidor said, smiling. "I know who you are now, green rider of Benden. Bless me, your Impression raised some eyebrows among the old boys hereabout. Well, boy, you didn't come all the way from

Southern to impress me with your dragonrider acquaintance—a joke, young lady. What have you to show me?"

"These," Dannen said triumphantly. He unfastened the tie around his carry-sack's neck and plucked out a fistful of plants. "The onions I was growing in the south."

Folidor took them from his son and examined them closely, his bushy eyebrows almost touching over his nose. The plants' leaves appeared to be wilted and their stems brittle. "Yes, yes, well grown, poor things. All dead. I see the problem. But where would they sustain such severe cold damage in the Southern Continent?"

Mirrim spoke up, feeling embarrassed for not insisting that it was a mistake to carry Dannen's precious specimens *between.* "We came directly from the growing ground, Master Folidor. On dragonback."

The eyebrows sprang apart. "Oho! That's where the frost set in. Frozen in a flash, you might say. Even you should know, lad, what the Harpers' tales say about the hideous cold of *between.*"

"At least I can salvage the seeds," Dannen said sadly. Mirrim blushed uncomfortably. *She* should have known.

*Turn to section 77.*

Turn to section 77.

* **58** *

*We must make haste,* Path reminded her. *Canth asks when we will be there? Elekith, Camuth, and two others wait for us. They say Thread is in sight over the sea.*

"I know, I know," Mirrim said, dragging the heavy fighting straps and a bag of firestone out of the stable to the impatient dragon. "Tell him I'm hurrying as fast as I can. I don't want to have to time it. No, don't tell him *that*." Taking one's dragon *between* times was still officially proscribed, though forgiven on important occasions. Mirrim knew well that F'nor expected her to be ready for Threadfall on time as ordered without having to rely on shortcuts. "Tell him we'll be there!"

She threw the mass of wherhide onto the cobblestones and began to straighten out the loops that would go around Path's neck. By all rights, she was supposed to go through a complete gear check before her flight, but that would take more time than she really had left. Mirrim bit her nails. F'nor would be furious if she arrived late. And she was still in disgrace with the Benden Weyrleaders.

*If Mirrim chooses to forego the preflight check, turn to section 82.*

*If Mirrim decides to go through with the preflight check, turn to section 79.*

## * **59** *

"It happened just after you left," Dannen said, trying to ease the suffering beastcrafter into a comfortable position. Brekke ran to Joras and examined his spine, shaking her head. The man's face was contorted into a pained mask. "His leg started kicking out all by itself. I tried to hold it down the way I've seen you do it, but it didn't seem to stop it."

"Did you hold down the knee?" Brekke asked.

"No," Dannen admitted, ashamed. "I only saw the end of the seizure Mirrim fixed."

"He's twisted his back. On top of the dislocation,

that's very bad. The nerves were reacting to the pain of the first injury. That happens sometimes," Brekke told Joras, soothing him with her voice. She held out a cup of fellis juice she poured from a skin in her bag. "Drink this. When you relax, they will relax."

"Will I walk again?" Joras asked, concerned. "I'm used to hunting on my own. I don't want to be crippled the rest of my days."

Mirrim knelt next to Brekke. "You'll be all right."

"Easy for you to say, dragonrider, you have legs other than your own on which you can rely," Joras said bitterly, draining the cup. When he drifted off to sleep, Brekke gave him a more thorough examination. Her eyes met Mirrim's, and they were not happy.

"Can't you do anything for him?" Mirrim asked.

"I'm afraid not," Brekke said regretfully. "It could take him a Turn to recover, or a sevenday, or not at all. Where does he live?"

"Southern Hold," Dannen answered.

"He should go back there. We'll rig a frame, and you can take him on Path. The Hold Healer is very good. I would take him to the Cove, but I don't know how much longer we will be staying with Master Robinton. Joras'll recover more quickly in a familiar surrounding."

Dannen gestured at the trees and hills and marsh. "This, to him, is a familiar surrounding. He lives outside almost all the time except in heavy rains or Threadfall. He won't be happy cooped up and forbidden to twitch a toe."

"I hope he *can* twitch a toe. That will mean the nerves weren't badly damaged."

Under Brekke's direction, they built a travois frame from tree branches and the rope from Mirrim's carry-sack. With a lot of grunting and hard work, they drew the fellis-fuddled man up to the plain where Path was waiting.

"It's an unfortunate accident," Brekke told Mirrim as she flew her *between* back to Cove Hold after depositing

Joras with the Southern Hold Healer. "But I think the original injury was one you could have taken care of yourself. You've had quite a bit of training. It was within your capabilities. It's a shame you didn't attempt to realign his back; he might have been back on his feet already."

Mirrim didn't look back at her foster mother's face. She didn't want Brekke to see the tears of frustration and anguish in her eyes. No Healer likes to lose a patient, even an unsuccessful Healer.

*Turn to section 52.*

## * **60** *

Mirrim thrust her lance into the wherry's breast. The wherry screeched and backed away. Mirrim was forced out from behind the reeds. She cursed; the damned thing was fast! The point of her spear jabbing it in the breast only made it furious. She had drawn blood on its dirty brown front, but it obviously was not mortally wounded. Wherries were stupid, and that made them doubly dangerous. when hurt, and this one was angry and in pain. Her only hope of escaping unhurt now was to kill it. Gritting her teeth, she stabbed again.

The wherry shrieked and dived at her, claws out. Its cry was answered by the three fire lizards, prepared to defend their mistress with their lives. Mirrim braced her spear.

**WHERRY**
*To be hit: 10   To hit Mirrim: 9   Hit points: 8*

## Section 61

*Roll for claws and beak each round. Claws do 1 D6
damage, the beak also does 1 D6.*
*Mirrim's knife/spear does 1 D6 damage.*
*After four rounds, if it is still alive, the wherry will flee.*

*If Mirrim kills the wherry, turn to section 40.*

*If she fails to kill it, turn to section 36.*

*If Mirrim's hit points reach 0, turn to section 29.*

* **61** *

"What do you think?" Mirrim asked Tolly, who had
elected to ride coiled around her neck. The brown fire
lizard cheeped drowsily. "You don't care, do you, unless
you get fed, is that it?" She scratched his little head with
a careful hand. He flattened his head on her shoulder,
surrendering to her caress, and making happy crooning
noises. "Oh, whatever. In spite of how it smells, I think
we'd be able to find what we're looking for on that
right-hand path. Numbweed grows in swampy land, but
that does me no good unless I'm planning to boil it, and I
haven't brought a kettle with me. And cresses and lily
bulbs grow in this area, too. Those would taste good with
roast wherry, or herdbeast stew, back at the Hold.
Brekke would like some." She raised a thin branch
blocking her way and stepped out. The fetid odor of
disturbed swamp mud made her wrinkle her nose. "But
will I need a bath later!"

The trail was not a wide one. If anyone had used it
lately, it couldn't have been more than one person
trailing a single pack beast. It was reputed that some of
the Holdless lived down here, rambling here and there,

living in a place only so long as it suited them. This vast continent with its tiny population suited the wanderers much more than the smaller, crowded Northern Continent.

And why not? Mirrim asked herself, looking around. It would be an easy life to stay down here. When she lived at Southern Weyr with Brekke, it had been all but effortless to feed and clothe themselves. The dragons dined on native wherry, far fatter and larger than those up north.

Wherries were marsh birds. They lived on tunnel snakes, water snakes, fish, marsh-dwellers, anything they could catch. Mirrim could see traces of the stupid scavengers' nests in pockets of earth and in overhangs cut out by a torrential rain or an aging riverbed. Wherry would make a succulent evening meal for Dannen and herself, with plenty of meat left for the fire lizards and the next day's midday meal . . . if she could kill one at all. The latter was not a foregone conclusion. Mirrim had only her belt knife with her, and wherries were fighters. Their forelegs could tear right through wherhide and flesh and she had left off her flying jacket. The dragon-rider decided even wherry meat wouldn't be worth the effort. There was too great a chance she'd be hurt.

Well, river fish and whersports were everywhere and much easier to catch. They'd still have meat for supper. Some of those lily roots would go down well, too; and windclocks were good, especially if she could find ones whose golden flowers hadn't turned to white yet. Mirrim concocted a tasty salad in her head as she moved along the narrow, slippery trail.

It was pleasantly cool in the underbrush. The brazen sun's light filtered through the deep blue-green leaves. Tall, jointed reeds loomed overhead, those whose hollow triangular cross-sections made them incredibly strong and light for use as ladders and scaffolding. Mirrim cut one with her belt knife and used it to poke at the ground before her feet. Here and there along the trail, she found blazings cut deeply into the trunks of trees. This path had been used for a long time, she decided. Some of the marks had grown up well above the ground, past the height of a tall man on the biggest trees, and fresh cuts made below them at eye level Turn after Turn. The lowest were very fresh. Mirrim measured with her hand, and decided that they must have been made within the last few days, and by someone just about her height, if this was his or her eye level. She knew her knowledge of woodcraft was limited. There was little need for the skill in weyrlife. The two green fire lizards returned from their reconnaissance and swirled above her head, creeling encouragingly. Mirrim smiled up at them and followed their lead.

The path took a turn, and continued on right through a shallow streambed: a useful natural highway. It was easy going, but the bottom was coated with sand as fine as dust, which built up into a thickly heavy mass around the soles of Mirrim's boots. She had to stop occasionally to clear them with her walking stick. Tolly protested sleepily every time Mirrim bent over, coiling his tail around her throat and scrabbling painfully up her arm with his claws to get back to a comfortable position. Mirrim looked ruefully at the bleeding scratches and wished that she had worn more than a sleeveless shirt under her riding clothes. Her skin was well scored with thin white scars from Turns of caring for fire lizards. They were always sorry they hurt her, but it didn't help the cuts heal any faster.

Lacy white flowerlets grew atop tall stalks that brushed Mirrim's shoulders. She recognized the plant and yanked one out of the earth. Yes, it was a wild finger-root. Garden roots had shorter, less flowery tops. The orange vegetable was good steamed or raw. These were young, shorter than her own fingers, which meant they were just right to be eaten. She pulled up several more and tied the stems together to make a bunch. Wild garlic grew nearby. Funny how certain root vegetables were always found together in the wild. Manora insisted that it was because they complemented one another: hardy ones breaking up the soil so delicate ones could grow, tall plants shading small ones. It was best to observe the survival techniques and plant natural pairs together for best yield.

Reppa and Lok sailed on ahead of them, and did a happy dance in the air. Mirrim squinted through the striped shadows to see what they were so excited about, but in a moment, her ears told her. The streambed was deeper here, actually enough so that at one bend it had formed a natural pond which, to judge by her fire lizards' reactions, held fish.

"Well, don't look at me, you lazy things! Catch them yourself. You're better built for fishing than I am." Even Tolly deigned to join the two greens splashing and diving. He closed his wings and arrowed down into the water. Mirrim sat down on a big boulder which rested half in and half out of the pond and pulled off her boots. There were water lilies growing on the surface; not only were they beautiful, but they had edible roots. Without actually climbing into the pool, she could reach a dozen of the white flower-cups. Only a few had to be discarded because they were too small or unhealthy looking.

She let the pond water flow over her feet, refreshing them. It was midday, but here in the shelter of the trees it was wonderfully cool, a relief from the scorching temperatures she'd endured at Cove Hold. Behind her was an almost complete fence of reeds, their leggy shoots whispering in the wind. Spreading her palms behind her on the rock, she let her head fall back on her shoulders and closed her eyes. She checked for Path, but the green dragon was still asleep, baking in the sun on that hilltop. Her thoughts were no more than echoes from her dreams.

The fire lizards played, ignoring her. Mirrim could hear them squabbling over bits of fish or pretty stones they found in the stream. From the sharp note in Reppa's voice, Mirrim guessed that she might be ready to rise again soon.

The raucous complaints got louder and more frantic,

# Section 61

and Mirrim frowned, assuming she was going to have to dispense justice among her little charges, and opened her eyes to see what was going on. To her horror, a wherry had appeared, probably drawn by the smell of fish entrails from her friends' catches. She slid carefully off the boulder and crouched behind it.

The wherry was a big one with talons as long as her fingers. On the other hand, it was alone. Wherries usually flocked in groups of three or more. Mirrim thought hopefully of roast wherry. With the help of her fire lizards, she might be able to kill it, but with the meager weapons she had on hand, it would take more than just jumping out and slashing at it. Mirrim saw a fish on a small rock in the pond that might do for bait. Her fire lizards sailed through the air, confusing the wherry and shrilling war cries. Their voices were so high they hurt Mirrim's ears, but she ignored her discomfort. She had to plan. If she lured the wherry to a place where it would trap itself, she could kill it quickly. In any case, a human alone would seem easy prey to the wherry. There was little chance that she and her fair could get away from the scavenger now without killing it or at least distracting it first.

Carefully, she drew her walking stick to her. Mirrim held her breath as it grated on the pebbles at the water's edge, but the noise didn't attract the wherry's attention. She forced the handle of her knife into the end of her walking stick, and tested it to make sure it wouldn't fall out. The thin hide bindings around the haft that she used to keep the knife from slipping in her grasp filled the hollow end of the reed as if it had grown there. Now she had a solid lance.

At her whistle, the fire lizards veered away from the wherry and vanished *between,* reappearing above her in the thicket, big eyes whirling. They stopped creeling and clung to young tree boles, and watched Mirrim prepare to move.

*If Mirrim tries to sneak away without the wherry seeing her, turn to section 47.*

*If Mirrim decides to attack the wherry, turn to section 60.*

*If she tries to bait and kill it, turn to section 56.*

## \* **62** \*

"Forgive me, journeyman," Mirrim said, lowering her voice from the tone of strident command she knew it'd reached. "I didn't mean to make a scene." She smiled winningly at the merchant, who peered closely at her, trying to decide if she was sincere.

*Roll 3 D6.*

*If the total is less than or equal to Mirrim's value for Charisma, turn to section 63.*

*If greater, turn to section 66.*

## \* **63** \*

"Forgive *me*, dragonrider, for allowing such a misunderstanding to grow between us. I always seek to assist the Weyr in any way I can. My supply trains bring Hold goods to every Weyr each Turn."

"Then may I see the stylus?" Mirrim asked again.

"I'm sorry, but that's out of the question," the trader said, just as firmly. "Weaver Timon and I are in the midst of a dicker over it. You wouldn't want to interrupt an honest bargain, would you?" He smiled, knowing that Mirrim had done just exactly that.

"No," Mirrim acknowledged, losing momentum.

"Should he decide to forego the joy of owning that little treasure, I would consider it an honor to offer you the next chance. Until then, I must bid you a good afternoon." Smoothly he gestured the weaver to a seat, and resumed his bargain without another glance at Mirrim.

The young dragonrider goggled at him, but she noticed the others in the hall were still watching her. Crimson, she fled outside the Hold and called for Path. Dannen followed her, and caught hold of her arm.

"Wait!" he pleaded. "Mirrim, don't rush off."

"I have to," Mirrim forced out, keeping her lips taut so as not to burst into frustrated tears. "Thread falls soon. I must get back to Cove Hold. Are you ready?"

Dannen shook his head. "I'm not coming with you."

"Why not?" Mirrim demanded, the tears leaking out of the corners of her eyes.

"I think I can find out more about that trader if I stay here. I'll see you at the wedding in Southern Hold in a few days. Just remember to save at least six dances for me. Is it a bargain?"

"But what if I can't go?" Mirrim asked, pausing in spite of the growing fear that she'd have to answer to F'nor for being late to Threadfall.

"You'll be there," Dannen assured her. "I know it." In an impulsive motion which surprised them both, he pulled Mirrim close in his arms and kissed her soundly on the mouth. "That seals the bargain," he told her, his blue eyes merry and warm. He glanced upward. "You'd better go. Here comes Path. Good-bye, Mirrim, and good luck!"

Mirrim stood motionless for a moment in the center of the courtyard staring after Dannen as he dashed away.

*Let us go,* Path called to her as the green dragon swept down from the Hold's fire heights. *They are waiting for us.*

With a rueful scowl on her face, Mirrim came out of her trance. "Oh, I know. And we'd better hurry."

*Turn to section 58.*

* **64** *

The apprentice lunged at her, taking advantage now that the attention of the rest of the room was on his master.

"Dannen!" Mirrim cried, though she had little hope of being heard over the Holders' voices. She backed away from the burly young man, who had assumed a hunched-over stance and was edging cautiously toward her, hands out, much the way that a spider-claw approached its prey. Mirrim swallowed. She, too, bent over into a fighter's crouch, and hoped that someone would realize what was going on and stop it. Her strength had not yet been restored from her strenuous adventures of the last few sevendays.

Her assailant knew he didn't have much time before the attentions of the room returned to the other protagonist in the argument. Mirrim wondered why the traders were so eager to silence her. Was this thievery more widespread than she knew? Did they fancy that the removal of rare objects was going unnoticed? She warily watched the apprentice's eyes. If she could judge where he'd strike at her next, she might counter his move. One of the training games young weyrlings were taught was unarmed combat. As the only female weyrling Mirrim had been forced to learn quicker and achieve more than her male counterparts, even the ones twice her size. All she needed was for this big oaf to make one good mistake.

Mirrim ducked as the apprentice's right fist went whistling above her head. With a grim smile, she moved in to swing a punch at his jaw, and intercepted his left fist, jabbing in and catching her right in the throat.

Coughing, she staggered backward. Mirrim cursed inwardly. He was a good infighter, damn him. She wasn't going to be able to read him in the same way she could read the weyrlings or the Weyrlingmaster. She took two strides forward, catching his hand on the way past him. With a quick foot, she pushed and pulled, flipping him over onto his back. As she'd been taught, she stooped to knock him unconscious with a flat-handed chop across the windpipe, but her attention was distracted at that instant by the appearance of three screaming fire lizards. Hers. They had sensed her danger and appeared from *between* to defend her. Her punch hit the apprentice in the jaw instead.

As she looked up to order them to silence, the apprentice's hands clamped onto her wrist and throat and she was hurled to the floor. His mouth was bleeding copiously from where she had bashed his lower lip into his teeth. Before she could react, he had one large knee in her chest, and was knocking her head repeatedly against the floor. Fortunately for her addled brains, the room had been well strewn with rushes, and she wasn't immediately knocked senseless. Instead, she had time to scream when she saw Dannen's face appear over the apprentice's large shoulder.

Dannen leaned over and wrapped a long arm around the apprentice's throat, locked the other one across his elbow, and lifted. Immediately the trader's hands fell from Mirrim's tunic front, and scrabbled at Dannen, trying to free his windpipe from the vise into which it had unaccountably become clamped. His face grew red and distorted the longer Dannen held on. His arms and legs flailed and kicked in the effort to break free, but the young farmcrafter was much stronger and had the advantage of position besides. With a grateful glance at Dannen, she started to rise to her feet, but a wild kick from the struggling apprentice took her just over the ear. She dropped to her hands and knees, shaking her head to clear it. The room was spinning around and around before her eyes.

It had taken the holders in the dining hall some time to realize that a fight was going on behind them, but they reacted swiftly enough once they saw what was happening. One man stepped up behind Dannen and peeled his arms away from the apprentice's neck and held him. Another pulled the youth upright, turning him so his hands were pinioned behind his back. "Now," the first one said amiably, "what's going on here?"

"See to Mirrim," Dannen pleaded, trying to pull away from his captor.

Two more men jumped forward and helped Mirrim to her feet. She batted away their hands. "I'm all right," she protested, though she could barely hear her own voice over the roaring in her head. There was a blackness growing at the edges of her vision, making it impossible to see to either side unless she turned her head, and it hurt to do that.

A face introduced itself into her narrowed field of vision. It was the plump steward. "We'll get the healer for you, rider. When you're more fit, the Lord Holder will want to hear what all this brawling was about."

"No," she said. "Please." She sought around for the apprentice and finally spotted him in the hands of a thick-set farmer. There was blood on his chin and chest.

"I'm sorry, rider, but it's a matter for the Lord Holder. If you were of this Hold, I could settle your disagreement, but I have no jurisdiction over the Weyr or a trader from another Hold."

Mirrim's heart sank, and she felt herself weakening. She would have a chance to exonerate herself before Lord Larad, but nothing would protect her from Lessa's wrath or help her to restore her lost honor. She'd be banned from the wedding, the digging site, and probably Telgar Hold until the angry Weyrwoman forgot about Mirrim's transgressions. Mercifully, she felt that she was drifting into unconsciousness. She could worry about her problems later.

*Turn to section 29.*

## * **65** *

Surprised, Mirrim realized that the trader's apprentice must have followed her from the hall. Before she could get away from him, he swung a wide punch and caught her hard in the side. She staggered and fell to the ground on the slippery, straw-covered floor, the breath to call for help knocked out of her by the blow. Not so hampered, Reppa, Lok, and Tolly shrilled war cries as they dove at the big youth. Their mistress was being attacked! The apprentice swatted at his biting and scratching assailants. He aimed another punch.

Mirrim didn't wait for him to hit her again. Luckily, most of the first blow had been absorbed by the thickness of her wherhide jacket. Her ribs hurt, but her movements were not much hampered. She rolled to her back and bent her knees, cocking her legs against her chest. As soon as the apprentice was close enough, they sprang out rigid, catching him in the belly. He was thrown back against a stall and thumped down on the floor. Straw flew in every direction, and the fire lizards screamed.

Swiftly, Mirrim flipped over, got to her knees, and then to her feet. The apprentice got up, too. Assuming a fighter's stance, he growled at her. He spat on his hands and rubbed them together. Mirrim could tell by the stubborn look in his eyes that she couldn't hope to get away while he was still conscious. He meant to beat the life out of her, and he was bigger than she was. No matter

©1987

what his instructions had been, his pride was hurt now. Mirrim couldn't hope to beat him in a fair fight. Where were the beastcrafters who worked here?

*Mirrim! What is happening? Are you in danger?* Path called to her.

She strove to keep her tone level. "I'll be all right for now, Path. But please ask Berelth to ask S'tarl to get to the stable. Tell him to hurry!"

*I will come!*

"No! Lord Larad's runners are in here. They'll tear themselves to pieces if they see you. Get S'tarl!"

She stood, warily watching the apprentice's eyes. If she could judge where he'd strike at her next, she might counter his move. One of the training games young weyrlings were taught was unarmed combat. As the only female weyrling Mirrim had been forced to learn quicker and achieve more than her male counterparts, even the ones twice her size. All she needed was for this big oaf to make one good mistake.

Without looking down, the apprentice dived forward, clutching Mirrim's knees and knocking her flat on her back. Mirrim cursed. He was a good infighter, damn him. She wasn't going to be able to read him in the same way she could read the weyrlings or the Weyrlingmaster. She wriggled in his grasp, turning over and clawing her way through the straw, trying to get to the door. The apprentice handed himself up her back, grappled one arm around her neck, and started to squeeze. Mirrim's cry for help was cut off.

Outside, she could hear Path roaring. *Berelth! We must save Mirrim! She is in danger!* The two dragons were setting up a racket, echoing Mirrim's distress. It was too late to think of the runnerbeasts. Frightened by the dragons' trumpeting, they were whinnying in fear and kicking at their stalls. In another moment, the green dragon would shove her way inside, through the bronze doors, the stone walls, and anything else keeping her from rescuing Mirrim from her assailant. With all her strength, the dragongirl pressed herself up onto her hands and feet, dislodging the big youth so that he lost his grip on her throat. Clambering to his knees, he reached for her again.

Tolly took the opportunity to fly in the apprentice's face and claw at his eyes. The man covered them with both hands and staggered up and away, moving toward the door. Mirrim, free from his attention, scrambled to a wooden pail, picked it up by its handle, and swung it in an arc, impacting against the side of the man's head. He collapsed groaning onto the straw, his face bleeding from a double-handful of scratch marks left there by the lizard's attack.

Mirrim stood slack against a stall door, panting, the pail dangling from her fingers. Outside, the roaring stopped. In a moment, two men—one wearing Telgar Hold's insignia and a Beastcraftmaster's badge, and the other a tall, slender man in wherhide riding breeches—stepped inside. "Dragonrider?" called the beastcrafter, squinting into the dark. "Are you all right? Your dragon wouldn't let me through. I think she was about to come in here."

With a rueful half smile that hurt because she had bashed that side of her face on the stone floor, Mirrim dropped the pail with a thud. "I'm all right," she said, brushing straw from her hair and clothing.

"Mirrim?" the other asked, coming forward with a teasing grin on his narrow face. "I'm S'tarl. I don't know if you remember me, but we've met at Benden Hatchings. That's my dragon out there with yours. Path must be pretty persuasive. That lazy sack of blue bones hardly moves except when he's hungry or when Thread falls. Both of them have been setting up the biggest racket."

"Oh, no," Mirrim groaned. She hastened outside to reassure Path, who was crooning through the door and terrifying the tethered beasts. She clutched the great green head to her and stroked above the sensitive eye ridges. The croon swiftly changed from a whine to a purr.

*I was worried,* Path explained, her eyes whirling red.

"I know, dear, but what will Lord Larad say when he hears all his prize beasts are foaming at the mouth because of you?"

"What will he say?" S'tarl asked, following her out of the stable. He and the beastcrafter had the trader's apprentice in tow. "It depends on what this ruffian has to say, about how he stealthily attacked a dragonrider, an honored guest of this Hold!"

*Thread falls soon,* Path reminded her.

"I know," Mirrim replied. "S'tarl, we must leave. Thread falls over Cove Hold, and I must be there."

"I understand. Come back soon, Mirrim, and we'll share a cup of wine." S'tarl extended his palm, and Mirrim covered it gratefully. "Good flying, dragonrider."

*Turn to section 58.*

## * **66** *

"Forgive me, dragonrider, for allowing such a misunderstanding to grow between us. I always seek to assist the Weyr in any way I can. My supply trains bring Hold goods to every Weyr each Turn."

"Then may I see the stylus?" Mirrim asked.

"I'm sorry, but that's out of the question. Weaver Timon and I are in the midst of a dicker over it. You wouldn't want to interrupt an honest bargain, would you?" He smiled, knowing that Mirrim had done just exactly that.

"No," Mirrim acknowledged.

"Should he decide to forego the joy of owning that little treasure, I would consider it an honor to offer you the next chance. Until then, I must bid you a good afternoon." Smoothly, he gestured the weaver to a seat and resumed his bargain without another glance at Mirrim.

The young dragonrider glared at him, but she noticed the others in the hall were still watching her. Crimson, she fled outside the Hold and called for Path. Dannen followed her. As soon as they were gone, the journeyman trader caught his apprentice's eye, and nodded coldly after Mirrim. The apprentice smiled nastily and left the room. On either side of him, the people in the hall were going back to minding their own business.

Dannen caught up to Mirrim on the threshold of the main entrance. "Wait!" he pleaded. "Mirrim, don't rush off."

"I have to," Mirrim forced out, keeping her lips taut so as not to burst into tears. "I must get back to Cove Hold. Thread falls soon. Are you ready?"

Dannen shook his head. "I'm not coming with you."

"Why not?" Mirrim demanded, the tears leaking out of the corners of her eyes.

"If I stay here I think I can find out more about that trader. I'll see you at the wedding in Southern Hold in a few days. Just remember to save at least six dances for me. Is it a bargain?"

"But what if I can't go?" Mirrim asked, pausing in spite of her growing fear that she'd have to answer to F'nor for being late to Threadfall.

"You'll be there," Dannen assured her. "I know it." In a surprising impulsive motion he pulled Mirrim close in his arms and kissed her soundly on the mouth. "That seals the bargain," he told her, his blue eyes merry and warm. "Good-bye, Mirrim, and good luck." He waved cheerily and slipped back into the Hold.

Feeling a glow of joy, Mirrim wandered slowly back toward the stableyard to pick up her gear. The stone cobbles under her feet felt as soft as air. She called to Path and woke her from her nap on the fire heights. "Come on, lazy. Thread falls over Cove Hold soon!"

*I know,* Path informed her petulantly, indulging in a good stretch. *Berelth is a kind host.*

"Well, thank him for me, and get down here! I'm borrowing a bag of firestone. Tell Berelth to inform S'tarl, and I'll pay them back sometime." She smiled at Path's luxuriously indolent thoughts, and called her fire lizards together as she gathered up her gear in the cool darkness of the beasthold. "We're back to the Hold. Why, what's the matter with you sillies?" she asked, wondering at their sudden panicked creeling. She spun around just as the apprentice lunged for her.

**TRADER'S APPRENTICE**
*To be hit: 11   To hit Mirrim: 11   Hit points: 8*
*Fists do 1 to 6 points damage.*

*If Mirrim wins the fight, turn to section 65.*

*If Mirrim loses, turn to section 69.*

## * 67 *

The weaver held the object out farther to examine it more clearly. It was small and resembled a stylus, except that the stem was clear as glass, with a smaller, nearly transparent vein or cylinder running up the center inside. The end of the stylus was bronze in color, but duller than polished metal. If it was a stylus, she didn't know who had fashioned it so: the point didn't look hard enough or sharp enough to mark slates easily. Another quick glance, and then she stared into her glass to ponder. Folidor took the inclination of her head to mean that she wanted a refill, and picked up the wineskin.

She risked another look at the item. While Folidor

poured wine for her, she peeked around her raised wine cup at the others. It was then she noticed and recognized the little white dot painted on its side near the bronze point. Mirrim gasped.

"No!" she breathed, balling her fists on the tabletop.

"No more wine, Lady Mirrim?" Folidor asked solicitously.

"Dannen!" Mirrim reached across the table and grabbed the shoulder of the young man's tunic. With the strength built over the Turns of hauling sacks of firestone and caring for a steadily growing dragon, she pulled him toward her and spoke urgently into his ear. Dannen looked surprised, but he wrapped a hand gently around her wrist. Crimson, she realized what she was doing and let go of him. "That little thing there, in the trader's hand. It's one of the artifacts missing from the site."

Dannen peered over at the plump man who had reclaimed his merchandise in order to point out some other facet of it with enthusiasm. The face of his potential client still showed him to be unimpressed. "Are you sure?"

"Yes," Mirrim said firmly, standing up. "It's marked. There's a white dot with numbers painted on its side. Excuse me," she interrupted the trader. "Forgive me for intruding, but may I ask where you got that little stylus?"

The trader journeyman's eye was cold, but his voice remained jovial. "Perhaps you're interested in buying, young lady?"

"No. I see that it has a mark on it, similar to the ones that are being applied to the things found in the Ancient Timers' site in the Southern Continent. May I see it?"

The weaver goggled fish-mouthed, but the trader's face didn't change. Instantly the little item vanished into the man's sleeve. "There is no such mark on it, young lady."

"But I saw it," Mirrim insisted.

The trader beckoned, and his two apprentices stepped forward. One of them, a burly brute with thick black eyebrows, bent down, and the journeyman spoke into his ear. The apprentice straightened up, and his eyes met

Mirrim's. She blinked. *He* looked familiar. She'd seen him before, but where? Somehow she felt that he'd had something to do with the Weyr. Supply trains? The young man studied her for a moment, and bent down again to whisper to his master. The man lost his cheerful expression for one moment, then it flashed back again. He nodded, and the apprentice left the hall. Yes, she knew him. He'd been at the site at least once. "You wouldn't be suggesting that there is anything amiss about my merchandise, would you?"

Mirrim brought her gaze back to the journeyman, and suddenly realized that everyone in the room was staring at her. Behind her, Folidor was demanding of Dannen, or anyone who would listen, what all the bother was about. The remaining apprentice looked like he'd be capable of some dirty fighting, and that he might not stick at brawling with a girl. Also, if she didn't do something, she was going to lose track of the stylus, and she felt sure it could help her clear her name with Breide.

*If Mirrim chooses to apologize to the trader, turn to section 62.*

*If she stands her ground, turn to section 70.*

## * **68** *

Taking advantage now that the attention of the rest of the room was on his master, the apprentice lunged at her.

"Dannen!" Mirrim called again, though she had little hope of being heard over the holders' voices. The burly young man had assumed a hunched-over stance and was edging cautiously toward her, hands out, much the way that a spider-claw approached its prey. Mirrim backed away and swallowed. She, too, bent over into a fighter's crouch, and hoped that someone would realize what was going on and stop it. Her strength had not yet been restored from her strenuous adventures of the last few sevendays.

Her assailant knew he had little time before the attentions of the room returned to the other protagonist in the argument. Mirrim wondered why the traders were so eager to silence her. Was this thievery more widespread than she knew? Did they fancy that the removal of rare objects was going unnoticed? She stood, warily watching the apprentice's eyes. If she could judge where he'd strike at her next, she might counter his move. One of the games young weyrlings were taught was unarmed combat, so that disputes that could endanger a rider's life and his dragon's could be solved without bloodshed. Mirrim had been forced, as the only female weyrling, to learn quicker and achieve more than her male counterparts, even the ones twice her size. All she needed was for this big oaf to make one good mistake.

They maneuvered around one another, hands out. Mirrim watched for a way in which she could dodge past the young man so she could get away. She had no wish to be caught in those huge, seamed hands. He looked like he could draw a gather-wagon all by himself, if he hadn't already.

Dannen was taking too long to come to her rescue. If she couldn't keep the man at bay, she might be in for a pulping. She took a very quick glance to her left, where she had last seen the farmcrafter's wispy silver hair over the heads of the others in the room. As quickly, the apprentice bounded toward her, a fist drawn back to his ribs. The hand shot out, straight at her face. Mirrim jerked to the left, her attention returning just in time to save her. She spun around on one foot and kicked high, her boot clouting the apprentice over the ear as he went by.

He staggered, his boot heels squealing on the stone

floor. Mirrim stepped backward, watching him carefully. Always watch the center of the chest, her Weyrlingmaster had told her. That signals their next action.

To her dismay, the apprentice seemed to have had the same sort of instruction. He feinted to the left. Mirrim dodged. Just as she did, he dropped to his knees, grabbed her ankles, and pulled. With a yell, Mirrim toppled over, her hands slapping the rush-strewn floor before her back and head struck. The apprentice was on his knees beside her, hands reaching for her throat. She let out a squawk before her air was cut off.

There was suddenly wild creeling, and Mirrim's three fire lizards appeared from *between,* clawing and scratching at the apprentice. Mirrim struggled to her feet. Batting at his aerial assailants, the trader clambered up, and made another grab for Mirrim's throat. She tried to evade him and got a clout in the jaw.

"Stop this brawling! Stop it!"

Out of the midst of the crowd came Lord Holder Larad's plump steward. He pushed between Mirrim and the trader's apprentice with his hands out. Mirrim fell back, almost into Dannen's arms. He caught her around the shoulders and braced her up.

"Are you hurt?" he asked.

Mirrim wiped the back of her hand across her mouth and discovered her bottom lip was bleeding. "I'm glad I wear wherhide. My own hide would be shredded."

"Dragonrider, what is going on here?" the steward asked, looking around, and deciding on Mirrim as his best source of information.

She opened her mouth to tell him the story of the missing artifact, but decided that Lessa would never forgive her for airing the Weyr's disgrace. Mirrim shrugged. "I was talking with this man's master. Many people gathered while we were speaking. I guess this apprentice disagreed with what I was saying to his master. He attacked me. I did nothing to provoke violence, I promise you." A quick glance at the table revealed that the trader was no longer there. He had fled the room when the brawl started. Mirrim met the steward's eyes with as sincere a gaze as she could muster.

*Roll 3 D6.*

*If the total is less than or equal to Mirrim's value for Charisma, turn to section 72.*

*If greater, turn to section 75.*

* **69** *

The trader's apprentice must have followed her from the hall, Mirrim realized in surprise. She tried to get away from him, but he swung a wide punch and caught her hard in the side before she was out of reach. She staggered and fell to the ground on the slippery, straw-covered floor, the breath to call for help knocked out of her by the blow. Not so hampered, Reppa, Lok, and Tolly shrilled war cries as they dove at the big youth. Their mistress was being attacked! The apprentice swatted away his biting and scratching assailants and aimed another punch.

Mirrim didn't wait for him to hit her again. Most of the first blow had been absorbed by the thickness of her wherhide jacket. Her ribs hurt, but her movements were not much hampered. She rolled to her back and bent her knees, cocking her legs against her chest. As soon as the apprentice was close enough, they sprang out rigid, aiming for his belly. Mirrim missed her aim, and painfully landed with a thud at her full length on the ground. With a hissed intake of breath, the young man hopped back, arms spread for balance.

"You she-wher!" he growled, sweeping one leg around

and into her ribs. She tried to ward away the blow, but he kicked her hand away and stepped forward with the other foot, impacting solidly on target. Unfortunately, it was the side that was already bruised. Mirrim gasped at the pain of her side and her hand, which was tingling so fiercely she couldn't close it into a fist. Clenching her teeth, she rolled over and started to crawl for the door. To her horror, she saw that the apprentice must have closed it and shot the bolt when he followed her inside. She'd have to finish the fight before she could escape outside.

*Mirrim? What's wrong?* Path asked anxiously, picking up her distressed thoughts.

"I'm locked in the stable," she told Path silently, trying to concentrate both on her dragon and on outmaneuvering the trader's man. "There's a ruffian in here attacking me. Ask Berelth to ask S'tarl to get down here, and to bring some of the Warder's men. Hurry!"

*I will come down and help you!* Path announced firmly.

"No!" Mirrim ordered, and nearly said it aloud. "I don't want you frightening Lord Larad's runners to death. Get S'tarl!"

*Berelth!* Mirrim could hear Path's cry. *Mirrim is in danger. Summon S'tarl!*

"Why did you follow me?" Mirrim demanded, skirting a feed trough as she tried to stay out of the man's grasp.

"You threatened my master," the apprentice said. He had small eyes and a pushed-up nose that made him look like a stubborn, stupid herdbeast.

"I didn't threaten him! I only asked him where that stylus came from."

"He doesn't have to tell you where he gets his goods for trading."

"I know, though," Mirrim said officiously, taunting him, as she felt for a wooden pail she could see out of the corner of her eye. "It came from the Ancient Timers' Hold. I don't know how it got here, but I'll find out. And I won't be the one he has to explain to."

"No, you won't find out," he snarled, jumping forward at her. Mirrim lifted her arms and dodged to block him, but she'd forgotten how well he bluffed. She plunged practically into his arms. He crushed her against the stable wall, attempting to weaken her by cutting off her wind. In protest, she hammered at him with fists and feet. She still had the pail in her hand, and swung it as best she could in the restricted space she had, between her assailant and the stone wall. It hit him square in the kidneys. He let go of her with a roar of agony. Swiftly assuming the advantage, Mirrim dropped the pail to the ground, planted both hands on one of his shoulders, and swept her right foot under his legs, pushing him off balance.

Awkwardly the bully stumbled backward, tripping over the pail behind his heels. As he fell noisily to the floor, Mirrim turned again to run for the door, but the apprentice scissored his legs out, and tripped her up. Now Mirrim was at a disadvantage. She was pinioned face down in the straw. The trader chuckled maliciously. Desperately, Mirrim tried to rise to her hands and knees and scramble away, but she couldn't get any purchase on the slippery stone floor, and her hand was still tingling from having been kicked. She screamed for help. Her voice rang in the stone room, echoed by the shrilling of angry fire lizards, the frightened runners, and outside the stable . . . Path.

*S'tarl is with me,* Path called to her. *He is trying to find a way inside. Berelth says he asks you to hang on. He and the warders will be with you soon.*

"I . . . will," Mirrim panted. With a final burst of strength, she kicked free of the apprentice's grip on her legs and scrambled toward the door. She had reached the bolt and was drawing it back when the man charged toward her, swinging the wooden pail which she had abandoned only moments before. Flinging herself back against the bronze doors, she flung up her hands to protect her face. The pail swept up, catching her under the jaw and, as she slipped to the ground stunned, down again to crash onto the back of her skull. Mirrim dropped the rest of the way unconscious.

At the other end of the stable, a long pole had been inserted between the louvers of the metal shutters across the tall window. Its end flicked the latch up, and the window flew open. Two men—one wearing Telgar Hold's insignia and a Beastcraftmaster's badge, and the other a tall, slender man in wherhide riding breeches—stepped inside. "Dragonrider?" called the beastcrafter, squinting into the dark. "Are you all right?"

The apprentice stared at them, and then shot back the bolt on the door and fled outside. "See to her," the slender man called as he pursued the burly youth into the sunlit courtyard.

The beastcrafter stooped and lifted Mirrim up in his arms. Her booted heels dangled against his hip. "Oof. She's a good-sized girl, she is." Mirrim was already starting to stir. "Easy, rider. Can you hear me? It's over now."

*See, S'tarl,* the blue dragon called, where he and Path sat waiting, coiled on the cobblestones. *We have caught him for you.* Caged between the protective claws of the two dragons, the unfortunate apprentice lay cowering.

"Come on, you," S'tarl snapped, yanking him to his feet with seemingly effortless strength. "How you dared to assault a dragonrider and an honored guest of the Hold—? Never mind. Lord Holder Larad will want to talk to you himself. Good work, Berelth." S'tarl smiled, scratching the angle of his friend's jaw. "And you, too, Path. Mirrim will be all right. The healer will see her, and then she's just going to need to rest for a while."

*Turn to section 29.*

## * **70** *

"It isn't your merchandise if it came from the digging site. It belongs to all Pern!" Mirrim stated firmly.

All around her, people were listening. If she was making a mistake, she would never be able to recover face now, not after causing a very public disturbance and accusing a trader.

"Well, now, young lady," the trader said, standing up. "I don't think you should be the one to accuse me. Or don't your fine friends over there know that you're a proven thief? Also accused by Southern Hold?"

Mirrim turned white. How could he know about that? Furious, Dannen stood up. "Watch your accusations, journeyman. You question a dragonrider's honor?"

Several others in the hall got to their feet. "Yes, name your grudge, trader," one man said, moving closer.

"Wait," said another. "Why does the dragonrider accuse a crafter? What evidence does she have against him?"

"If you ask me, I say it's a private matter, Holders. Shall we let them handle it alone, without interference?" Folidor came forward, trying to push between the two men. Mirrim found herself on the outside of a crowd, unable to get close to the trader.

"See here, a man has a right to barter what he chooses," a tall woman said, barging forward.

The trader caught his student's eye and nodded at him. "So I have always believed, good folk."

"My master is an honest man," the apprentice protested, pushing through the crowd, which closed behind him, immersed now in its own arguments. A sinister expression crossed his face, and he called back over his shoulder. "Just because we are strangers here . . ."

The trader picked up the theme from the center of the crowd. "Yes, forgive me, good folk, but I am surprised that in Telgar, a Hold renowned for its sense of justice that we should be suspected so."

There was an outcry of protest from the folk, just as the apprentice moved forward to grab for Mirrim.

"Dannen!" she screamed, and sought to sidestep the angry trader.

**TRADER'S APPRENTICE**
*To be hit: 11    To hit Mirrim: 11    Hit points: 8*
*Fists do 1 to 6 points damage.*

*The fight will go on for three rounds until it is stopped.*

*If Mirrim runs out of hit points, turn to section 64.*

*If Mirrim wins, turn to section 71.*

*If neither wins, turn to 68.*

## * 71 *

The apprentice lunged at her, taking advantage now that the attention of the rest of the room was on his master. "Dannen!" Mirrim called again, though she had little hope of being heard over the Holders' voices. She backed away from the burly young man, who had assumed a hunched-over stance and was edging cautiously toward her, hands out, much the way that a spider-claw approached its prey. Mirrim swallowed. She, too, bent over into a fighter's crouch, and hoped that someone would realize what was going on and stop it. Her strength had not yet been restored from her strenuous adventures of the last few sevendays.

Her assailant knew his chance would be brief before the attentions of the room returned to the other protagonist in the argument. Mirrim wondered why the traders were so eager to silence her. Was this thievery more widespread than she knew? Did they fancy that the removal of rare objects was going unnoticed? She stood, warily watching the apprentice's eyes. If she could judge where he'd strike at her next, she might counter his move. One of the training games young weyrlings were taught was unarmed combat. As the only female weyrling Mirrim had been forced to learn quicker and achieve more than her male counterparts, even the ones twice her size. All she needed was for this big oaf to make one good mistake.

Breaking stance suddenly, the apprentice lunged forward, shooting a one-two punch at Mirrim's midsection and jaw. Quicker than thought, Mirrim wove from one side to the other, completely avoiding his fists. She danced to one side, tilted her body and shot her leg out in a snapping kick. It took the apprentice completely by surprise in the belly. He staggered back, off balance. Mirrim followed up her advantage by twirling around and kicking him on his other side with the heel of the same foot. The heavy boot must have hurt a lot where it struck, for the apprentice's face contorted into a red mask.

All technique and control fled from him. He rushed her with both hands clenched into fists, intending to pound whatever part of Mirrim that presented itself. Mirrim judged that he must be a nasty infighter, but the Weyrlingmaster had taught her a lot of very dirty tricks to use if her opponent abandoned honor during a fight. She didn't dare let the apprentice touch her. If he could, he'd pound her into a pulp; she could see that in his eyes.

Keeping her eyes on his chest, the center of all movement in a fight, she continued to back away from him. Suddenly she bumped into something large and soft behind her. It was one of the farmholders. She turned her head to apologize. That was all the advantage the apprentice needed. He reached out, seized her by the collar, and raised his fist to slam her across the jaw. Mirrim braced herself for the inevitable blow, but the trader's attention was distracted at that instant by the appearance of three screaming fire lizards. Hers. They had sensed her danger and appeared from *between* to defend her. His blow fell, but it lacked most of its strength and certainly all of its aim, hitting her in the collarbone, which fortunately was well padded by her fleece-lined jacket.

While Reppa and Lok hung in the air and shrilled war cries, Tolly dove into the man's face, scratching down his cheeks with sharp little claws. He flapped his arms at the little fire lizard and covered his eyes to protect them.

That was all the opening Mirrim needed.

"Up!" she ordered Tolly. The fire lizard soared for the ceiling beams, his voice joining Reppa's and Lok's. Shifting all her weight to her bent right leg, she shot her foot out sideways, and took the apprentice right under the jaw. He fell backward, measuring his length among toppled benches.

It had taken the Holders in the dining hall moments to realize that a fight was going on behind them, but the voices of the fire lizards were impossible to ignore. The Holders reacted swiftly enough once they saw what was happening. Two men pulled the youth upright, slapping his face to bring him back to consciousness. "Now," the first one said amiably, "what's going on here?"

"He attacked me," Mirrim explained, panting a little. "I was talking to his master . . . he's gone." She looked around, but the trader had removed himself from the hall, probably as soon as the fray began. "I had to defend myself."

"Never mind," the man said. "He'll do all the explaining that'll need to be heard. Attacking a dragonrider's a serious offense. The Lord Holder'll have a lot to say to him, and to his master."

# Section 71

"The dragonrider needs to get back to Cove Hold for Threadfall," Dannen announced, stepping forward and taking her arm. Respectfully the Holders parted, leaving an aisle for them.

"Thank you," Mirrim told him, hurrying out beside Dannen. She called Path down from the fire heights. "I didn't know how I would get out of there quickly. I haven't got long. It's a good thing Path can go *between*. Did you say good-bye to your father?"

"No. I'll be staying here with him for a while."

Mirrim stopped and stared at him, disappointed. "Aren't you coming back with me? What about your runnerbeast?"

He grinned at her. "I'm going to stay around and see if there's anything I can't dig up about those traders for you. My runner will be safe at Cove until I get back for him. I'll see you at the wedding. Just remember to save at least six dances for me. Is it a bargain?"

"But what if I can't go?" Mirrim asked helplessly.

"You'll be there," Dannen assured her. "I know it." In an impulsive motion which surprised them both, he pulled Mirrim close in his arms and kissed her soundly on the mouth. "That seals the bargain," he told her, his blue eyes merry and warm. "You'd better go. Here comes Path. Good-bye, Mirrim, and good luck!"

Mirrim stood motionless for a moment in the center of the stableyard staring after Dannen as he dashed away.

*Let us go,* Path called to her as the green dragon swept down to meet her in the stableyard. *They are waiting for us.*

With a rueful scowl on her face, Mirrim came out of her trance. "Oh, I know. And we'd better hurry."

*Turn to section 58.*

# * **72** *

"That's right," said one of the men in the crowd. "I saw him swing his fist at her. She was only defending herself."

The steward stared at the apprentice, who was half sprawled on the floor at his feet. The young man scowled defiantly at him, not bothering to speak in his own defense. "That'll most likely mean a fine for you, and for your master. On your feet! The Lord Warder will want a word with you!"

While the Warder was berating the now-chastened bully, Dannen grabbed Mirrim's hand and hustled her out of the hall and out the main Hold entrance. "You must get back to Path. Never mind them. If any speaking needs to be done, I will speak for you. My father will stand with me. He may be hard to live with, but he is fair. When is Thread expected?"

Mirrim squinted at the sun and began to calculate the difference in hours between Cove Hold and Telgar. "Oh, no!" she cried, and started to run back toward the stableyard. "Not more than half an hour."

Dannen ran after her, his longer legs keeping up at an easy pace. "Wait," he said, catching her arm. "It'll be all right. You'll be on time. I'm staying here with my father."

Mirrim looked at him, disappointed. "Aren't you coming back with me?"

He grinned at her. "I'm going to stay around and see if there's anything I can dig up about those traders. My runner will be safe at Cove until I get back for him. I'll see you at the wedding. Just remember to save at least six dances for me. Is it a bargain?"

"But what if I can't go?" Mirrim asked helplessly, all her troubles coming back to her, on top of the growing fear that she'd have to answer to F'nor for being late to Threadfall.

"You'll be there," Dannen assured her. "I know it." In an impulsive motion which surprised them both, he pulled Mirrim close in his arms and kissed her soundly on the mouth. "That seals the bargain," he told her, his blue eyes merry and warm. "You'd better go. Here comes Path. Good-bye, Mirrim, and good luck!"

Mirrim stood motionless for a moment in the center of the stableyard staring after Dannen as he dashed away.

*Let us go,* Path called to her as the green dragon swept down from the Hold's fire heights. *They are waiting for us.*

With a rueful scowl on her face, Mirrim came out of her trance. "Oh, I know. And we'd better hurry."

*Turn to section 58.*

*Turn to section 58.*

* **73** *

"I can't take you directly *between* to Telgar," Mirrim explained the next morning as they bathed and oiled Path. "Living flesh can stand *between* because the blood circulates to warm the body up again, but I'm sure that uprooted plants would freeze solid in seconds."

"I'm sorry I asked," Dannen said, kicking a rock, clearly not happy to have his ideas trodden on. "I just wanted my father to see my work."

"I'm not saying he can't," Mirrim answered, exasperated that he was letting ego get in the way of reality. "Master Idarolan should be docking in Cove Hold or the Ship Meadow bay very soon. We can ask him to take your bag of plants to Telgar, and keep out a few examples to show your father. It will take a sevenday or so, but at least they will reach your father alive. Then I *will* take you *between* to Telgar."

"Thank you, Mirrim," Dannen said, his good humor returning. "I should have trusted you to have a good reason."

Mirrim smiled. "I won't be able to stay too long. Thread falls later today over Cove Hold, and I must be back on time."

They found Master Idarolan's three-masted ship in the harbor at Cove Hold when Path circled in to land on the ridge overlooking the dock. The Masterfisherman himself was in the Hold being served wine by Brekke. His sun-seamed face crinkled into an expression of pleasure when he saw Mirrim. "Well met, young Mirrim. How are you?"

"Very well, sir," Mirrim smiled. "May I present Journeyman Farmcrafter Dannen?"

"And what may I do for you, Journeyman Dannen?"

The fair-haired crafter explained his errand, and asked if Idarolan could find room for his bag of onions. He held out the smaller parcel, picked out from his huge sack of gleanings.

"I'd be happy to," the Masterfisherman said, smiling. "Will you be able to pay the fare for shipment?"

Dannen swallowed. "How much will that be, sir?"

"Oh," Idarolan hefted the bag. "It is usually by weight that I calculate the cost. So"—his eyes twinkled—"it should cost just under a thirty-second of a thirty-second. But as I've not change for a thirty-second piece, I'll have to waive it. I'm teasing you, son!" the Masterfisherman laughed, and Dannen looked relieved. "Just write out a hide tag saying its contents and destination, and I'll ask around if anyone in Big Bay will carry it northwards to Telgar for me."

"Thank you, sir!" Dannen exclaimed.

"Nothing to it," Idarolan assured him. "Any friend of young Mirrim is a friend of mine."

They bid Idarolan and Brekke a courteous farewell and returned to Path. The green dragon moved to the edge of the hilltop and sprang upward, using the extra depth of the slope to give herself wingspace on the narrow crown. Dannen clutched Mirrim nervously as they flew high and slipped into *between*.

Mirrim gasped as they came out of *between*. It was full spring here in the north, but the temperature was far below that of the hot tropical morning they had just left.

The blue watchdragon on the fire ridge of Telgar Hold warbled a challenge, and Path answered with her name and Weyr affiliation. *Berelth says welcome, and S'tarl sends his greetings.*

"Good," Mirrim said. "Give him mine, please, and tell him we're visiting Farmcraftmaster Folidor in the Hold."

*He says I may stay up on the fire ridge with Berelth, and he will tell Lord Larad we are here.*

Mirrim stripped the flying straps from Path's neck and put them on a hook on the wall of the stable. As soon as her passengers had dismounted, Path spread her wings and bounded upward. Berelth, on the heights, trumpeted cheerfully to her. The fire lizards soared off in a colorful explosion to join the fairs of local fire lizards already coming to greet them.

"Come on," Dannen said. "I'll take you to meet my parents."

Telgar Hold was one of the handsomer habitations on Pern. The prow-shaped cliff face out of which the central Hold was hewn had a sheer, smooth facade marked along five levels with broad bronze-shuttered windows. Brightly painted designs decorated the colored eaves of each stone cothold, and the people wore clothing dyed in the vivid hues imported from Southern Boll and Igen. Mirrim, in her wherhide, felt quite drab by comparison.

A train of small wheeled carts pulled by canines passed by them. Each cart was piled high with a different sort of vegetable, all familiar to Mirrim—redroot, tubers, greens, orange finger-roots, river grains in sacks, and the like; and a plump, berobed steward standing at the door with a slate and stylus checked the produce in. He barely noticed them as they went by him after the last cart.

Master Folidor was not to be found in the family's sleeping quarters. Instead, a drudge directed them to a small building outside the main Hold, where they came upon the Masterfarmer doling out quantities of seeds to his journeymen. He was a round-bellied, heavy-jowled man with gray hair and thick black eyebrows sketching surprised arcs on his forehead. Mirrim decided Dannen must look like his mother.

"Those are to be monitored, mind you," Folidor insisted. "Have the Holders *count* every seed they put in the ground, and count every one that comes up. Or doesn't come up. We will see to calculating the yield. Well, hello, boy," the Masterfarmer said, turning away from his work. "This is a pleasant surprise. Have you seen your mother?"

"Not yet, sir," Dannen said, embracing his father. "May I introduce Mirrim?"

"Charmed, dragonrider. M'rim, is it?" He put out his hand palm up, and she covered it with one gloved hand. Folidor looked down at her glove quizzically, one eyebrow up.

"Forgive me," Mirrim said, and pulled off gloves and flying helmet.

"Well met, indeed," Folidor said, smiling, watching her braids tumble down her back. "I know who you are now, green rider of Benden. Bless me, your Impression raised some eyebrows among the old boys hereabout. Well, boy, you didn't come all the way from Southern to

# Section 73

impress me with your dragonrider acquaintance—a joke, young lady. What have you to show me?"

"These," Dannen said triumphantly. He unfastened the tie around his carry-sack's neck and plucked out a fistful of plants. "The onions I was growing in the south. One season to edible roots, two to seed."

Folidor took them from his son and examined them closely, his bushy eyebrows almost touching over his nose. The plants' leaves appeared to be wilted and their stems brittle. "Yes, yes, well grown, poor things. But they're dead! Where would they sustain cold damage in the Southern Continent?"

Mirrim spoke up. "We came directly *between* from the growing ground, Master Folidor. On dragonback."

The eyebrows sprang apart. "Oho! That's where the frost set in. Frozen in a flash, you might say. You know what the Harpers' tales say about *between*."

"That's why we have only these few," Dannen added. "The rest will be here when the *Dawn Sister* returns to the north."

"Good, good. I'll keep an ear cocked. Meantime, I'll see if I can start any of these seeds in a sheltered bed." Folidor smiled down at the handful of round black pips. "Well grown, well grown indeed. Only my native impatience keeps me from calling a celebration. I want to see these plants mature for myself!"

*Turn to section 77.*

## * **74** *

With one hand, she steadied the top of the bench on its rocking legs, and slid carefully closer. At last, she could understand what the trader was saying. "Of course, our sources guarantee the authenticity of this little treasure," he was saying. "It is one of a kind."

"And from which Turn do you think this comes?" the weaver inquired.

"This is of unknown age, sir. I cannot guarantee, but I assume that what you hold right now was once held in the very hands of one of our Ancient ancestors." Mirrim's mouth fell open, and she strained to see out of the corner of her eye what the item was.

*Turn to section 67.*

## * **75** *

"That wasn't at all like it happened," one of the men spoke up. "The dragonrider accused his master. I heard her. She said he'd thieved something from the Old-timers."

"My master never stole anything from the Oldtimers," the apprentice smirked. The witness's mishearing of Mirrim's statement suited his lie well.

# Section 75

"I didn't say he stole from the Oldtimers," Mirrim protested. "I said he had something that belonged to the Ancient Timers. The ones who lived on the plateau in the Southern Continent thousands of Turns ago."

"Yes, but they're long dead," the steward said, wrinkling his forehead. "Doesn't that throw off the question of ownership?"

"Lord Toric and Lord Lytol have instructed that nothing is to be removed from the place where it was found," Mirrim tried to explain. Just as quickly, she tried to swallow her words. There she went again, putting herself into the middle of things. Lessa would be angry. It would have been better if she had kept her mouth shut and informed the Weyrleaders about this trader. Obviously, if he had received that stylus here in Telgar, there was some kind of network in operation, which took whatever pieces looked interesting to them from the site.

"Then it's a matter for the Council of Lords," the steward said, signing to a couple of burly Holders to haul the apprentice to his feet. "You can explain it all to Lord Larad. He'll sort it out, and, if necessary, take it into Council or call in the Weyrleaders. None of my business. It's beyond my authority."

"But . . ." Mirrim sputtered, but he wasn't listening to her. With a firm hand, he guided her out the door, and steered her toward Lord Larad's quarters. She looked over her shoulder at Dannen, who shrugged his shoulders helplessly as she was led away. She would be in disgrace now until her last day. Lessa would never forgive her for involving the Lord of another Hold in Weyr matters.

*Turn to section 29.*

## * **76** *

With one hand, she steadied the top of the bench and slid carefully closer. To her dismay, the bench rocked back and forth on its standards and creaked alarmingly. The movement halted the trader's eloquence, and he turned toward Mirrim, his eyes meeting hers. She turned scarlet and hastily averted her face.

The two men resumed their conversation, and Mirrim strained to overhear them. The phrases, "one of a kind," and "of unknown age," rolled by, but she was unable to understand more.

*Turn to section 67.*

## * **77** *

"Come and have a drink," Folidor offered, standing up when the last of his apprentices and journeymen had been given their tasks. "There's good wine to be had in the dining hall. Winemaster Ollag's a friend of mine, and he saves me a bit of the best for special occasions such as this."

He led them to the hall, deep inside the Hold complex. Others had the same idea as Folidor, taking time out of the middle of a busy day to share wine in a friendly atmosphere. There were tables full of crafters and holders lingering over the remains of their midday meal or a brimful goblet. In the warm air stirred by the hearthfires, Mirrim could smell the heady fragrance of the wines being poured even as she came in. Not a bad bouquet, but in pride she assured herself it couldn't compare to a Benden wine.

Folidor confessed that the spring in Telgar, too, had been unseasonably hot. "All to the good, though, speaking as a farmer. I'm not protesting that. No ill happens which cannot be turned to good. Even soured wine has its uses, as I always say. In fact, we're to have a large crop surplus at harvest time because of the heat. A lot of it will go to the Weyr. Right and proper, I think. Not that I didn't have to have it proved to me, Turns back before Thread fell. To my own credit, I must protest I didn't need it explained twice, not like some in this Hold. Dragons are living animals, and animals need fodder!"

Mirrim had to consider whether she thought it an insult to have dragons called mere "animals," but decided it was just the Farmcraftmaster's way of distinguishing dragons from plants, which they most assuredly were not.

The three of them made themselves comfortable at one end of a long table with wooden benches pulled up close. The tabletop was a thin slab of stone balanced on trestles of metal, as were the seats of the benches. That Lord Larad could afford wooden seats in the very Hold dining hall where drudge and Lord Holder alike ate spoke eloquently of his Hold's wealth. Wood, though more common everywhere, was still dear. The bench rocked slightly as Mirrim sat down. Folidor raised a hand and attracted the attention of a drudge, who pointed out the Telgar Winecraftmaster's nook to him. The drudge was sent for meatrolls while Folidor went over to chat with his friend.

In a short time he returned with a full wineskin and three earthen goblets. "Ollag was generous. He says welcome back to you, Dannen, and greetings to the dragonrider, Mirrim. This is one of his specials. I've no idea of the year it was pressed, nor how he gets it just so. He claims that sort of secret is trade talk among winemen alone." He poured for all of them and set the skin on the table. To Mirrim's surprise, the wine was pink, not the usual white-gold of Benden wines.

"There," Folidor sighed, setting down the glass after a long draught. "There's tasty." Mirrim sipped hers and had to agree. It was good, potent wine, even a little stronger than what she was used to at the Weyr. "So," Folidor urged, "indulge an old man's curiosity. How did the two of you happen to be hunting greens together?"

Mirrim glanced sharply at Dannen, but he gave her a reassuring nod. "I all but missed harvesting my experimental crops when I staggered into Cove Hold with some gifts for the Master Harper. The lady Mirrim kindly offered to fly me back to my patch. Thread falls later today, so her visit won't be long, but she was kind enough to bring me here so I could see you."

The big man slapped the table and guffawed. "And there're those who say the dragonriders'll not stir from their Weyrs between Threadfalls. I'll tell them dragonfolk'll not stick at helping Holders. That will shake a few composed minds, it will."

"Mirrim is . . . Brekke's fosterling, Father." The cautious way in which he spoke her name told Mirrim that he'd remembered what had happened to Brekke and Wirenth.

"What? What's that you say?" Folidor humphed softly in his throat. "Well, small wonder then that her fosterling has learned kindness to others. She was always such a considerate child." He took another swallow of wine, cleared his throat. "That aside, boy, tell me what you've been doing!"

Though she tried to pay attention to their conversation, Mirrim felt her eyes begin to glaze over with the technical terms the two farmcrafters shot over her head as Dannen and his father fell into a deep discussion of germination periods and crop yield. Soon, they forgot that she was there. To clear her mind, she ignored their conversation and studied the others in the chamber. Three large and dusty men, farmholders by their garb, were chatting over a pitcher of ale. One of them had a new white bandage wound around his arm, which he held stiffly. Professional curiosity made Mirrim want to go over and ask what had happened to him and see if she could ease the stiffness. If she listened intently, she could almost hear what the man was saying.

At the other end of the table where Mirrim sat, a trader with a journeyman's knot on his shoulder was bargaining glibly with a prosperous-looking weaver as the trader's apprentices watched quietly. It was evidently a lively dicker, and it wouldn't be long before that journeyman walked the tables to mastership, if this was any sample of his skill. She shifted her bottom slightly closer on the bench toward them, hoping she wouldn't be noticed. It wasn't polite to eavesdrop, but the man's animation, and the rise and fall of his voice, were hard to ignore.

*Roll 3 D6.*

*If the total is less than or equal to Mirrim's value for Dexterity, turn to section 74.*

*If greater, turn to section 76.*

## * **78** *

When they were high enough over Telgar, Mirrim signed to Path to go *between* to Cove Hold. Instantly they vanished from the sunlit sky of the north and plunged into the cold blackness of *between*. Mirrim could feel no part of her body, nor the neck of the dragon she sat astride, but she still had the bond that existed between her whole being and Path's, that let her know she was not alone in the void. To go from one place to another took only the time it took one to cough three times, and yet it always seemed like an eternity to Mirrim.

They emerged into blazing daylight over Cove Hold. Mirrim's body thawed out from the cold of *between* in the tropical heat. As they descended into place in the formation, Mirrim threw a high sign to F'nor. The knot of concern between the Wing-second's brows undid itself, and he waved back.

*Canth says F'nor is relieved you are here, but you must be on time next time,* Path told her. Mirrim swallowed, knowing that she was guilty of a breach of discipline. She resolved to be more conscientious in the future.

The leading edge of Threadfall was well in sight, only two hands of minutes from the Hold. Mirrim reached for the sack of firestone, leaning well forward against the secure hold of the fighting straps.

"I hope you can chew quickly," she warned Path. "It's almost upon us."

With a loud report, the rear strap split on both sides. Mirrim threw herself forward, tightening her knees and wrapping her arms as far as she could around Path's

neck. It couldn't save her. As soon as she moved he
weight, the front loop split, too. Mirrim was so surprised
she lost her grip on Path. She scrabbled to get some sor
of hold on a neck ridge, but the unraveling ends of th
neck loops dashed her hands away. Mirrim tumble
backward, off the last neck ridge, down the smooth
length of Path's spine between the wings, and plum
meted off the base of the dragon's tail into the sea.

Bugling alarm, Path dove out of the sky after her
Mirrim was far below the surface, fighting to get free o
the hide straps, which wove about her like a sea monster
threatening to surround and engulf her with its tentacles
She was horribly hampered by the heavy wherhide ridin
garments which ballooned around her under the water
Realizing that she needed fresh air desperately *now,* she
kicked off her boots and struggled toward the surface.

*Mirrim! Mirrim!* Above her, the girl saw a huge, dark
shape bearing down on her. She shied momentarily a
the obstruction, losing precious air in a panicked gasp
then caught blurry sight of Path's luminous eyes, whirling red behind their protective third lids. Mirrim realized she couldn't last much longer, and kicked with the
last of her strength toward the green dragon. With the
edge of her water-logged glove, she managed to catch
hold of a clawed toe, and pulled herself toward the foot
Path scooped her rider in with her massive foreclaws and
shot upward toward the air.

"Get ashore!" F'nor's shout met them as they broke
the surface. Mirrim, vision nearly blackened from lack
of oxygen, nodded an exhausted acknowledgment, and
clutched Path as the lithe green dragon swam toward the
beach.

Mirrim all but crawled ashore, to be met by Brekke,
who must have heard from the dragons what happened,
and Lytol. The Lord Warder drew his knife, slit the belt
straps, and pulled Mirrim inside as the sodden mass
dropped in a heap on the sand.

"What happened?" Brekke demanded, throwing a

drying cloth around Mirrim's shoulders, and helping the girl to take off her gloves and belt.

"The straps broke," Mirrim said. "First one, then the other. Thank the Egg that it happened after I went *between* instead of before! I could have been spilled off over Telgar Hold." She shuddered, and went on removing her flying gear.

Brekke's forehead creased with worry as she rushed to the kitchen for hot klah. Robinton sat down beside Mirrim, resting his elbows on his knees. "I thought that was new leather, my dear."

"It was!" Mirrim exclaimed, then realized she was missing Threadfall. "I must go! F'nor needs me." She threw off the drying cloth and ran toward the door.

"Mirrim, wait. You can't fight Thread with soaking wet gear. You'd be frozen solid the first time Path went *between*," Robinton said reasonably, laying a hand on her arm. "You and I will just have to sit this one out behind shutters."

The trader's apprentice made his way back to the quarters which he shared with his master and the other apprentice. "Did you . . . take care of the dragonrider?" inquired the journeyman trader.

"I did, Sotessi." The young man grinned, a mirthless showing of teeth. "She got lucky, though. Nothing happened. Maybe it'll just scare her into leaving us alone."

"Perhaps," Sotessi agreed thoughtfully. "I doubt we've heard the last of that young lady. Never mind. She hasn't heard the last of us, either."

When Fall had ended, Mirrim joined the others doing a sweep of the ground for any traces of viable Thread. They knew that it was largely unnecessary in Southern, but as Robinton voiced for all of them, "Habits, especially survival habits, are very hard to break." When the others had gone inside for a meal, and the dragonriders took their beasts into the sea to get cleaned up, Mirrim dragged her fighting gear from the beach to the stone porch of the Hold. She wanted to make a close examination of the hide. How could nearly new gear disintegrate like that? Had she neglected any scores left by the last Threadfall? Was it actually weak hide that she had mistaken for strong?

When she spread the straps out and looked at the torn edges, the real answer was much more chilling. The straps had been cut. Not all the way through, only enough so that they would look whole on cursory examination, but would withstand only a tug or two before they broke apart. She thought hard about where the damage might have occurred over the next two days, repairing her straps and waiting for Thread to fall again.

*Roll 2 D6 and return the total to Mirrim's hit points.*

*Turn to section 84.*

## \* **79** \*

*We must hurry,* Path urged her.

"Oh, I know," Mirrim grumbled. "Don't be a nag. I have to check everything. You know that."

*But Thread falls! Canth calls us.*

Mirrim swallowed and glanced at the sky, fearing that the menacing silver strands were falling down on her here, half a world away. "We can time it if we have to. F'nor will be angrier if I show up sloppy."

With deliberate hands, she felt around her tough wherryskin belt, feeling inside for the thick padding of fleece that cushioned her from midair jolts when Path would abruptly change course during Thread-fighting, and protected her kidneys and lower spine from the cold.

She pulled on the four straps depending from it and checked the fastenings that clipped onto Path's fighting straps. Check. Her scarf was in place over her face and neck, her close-fitting hide helmet properly fastened. The thick wherhide jacket was done up, and met the tops of her strong boots over the legs of her wherhide pants. All check. Path crooned a song of worry. Mirrim shot her a perturbed look, and the green dragon subsided. "This is for your well-being as well as mine," she said. "You know what ill-fitting straps feel like."

*I know,* Path replied humbly.

Feeling rushed and fumble-fingered, Mirrim let the neck loops slide between her fingers, tugging at the material to test their strength. Just then, at the side of the rear loop, she felt an out-of-the-ordinary *give* in the hide at the point which would rest on the left side of Path's neck. She peered closely at it, and discovered a tiny slit through which she could see daylight. "Uh-oh," Mirrim said, turning the strap over. "Feels like this one's ready for repair. Will you bespeak F'nor that I'll be a little delayed. He won't be happy . . ."

Her voice died away as she saw the underside of the strap. It was as if someone had taken a knife and drawn from one side of the hide to the other, leaving only the thinnest layer of top leather to hold it together. "Now how under heaven could that have happened?" Mirrim asked. "I only made these straps a few sevendays ago."

She seized the forward strap and began to examine its underside, searching with anxious fingers. To her horror, that one was cut almost all the way through, too, on the side which would be to the right of Path's neck. Those straps were new! The only way they could have given out so quickly was if they were—no, it was too much to contemplate. "These would not have withstood more than one or two strong tugs. I couldn't have done that by accident. Someone cut them on purpose!" Mirrim said definitely, but her eyes were puzzled. "But why? I couldn't fly with these. I might be killed."

*F'nor IS cross,* Path informed her. *But I have explained what has happened, and he is happy you did the check properly. He would rather have you late than badly hurt. Can we get there before the end of Fall, he asks.*

*If Mirrim decides to make temporary repairs, turn to section 80.*

*If Mirrim decides to get them fixed for sure, turn to section 86.*

## * 80 *

"Yes," Mirrim said firmly. "I'll patch these, and we'll be on our way. It won't take long at all. Tell F'nor we'll be there soon."

She set to work with haste, unwinding thongs from Path's neck sacks. With her belt knife, she pierced rows of holes along the torn edges. Licking the end of a doubled thong, she threaded it through the first set of corresponding holes, knotted it fast, and repeated the process across the width of the straps. When she finished, she made several knots in the ends and cut them short.

"It's not the best, but it'll have to do. We must get there!" Mirrim declared. She held up the straps for Path, and helped settle them at the base of the green dragon's neck.

*They are not comfortable, but they feel secure.*

"Good!" Mirrim stepped up onto Path's foreleg and jumped into her place between the neck ridges. With quick movements, she fastened the belt ties to the straps. "Let's go!"

## Section 81

Path spread her great wings and bounded into the sky.

She and Path got to Cove Hold in time to meet the other dragonriders as Threadfall was ending. She stood uncomfortably studying her boot-tops as F'nor tore strips out of her for being late to her duties and for neglecting her gear. Mirrim didn't tell the angry brown rider that she suspected her straps had been sabotaged. Abashed, she spent the next two days shoring up her fighting gear, and when Thread fell again, she was ready on the dot.

*Roll 2 D6 and return the total to Mirrim's hit points.*

*Turn to section 84.*

## * 81 *

As she and Path circled high above the Hold, Mirrim pictured the coordinates for Cove Hold. She intended to appear just over the dock, protecting the Hold and wherry pens as had been her duty before. Path caught an updraft under one wing and turned. To Mirrim's horror, the front strap split with a loud *snap*, jostling her to one side. Unrestrained, the second strap began to turn, and coming right into her field of vision, Mirrim could see a split forming in the back strap. She scrabbled to hold on to the neck ridges, but the moving straps knocked her hands away. "My straps have broken! Path!" She unlocked the short ties holding her to the big loops and watched with a sick feeling as they slid off Path's back and spiraled down to hit the stones far below. "Get us down!"

Bugling in alarm, Path began to descend, calling to Berelth. *Mirrim is falling! Help me save her!*

The blue dragon leaped upward from his perch on the fire heights. He began as a tiny figure in Mirrim's field of vision, but he grew quickly as he stroked the air with his strong wings, hurrying toward them. Mirrim felt herself slipping. On command, Path canted her angle of descent so that Mirrim could flatten herself between the neck ridges. They continued along a very slight downward slope.

With both arms wrapped as far around Path's neck as she could reach, Mirrim hung on, a grim expression on her face. Those straps were new! The only way they could have given out so quickly was if they were—no, it was too much to contemplate. Who hated her so much as to want to kill her? And why? But whether by accident or sabotage, she was in mortal danger.

Berelth matched their angle of descent and flattened his great back below her, making a broad platform to break her fall just in case. From *between*, two other dragons and riders appeared above them in response to Berelth's call for help, and arrowed down toward the imperiled Mirrim.

Path was frantic, trying to smooth her flight so her rider wouldn't fall. She had her wings open to their maximum stretch, avoiding more than the most cursory wingtip flutters to maintain her easy course. The two other dragons, a bronze and another green, maneuvered to cover the area around Berelth.

"How did it happen?" one of the other riders asked, bespeaking Mirrim through Path.

"My fighting straps broke," Mirrim strained out through her teeth. She could no longer see the ground below because of the other dragons, but it seemed to be taking Path an incredibly long time to land.

"You tried to fly with unsafe straps?"

"*No!* I mean—" Mirrim's abashed reply was cut off when an updraft hit them as they passed over a forest.

Path, unable to keep from responding to it, turned into the wind for stability. Mirrim was so surprised, she lost her grip on Path. With a scream, she tumbled backward, off the last neck ridge, down the smooth length of spine between Path's wings, and plummeted off the base of her dragon's tail.

*Roll 2 D6.*

*If the total is five or under, turn to section 83.*

*If the total is six or greater, turn to section 89.*

# * 82 *

*We must hurry,* Path urged her.

"Oh, I know," Mirrim grumbled. "All right." She held up the great loops and Path put her head through them, throwing them back to the last ridges on her neck. "Firestone, do I have enough firestone?" Mirrim asked herself frantically, sure that she'd picked up a sack of Cromcoal instead of the right stuff. Sneaking a quick glance in the bag, Mirrim gave a relieved sigh. "It's firestone all right," she affirmed, tying the bag to Path's neck straps. That was the last check she could make. There was no time to see to her flight gear. She could only hope that she had fastened on her belt correctly, and that not another square fingertip of skin was exposed than needed to be. Most experienced Threadfighters had scores on their faces and necks. As she climbed up on Path's neck, she patted the scarf that covered her face from the bridge of her nose down to the base of her throat, adjusted her protective goggles and helmet. With deft fingers, she attached her fighting straps to Path's.

"Ready!" she called out.

Path opened her great wings and bounded upward, forcing back the ground suddenly far below them.

*Roll 3 D6.*

*If the total is less than or equal to Mirrim's value for Wisdom/Luck, turn to section 78.*

*If greater, turn to section 81.*

## \* **83** \*

The wind hit her squarely, tumbling her over and over, rendering her weightless. Path's frightened bawling cut right through the rush of air. She didn't know which way she was falling until a pair of arms hit her across the back of her neck and knees. She bounced off them back into the air. Screaming, she clutched at an arm, tunic edge, until her hands locked fast onto the belt ties holding the rider to his bronze dragon's neck straps. Wide-eyed, she kicked out for a foothold, found none on the dragon's smooth neck. Relief flowed through her when the man clutched her upper arm and hauled her bodily upward. She felt something in her arm tear, but she had no time to think about pain as the rider swept her up and settled her between the neck ridges before him. Wrapping an arm around her waist, he gave the signal for the dragons to descend.

"Got you, my daring green rider! I'm D'or, Ramelth's rider." Mirrim looked back at the grinning face of the man holding her. He was a broad-chested youth with strong white teeth and the end of a red curl escaping from under his helmet's edge. Ramelth peered back at them over his shoulder as he made for a landing spot in among the trees.

"Mirrim, rider of Path," she managed to croak out, through a throat dry with fear and relief.

"You were lucky, Mirrim, that some of us were instructing weyrlings at the time Bereth called for help, otherwise no one in Telgar would have been scrambled! We've just finished with our latest Fall. It's a funny thing, being called out by your own dragon." He was silent for a moment, giving instructions, and Ramelth landed in a small field bounded by young saplings. Path landed beside them, and hurried to Mirrim, crooning deep in her throat. Mirrim hastened off Ramelth's neck with thanks, and ran to her dragon to reassure her.

"I've sent V'tor for your straps. I think we'd spotted where they fell. We'll do a proper patch on your gear at the Weyr, and send you home to Benden."

Mirrim reddened, but D'or didn't seem to notice. "I'm at Cove Hold for now."

"Ah!" D'or obviously didn't think that constituted exile. In fact, he appeared to envy her. "With the Master Harper? How does he?"

"Very well." She opened her mouth to say something about the Ancient Timers' dig, and thought better of it. Then, she started to mention the wedding in Southern that was bare days away. . . . In the end, she remained silent, stroking and caring for Path, who was still upset about the near-disaster. But Mirrim was nearly swaying on her feet from shock.

"We'd best get you to the Healer, Mirrim. You're pale."

"I'm all right," Mirrim protested. D'or swept her up.

"Path and I will fly direct to the Weyr." He signed to the others to go *between*. Path took wing, staying close to Ramelth.

The bowl of Telgar Weyr had a natural lip like a thumb that rose at its northern end, dividing the winds which blew down on it from the Northern Barrier Range. In the notch at its southern end, pointing the way down the Central Mountain Range to Igen Weyr, perched a weyrling on watch duty who waved them on in when they appeared from the southwest. Mirrim didn't see much of the rest. Ramelth landed them close to the living caverns, and she was hurried in to see the Healers. Before she knew it, she was flat on her back on a rush-stuffed bed, and two women were examining her. The elder, a brown-skinned woman with an ageless face and a wonderful braid of gray hair that swept the hem of her sleeve, felt gently along Mirrim's collarbone. Her hands smelled of redwort and comfrey. Mirrim found the aroma comforting.

"Only dislocated," she declared, signing to her assistant, who slathered numbweed on Mirrim's neck and upper chest. The pain-deadening salve worked immediately, and the red-hot pain, of which Mirrim had been scarcely aware, receded. She felt herself relaxing, and settled into sleep while the Healers worked. She could rest here.

*Roll 1 D6 and remove the number rolled from Mirrim's hit points.*

*If her hit points are reduced to 0, turn to section 29.*

*If she still has hit points, turn to section 85.*

## * **84** *

Mirrim watched Path pick a third and then a fourth wherry out of the pens behind the Hold on the morning before Threadfall was due. "Don't gorge yourself, or you won't feel like flying later," Mirrim admonished her.

*I am very hungry,* Path answered simply, carrying the bird back to her wallow. *I will fly well when I have eaten.*

Mirrim sat down with a sigh, and began to shine her boots again. These were old ones; her new ones had been utterly ruined the day of the last Fall. This pair was already as neat and shiny as glass, but she wasn't satisfied. Nothing she did today could make up for the disaster of failing in her responsibilities. For two days she had worked like a whirlwind, cleaning and scrubbing and sanding Path until the dragon pleaded that she was clean enough. Her gear was spotless and oiled to a suppleness almost equal to that of the living wher from which the hide had come.

"Mirrim?" Brekke appeared beside her with a pitcher of fruit juice. "Would you like some? You haven't eaten anything yet today."

"I have to finish preparing my gear," Mirrim explained, holding up the brush and the boot she was working on. "And take care of Path."

"You can't neglect the rider," Brekke said gently.

"I'm not," Mirrim protested sharply. But she did accept a cup of juice. It was freshly squeezed, and tasted sweet and tart at once. When she drank it, she realized how empty her stomach was. She looked hopefully over her shoulder at the kitchen door. Brekke smiled, her thin face lighting up. She squatted beside her and rested an arm around Mirrim's waist.

"Well, the rest of us are taking a meal now. You can leave the boots until later."

Staring down at the flagstones, Mirrim laid down the brush and followed Brekke inside.

She found little to say during the meal, though everyone present, F'fej and D'dot, F'nor, Lytol, Robinton, and Brekke herself, tried to bring her into the conversation. Mirrim was determined not to give offense again. Even to teasing she responded with forced gaiety and solemn eyes. F'nor encouraged camaraderie among his riders since they'd be going into dangerous situations and needed to rely upon one another.

They were joined this time by three more junior riders, and, to Mirrim's chagrin, F'lessan and his bronze Golanth, who would act as Wing-second to F'nor over the second three. Not that she didn't like the Benden Weyrleader's son, but he served as more of a reminder of her disgrace. She was closer than she had been before to discovering who had actually stolen from the Ancient Timers' site, yet not a step closer to clearing her name. She had suspicions, but no evidence that she could use.

After the meal was finished, Mirrim went out to Path's wallow, and put the patched fighting straps around the dragon's neck. When she was satisfied as to their fit, she began the safety check, not missing a single detail.

Sensing Mirrim's internal agitation, Path crooned sadly, and the girl hugged the great green head to her. "I'm fine," she whispered, scratching the soft hide around Path's head knobs. Path forgot about the pervasive sense of worry, and let her eyelids drift closed in ecstasy. The other dragons were being prepared now, and the riders ignored them, concerned only with their own dragons and safety checks.

F'fej ran back to the wallows, heading for Camuth. "Leading edge is in sight!" He put a foot on the blue's outstretched foreleg and vaulted into place on the neck ridges. With a mental command to Path, Mirrim climbed up and fastened her ties down.

On F'nor's command, the eight dragons bounded off the rock ridge and into the sky, arraying themselves to his direction. Golanth, the only bronze present, hung glittering in the sky like the sun at twilight, though he was much the same size as brown Canth. Admittedly, Canth was the biggest brown dragon on Pern. Though it was no disgrace for a bronze to meet his size, it seemed somehow curious that the Weyrleader's son wouldn't have a dragon as large as the Weyrleader's. Still, he was beautiful. F'lessan spent hours grooming his dragon every day. Now he sat smugly in place, his endlessly long legs dangling astride Golanth's neck. Mirrim hoped only that Path looked as clean and shimmery to the others as his did. To her, Path was perfect, but Mirrim might have missed some small place that would displease the Wing-seconds.

F'nor swept his gaze back at the hovering dragons. Golanth's wing consisted of two more greens and another blue. Path chewed chunks of firestone, and between the grinding and crunching of masticating rock, Mirrim fancied she could hear the rumble of building gases. F'nor raised a hand, and they swept forward to meet the leading edge of Thread.

Behind the scarf covering her face, Mirrim gasped as she always did, when she sized up their ancient enemy. Thread, the shimmering, dragon-long strands, which could suck the life out of any living creature or plant, seemed so harmless as it drifted on the wind. Clumps of Thread formed, broke apart, re-formed, and rained into the sea with a delicate hiss. The three large dragons—Canth, Golanth, and Elekith—soared upward to meet the greater patches of Thread, leaving the smaller ones for the five blues and greens. It was the sound which brought Mirrim out of her trance as Path drew nearer to their first target, a clump of Thread slowly elongating as it fell.

"To the left, Path. We'll sear this one from above."
Mirrim leaned to the left, and started violently as she
realized she was applying weight to the recently repaired
straps. They were holding as if they had been new, a
tribute to expert tannery work, and much careful glueing
by Mirrim. She relaxed, and dedicated her concentration
to fighting Thread.

Path angled her flight, gaining altitude as they moved
toward the patch of Thread. They were in the perfect
position—! "Now!" Mirrim cried.

*Roll 3 D6.*

*If the total rolled is less than or equal to Mirrim's value for
Dexterity, turn to section 90.*

*If greater, turn to section 87.*

* **85** *

With her arm in a temporary sling, Mirrim spent the
next several hours sitting in the workshop of the Telgar
Weyr tanner, who was only too happy to assist a Benden
dragonrider. "These were well made, but what did you
do to them to make them go like that?" the tanner, a craft
journeyman, inquired. "They look almost like they've
been cut!"

"I don't know," Mirrim admitted miserably.

The trader's apprentice made his way back to the
quarters which he shared with his master and the other
apprentice. "Did you . . . take care of the dragonrider?"
inquired the journeyman trader.

"I did, Sotessi. I cut her riding straps, but she got

## Section 86

lucky, sear the skin!" the sullen young man swore. "She
fell off but other dragonriders saved her. Maybe it'll just
scare her into leaving us alone."

"Perhaps," Sotessi agreed thoughtfully. "I doubt we've
heard the last of that young lady. Never mind. She hasn't
heard the last of us, either."

Mirrim arrived back in Cove Hold shortly after the
following edge was just out of sight on the sea. She faced
down a scolding from F'nor for missing her duties, for
not being around when expected, and for neglecting her
gear almost to the cost of her own life. The Wing-second
laced her up one side and down the other. Mirrim didn't
voice her suspicions to him that the straps had been
tampered with, but took her lecture with downcast eyes.
She spent the next two days shoring up her fighting
gear, and when Thread fell again, she was ready on the
dot.

*Roll 2 D6 and return the total to Mirrim's hit points.*

*Turn to section 84.*

* **86** *

"No," Mirrim sighed, letting the straps fall to the
ground. "They're hopeless. I'll have to borrow materials
from the Hold tanner to patch them. But this time I
won't let these straps out of my sight!" She knew she was
in for a terrible scolding, and she felt miserable and
guilty.

Mirrim spent the next several hours in the workshop
of the Telgar Hold tanner, who was only too happy to

assist a dragonrider. He even insisted on fixing Mirrim's gear himself. "I know what I owe to the Weyr, dear lady. You just sit right there. It won't take but a snap."

The shop was small but well ventilated, a building constructed right up against the cliff into which the Hold was built, with windows opening out onto a splendid view of the Telgar plainslands.

"Are you sure I can't decorate these for you, Lady Mirrim?" the tanner asked. He was a pleasant bronze-skinned man whose front teeth's bottom edge was set along a diagonal line, giving him a slight lisp. "We've some splendidly vivid green dye just in from Southern Boll. Match your Path's hide, only darker. For best contrast, of course."

Mirrim laughed, her gloomy face remolded into pretty delight. "No, please don't waste the effort. But thank you kindly. This is just a mend and patch job on a pair which won't last very long now. I'll have to make new straps almost right away."

The tanner turned the damaged straps over in his hands, which were stained with Turns' worth of colored dyes and fixatives. "These were well made, lady. You should have been in the Tannerscraft."

Mirrim just smiled, looking out of the broad window at Path, who was sunning herself on the cobbles. "No, I wouldn't have missed Impression for all the crafts on Pern. Oh, no offense."

"None taken, my lady." The tanner gave her an amused little grin and went back to stitching hide around the cut edges. Mirrim watched him for a while, and then turned her attention out the window. "There!" the tanner declared, bringing her back from *between*. He plumped the straps down on the table. He snipped away an almost invisible length of resin-coated gut with a tiny pair of metal clippers. "Those'll do you well enough. Now don't go getting them cut up again."

"I'm not sure how they did get cut up," Mirrim muttered to herself, gathering them up. She bid the tanner thanks and farewell, and went out to Path.

\* \* \*

## Section 87

The trader's apprentice made his way back to the quarters which he shared with his master and the other apprentice. "Did you . . . take care of the dragonrider?" inquired the journeyman trader.

"I did, Sotessi. I cut her riding straps, but she got lucky, sear the skin!" the sullen young man swore. "Nothing happened. She must've discovered the cuts before taking flight."

"Perhaps," Sotessi agreed thoughtfully. "I doubt we've heard the last of that young lady. Never mind. She hasn't heard the last of us, either."

Mirrim arrived back in Cove Hold shortly after the following edge was just out of sight on the sea. She faced down a scolding from F'nor for missing her duties, for not being around when expected, and for neglecting her gear almost to the cost of her own life. The Wing-second laced her up one side and down the other. Mirrim didn't voice her suspicions to him that the straps had been tampered with, but took her lecture with downcast eyes. She spent the next two days shoring up her fighting gear, and when Thread fell again, she was ready on the dot.

*Roll 2 D6 and return the total to Mirrim's hit points.*

*Turn to section 84.*

*Turn to section 84.*

* **87** *

Path opened her mouth and breathed. The twisted filaments belled out away from her flame, and only part of the clump dissolved into a puff of black dust. No command was needed from Mirrim to send Path *be-*

*tween* to avoid the rest of the Thread that continued its downward drift toward them. They would be in the middle of it if it hadn't been for the dragon's skill at vanishing *between* just at the right moment.

When they emerged from the blackness a heartbeat later, her wingman had reduced the clump to black mist which dusted the sea. F'fej, on Camuth, had been hovering right behind and above her. She felt mildly perturbed that he assumed she might fail, but she said nothing. After all, it was standard procedure to back up your wingman, she chided herself. No doubt she was just feeling edgy. She threw a little wave at him and flew after another mass of Thread. There was no time to waste.

*Turn to section 91.*

*Turn to section 91.*

## \* **88** \*

Mirrim felt the heat through the legs of her wherhide trousers as Path belched a long gout of flame up at the Thread. The clump shriveled upward, curling in on itself, becoming a small black ball that broke apart on the wind. There was a satisfaction to destroying individual Threads, but it only reminded her that each Thread needed to be similarly treated, and there was an endless supply of the menace. She found herself wishing Dannen could be here to watch Thread-fighting. It was too bad that he decided to stay behind in Telgar with his father. Reaching forward, she stuck her hand in the carry-sack for another chunk of firestone for Path.

"Uh-oh, we're out," she told Path. "Tell Camuth we're landing to get more firestone, and to cover for us."

*He asks will you bring him some, too?* Path responded.

## Section 89

For answer, she waved a hand over her head, and Path wheeled to wing down to the beach.

*Turn to section 102.*

* **89** *

The wind hit her squarely, tumbling her over and over, rendering her weightless. Path's frightened bawling cut right through the rush of air. She didn't know which way she was falling until a pair of arms hit her across the back of her neck and knees. She bounced off them back into the air. Screaming, she clutched at an arm, tunic edge, until her hands locked fast onto the belt ties holding the rider to his bronze dragon's neck straps. Wide-eyed, she kicked out for a foothold, but found none on the dragon's smooth neck. The rider, surprised at her sudden fall, seized her arm and stretched out his other hand to gather her up. Mirrim felt the bones in her wrist sliding between the rider's fingers, and tried to get a better handhold. She grabbed for a neck ridge, and her movement finally dislodged her wrist from the dragonrider's grasp.

"Ramelth! She's falling!"

Before the man could move to catch her, she slipped over the side of the bronze's neck, past the claws outstretched to rescue her, and plummeted toward the treetops less than a dragonlength below them.

She landed among the branches, impacting with some force against the bole of a needle-leaf. Her shoulder exploded in pain, and she was battered into a stupor by the branches as she fell through them. Mirrim huddled as small as she could to protect her face. She slammed to the ground in a cloud of brown needles on the dark forest floor. Her hip had taken the greatest part of the shock. It was in agony. She lay at the base of the tree panting, blinking to clear tears from her eyes. Where was she?

"Path?" When Mirrim looked up, she couldn't see the sky through the thick foliage. Where was her dragon?

*D'or says to stay where you are!* Path said. *You are not to move. We will find you. We will help you to stop hurting.*

"I'm going to be all right," Mirrim assured Path, who sounded horribly worried. "There's nothing to be alarmed about. Here!" she shouted when she heard rustling in the trees not far away. Mirrim fell back to cough. Her voice was weaker than she'd hoped. Some of her ribs must also have been damaged.

*You were very lucky,* Path told her. *D'or said if you had not landed in the forest, you might have been killed. I do not like to think about that!*

"Neither do I," Mirrim confessed. "But I don't feel that lucky."

D'or, Ramelth's rider, and V'tor, rider of green Lodenth, appeared between the naked boles of the needle-leafs. In her dark brown wherhide, Mirrim was hard to distinguish from the heaps of forest debris until she moved to beckon them over.

"We'd best get you to the Healer, Mirrim. You're deathly pale," D'or observed. V'tor helped him turn her over onto her back.

"I'm all right," Mirrim protested. D'or swept her up gently, and V'tor supported her other side. Mirrim bit her lip to keep from crying out at the jostling to her injured limbs. She breathed in tiny, strained pants, concentrating on suppressing the fear that her hip was broken.

"To be sure, to be sure. We'll fly direct to the Weyr," D'or announced. "We're close enough not to need to go *between,* and it might be bad for you right now."

The bowl of Telgar Weyr had a natural lip like a thumb that rose at its northern end, dividing the winds which blew down on it from the Northern Barrier Range. In the notch at its southern end, pointing the way down the Central Mountain Range to Igen Weyr, perched a weyrling on watch duty who waved them on in when they appeared from the southwest. Mirrim didn't see much of the rest. Ramelth landed them close to the living caverns, and she was hurried in to see the healers.

Before she knew it, she was flat on her back on a rush-stuffed bed, and two women were helping her off with her riding gear and examining her. The elder, a brown-skinned woman of indeterminate age with a wonderful braid of gray hair that swept the hem of her sleeve, felt gently along Mirrim's collarbone. Her hands smelled of redwort and comfrey.

"Only dislocated, Canidan," she declared, signing to her assistant, who slathered numbweed on Mirrim's neck and upper chest. "As for the hip, I don't know yet. I think you're going to be with us for a while, my child. Just relax. Your dragon is fine, and you're going to be fine."

The nerve-deadening salve worked immediately, and the red-hot pain, of which Mirrim had been scarcely aware, receded. She felt herself relaxing, and settled into sleep while the healers worked. She could rest here.

*Turn to section 29.*

## * **90** *

Path opened her mouth and breathed. The twisted filaments turned from silver to gold to black, and shivered into dust in the heat of Path's flame. Their angle carried them through the dust cloud, and Mirrim shut her eyes to avoid getting any of the crackdust in them.

"Nicely done!" F'fej called, hovering just behind her, ready to sear the clump if she missed. She knew why he was there, and was mildly perturbed that he automatically assumed she might fail, but she said nothing. After all, it was standard procedure to back up your wingman, she chided herself. No doubt she was just feeling edgy. She threw a little wave at him and flew after another mass of Thread. There was no time to waste.

*Turn to section 91.*

## * **91** *

Her next aim was a small patch that had split off from a greater clump Canth had just seared. The brown dragon was already high above them, busy with other targets. Path exhaled a bare streamer of flame at the patch as she flew over it and continued on, knowing that there was nothing left of that to threaten anyone on the ground.

## Section 92

The wherries screamed as Path's shadow crossed over them.

"The stupid things!" Mirrim exclaimed. "You're protecting them!" She turned her head toward the northeast and pointed. "There." A shimmering skein of Thread sailed down toward them.

At Mirrim's urging, Path flew up, ready to sear the Thread from below.

*Roll 3 D6.*

*If the total rolled is less than or equal to Mirrim's value for Dexterity, turn to section 88.*

*If greater, turn to section 92.*

## * 92 *

Mirrim felt the heat radiate through the bottom of her wherhide trousers as Path belched a long gout of flame up at the Thread. She wished Dannen could see her and Path fighting Thread. He would have been impressed; far more so than with her limited skill as a plant-gatherer. Of course, this was her craft. She watched intently as the flame searched out and touched the Threads. To her dismay, the clump broke apart on the winds, separating in two as the flame hit it. Mirrim, cursing herself for her momentary break in concentration, woke up to the danger. She urged Path to burn the clumps and then jump *between*. Path turned her head slightly and breathed again. The right-hand Threads were closer than Mirrim thought, reaching out obscene silver fingers inside the range of Path's flame. The left-hand group crackled away, but the right-hand ones stayed mostly intact. They wouldn't be burned away before Path and Mirrim were within range.

They vanished *between*, but not before a delicate filament of Thread charred a stripe across one leg.

*Roll 1 D6.*

*If the roll is 1 to 4, Path has been laced by Thread. Mark it on the record sheet.*

*If 5 or 6, Mirrim has been laced. Roll 2 D6 for damage; subtract the total from her hit points on the record sheet.*

*If Path has been laced, turn to section 93.*

*If Mirrim has been scored and is now down to 0 hit points, turn to section 100.*

*If Mirrim has been scored but she still has hit points, turn to section 96.*

## * **93** *

Path squealed as they emerged from *between*. Mirrim could almost feel on her own leg the place where Path had been scored on hers. It was not a serious scoring, Path hastened to assure her, but it hurt!

"Do you want to land?" Mirrim asked Path, biting her lip in concern. How could she be so careless as to let her dragon become injured? If only she hadn't insisted Path try to sear those Threads *before* she ducked.

*No. It is only a small burn.*

"Well, all right, but as soon as Fall is over, I want to take a good look at your leg." She reached forward to get another chunk of firestone for Path to chew. "Uh-oh, we're out," she told Path. "Tell Camuth we're landing to get more firestone, and to cover for us."

*He asks will you bring him some, too?* Path responded.

For answer, she waved a hand over her head to F'fej, and Path wheeled to wing down toward the beach.

*Turn to section 102.*

## * **94** *

Mirrim emerged from *between* still beating at the place on her arm where Thread had landed. It had cracked off into dust *between*, leaving a finger-length gouge in the folded cuff of her glove, her sleeve, and in the skin below. Between the cut edges of hide, Mirrim could see, and feel, the angry red irritation of Threadscore. She had waited too long to go *between;* the filament should never have been allowed to pierce through so many layers. The smart made her eyes sting with tears, but she dashed them away with the back of the other glove and ordered Path to set down on the ridge for a short rest.

*Turn to section 108.*

# * 95 *

Mirrim shared the overwhelming anxiety of her dragon's pain as she looked at the injury she'd sustained. One of Path's left mainsails had been threaded. Red and black streaks overlay the transparent green of the pinions; though the sail wasn't tattered, it must still hurt horribly. Cringing in sympathy, she prepared to take Path down.

"Brekke has numbweed there for you, love."

*It's not that bad,* Path told her in a very small voice.

"All right, but you let me know if you can't go on, and for now let's set down on the ridge for a short rest," Mirrim said, sounding less sure of herself than before. Path was being brave for her sake. Mirrim felt worse and worse about her vow to be efficient, if it meant that her dragon got hurt.

*Turn to section 108.*

# * 96 *

Hissing at the pain, Mirrim emerged from *between*, clutching her knee between white-knuckled hands. That Thread had sliced a line nearly as fine as a hair through her trouser leg and into her skin before the jump *between* cracked it off. She breathed deeply, concentrating on subduing the pain. Counting slowly up to ten and down again, she strove to put it out of her mind.

*Are you scored?*

Mirrim stopped counting to tell her, "My knee!"

*Shall we land?* Path wanted to know.

"No! I can handle it. It isn't so bad." To prove that she could still function, she reached forward to get another chunk of firestone for Path to chew.

"Uh-oh, we're out," she told Path. "Tell Camuth we're landing to get more firestone, and to cover for us."

*He asks will you bring him some, too?* Path responded.

For answer, she waved a hand over her head at F'fej, and Path wheeled to wing down toward the cove.

*Turn to section 102.*

*Turn to section 102.*

## * 97 *

Mirrim shared the overwhelming anxiety of her dragon's pain as she looked at the injury she'd sustained. One of Path's left mainsails had been threaded. Red and black streaks were shot through the transparent green of the pinions; the sail was tattered. Deep green ichor dripped from it. It must hurt horribly. Cringing in sympathy, she ordered Path down.

"Brekke has numbweed there for you, love."

Path whimpered, treating the injured wing with much care as she glided back to the ridge. Brekke was already there, treating the blue dragon from F'lessan's wing, who had been severely scored across the tail. With a sympathetic glance at Mirrim, Brekke handed her a large pot of numbweed and rolls of bandages. "Treat Path, and I'll see to her as soon as I can, Mirrim."

"I'll take care of her," Mirrim said stoutly, running back to her dragon. "It's my fault she's hurt," she added under her breath.

Fall ended without other incident, and F'nor came to see to the two dragons that had been injured badly.

"We had fingertip scorings, F'lessan is patching up Golanth, and D'dot has to mend his jacket where Thread sliced through the hide. Hmmmm." He looked over Path's wing, spreading the damaged mainsail out deftly. Mirrim watched him anxiously as his brows drew down. "It'll be a few sevendays before she can fly again, you know."

Mirrim hung her head. His tone was gentle because they both knew what that meant. She couldn't fly Robinton to the wedding at Southern Hold if Path couldn't fly. With a sinking heart, she went on bandaging her dragon's wing.

*Turn to section 29.*

* **98** *

Her lizards disappeared *between,* and Mirrim didn't look to see if they reappeared. She felt bad for driving them away, but they had been so close to Path's flame, they could have been consumed, burned up, just like the Thread. Mirrim was proud of Path, the way that she had destroyed that clump, exactly as F'nor ordered. Path drove into it, flaming it from the inside out. The Thread expired in a broad hoop of smoke through which the dragon swept like a trained beast at a Gather. Mirrim enthusiastically thumped her on the side of the neck.

## Section 99

"Good flying, Path! You're the best, cleverest, most agile dragon in Pern's skies."

Path's tone showed pleasure at her weyrmate's praise. *We work together,* Path corrected her. *But I am getting a little tired,* she confessed.

"We'll go down for a short rest. Here comes Elekith back from his. He can cover for us."

*Turn to section 108.*

*Turn to section 108.*

*   **99**   *

Mirrim emerged from *between* still beating at the place on her arm where Thread had landed. It had cracked off into dust *between,* leaving a handspan-long gouge in the folded cuff of her glove, her sleeve, and in the skin below. Mirrim spread the cut edges of hide to look at her arm. The flesh had been sliced and cauterized as if by a hot knife, but it hurt ten times worse. She ignored the pain, as she had done before, but she couldn't ignore the fact that her hand refused to respond to her commands. The fingers wouldn't close all the way. She plunged the hand into the sack of firestone, and watched as the chunk she pulled forth dropped nervelessly out of her shaking hand into the middle of the wherry pen. The stupid birds, already half *between* with fear, exploded into hysterical activity, running around, throwing themselves against the walls of their corral.

"Path?" Mirrim croaked, her throat dry with pain. "Take me down." She was shaking so much she hardly felt the bump as Path landed on the rock ridge on the other side of the Hold.

The second blue dragon was already down, having been badly laced across the tail. Brekke left his rider to smear numbweed and tie bandages on his dragon, and then ran to help Mirrim down. She saw the extent of her arm injury, and made her sit down against Path's leg while she fetched salve and fellis juice.

"Drink this," Brekke ordered, handing her a cup of strong-smelling potion. "My heavens, that's a nasty one. You'll be all right though, dear. You'll need to rest for a few days, and keep from using the arm, but you'll be all right."

"A few days?" Mirrim said, her eyes already swimming hugely in her face from the fellis juice. "But what about the wedding at Southern?"

Brekke shrugged sadly. "I'm sorry, Mirrim. I don't see how you'll be well enough to go."

Mirrim felt tears leak down her cheeks, and she didn't have the strength to stop them.

*Turn to section 29.*

## * **100** *

Hissing at the pain, Mirrim emerged from *between,* clutching her knee between white-knuckled hands. That Thread had sliced a very fine line through her trouser leg and into her skin before the jump *between* cracked it off. She breathed deeply, concentrating on subduing the pain. Counting slowly, she continued to draw in air, and force it out, over and over, while Path demanded to know what the matter was. Mirrim stopped counting to tell her, "I've been Threadscored. My knee!"

# Section 100

*Shall we land?* Path wanted to know, but Mirrim ignored her, teeth clamped on lower lip, breathing faster and faster, until her head started to swim.

"We'd better," Mirrim panted, the tears starting in her eyes. "I'm hyperventilating. I can't stop."

The sunlight faded away as she started to black out. Brekke was there on the ridge, waiting with medical supplies for wounded dragons and riders. When Mirrim saw her, she realized she couldn't show her foster mother weakness when so many others might need her skills before the end of Threadfall. Using all her willpower, Mirrim unhooked her straps and stepped off Path's back.

Brekke came partway to meet her, but Mirrim gestured her back. "I'll be all right," she assured Brekke. "I'm fine." She took a step forward onto her injured leg, and the shooting pain dragged her the rest of the way down into unconsciousness.

When she came to, she was inside the Hold in her own chamber. The windows were open, so the Fall had ended. Mirrim reddened with shame for not having seen it all the way through. It was all her fault, pushing herself when she knew that she probably wasn't all the way up to strength from her recent adventures. Through the wide casement, she could see Path peering in at her, eyes whirling yellow with concern. Mirrim hastened to comfort her, reaching out of the window to scratch Path's head.

"See, I'm awake now. You can stop worrying."

*Threadfall was nearly over anyway,* Path said, hoping to console her rider. *You must rest for some days, Brekke says. We are going back to Benden soon.*

"And by then the wedding will be over with. But I won't be able to go." Feeling sorry for herself, she dropped back against the pillows, careful of her healing leg. "I'll ask them to say good-bye to Dannen for me."

Turn to section 29.

# * **101** *

Her lizards disappeared *between*, and Mirrim didn't look to see if they reappeared. She felt bad for driving them away, but they had been so close to the Thread, they could have been caught in it. Mirrim was proud of Path, the way that she had destroyed that clump, exactly as F'nor ordered. Path drove into it, flaming it from the inside out. The Thread expired in a broad hoop of smoke through which the dragon swept like a trained beast at a Gather. Mirrim enthusiastically thumped her on the side of the neck.

"Good flying, Path! You're the best, cleverest, most agile dragon in Pern's skies."

Path's tone showed pleasure at her weyrmate's praise. *We work together*, Path corrected her.

"From above!" F'nor's shout alerted them.

Mirrim looked up. Canth must have missed some of the Thread. There wasn't any way Path could turn on her tail fast enough to flame it. Camuth flew in flaming, still shedding crackdust from his last target. Mirrim ordered Path *between*, but she wasn't quick enough to avoid getting laced. As they disappeared into the cold void, Mirrim felt rather than saw Thread strike one of them.

*Roll 1 D6.*

*If the roll is 1 to 4, Path has been laced by Thread. Mark it on the record sheet.*

*If 5 or 6, Mirrim has been laced. Roll 2 D6 for damage; subtract the total from her hit points on the record sheet.*

## Section 102

*If Path has been laced only once, turn to section 95.*

*If this is the second time Path has been injured, turn to section 97.*

*If Mirrim has been scored but still has hit points, turn to section 94.*

*If Mirrim is now down to 0 hit points, turn to section 99.*

* **102** *

On the stone ridge, D'dot and some of the weyrlings had piled sacks of firestone, enough to supply all eight dragons through the duration of the Fall. Mirrim leaped off of Path's back and ran over to the heap. The bags were heavy, forcing Mirrim to make two trips. So much for her efforts to be efficient! She cursed extra seconds wasted as she undid the fastenings to her empty sack and tossed it aside onto the stack of others that had been discarded. With the new one in place, Mirrim slid the second bag across Path's neck and hopped up between the ridges. Snapping down her belt ties, she called to Path to take off again.

Path bounded high, fanning the air back with her great wings. When F'fej saw them coming, he dropped down a little to catch the bag Mirrim flung to him. "Thanks!" F'fej shouted. "Up there, coming your way!"

Path chewed stone and swallowed it, her fires regenerating themselves in plenty of time to dispose of a small patch of Thread, the remainder of one that Canth had just seared.

The clumps of Thread fell unevenly. At times, there would be a heavy concentration, and then nothing at all for dragonlengths. And a novice rider might think that Fall was ending; that was the most dangerous part of Threadfall to new fighters. Mirrim could see by the relaxed posture of the other blue rider that he hadn't seen the patch heading for him. She was tempted to swoop above him and wipe it out before his eyes, but she knew what F'nor would say to such showing off. Instead, she had Path bespeak the other dragon and watched with satisfaction as the wet-behind-the-ears weyrling snapped to attention and looked up. Blue wings spread to their uttermost span, the dragon climbed a thermal to crisp the small but dangerous patch that had all but landed on his tail.

"Mirrim, with me!" F'nor commanded, gesturing toward a dragon-sized clump of Thread floating downward on a vector that would have landed smack among the Hold's fruit trees, had they allowed it to escape them. It looked tricky, forming and re-forming from two to one to three masses as they approached it. As it separated into two bundles again, one on top of the other, F'nor ordered Mirrim to flame the lower one, leaving Canth free to sear the uppermost Threads.

"I'm angling fire down," F'nor said through Canth. "Look out!"

Mirrim cautioned Path to hang back. Her fire lizards, who had been behind and below the fighting dragons, were beside her, their little jaws flaming in a businesslike manner, ready to help destroy Thread.

"Stay out of the way, you sillies!" Mirrim shouted, though her warning was unnecessary. No fire lizard ever deliberately got in the way of a dragon flaming Thread. It just showed how on edge she was, screaming at fire lizards.

*Roll 3 D6.*

*If the total rolled is less than or equal to Mirrim's value for Dexterity, turn to section 98.*

*If greater, turn to section 101.*

## * **103** *

Almost before the word was out of her mouth, the Thread vanished, crisped from both ends by Path and Camuth. The flames ran toward each other along its length until there was a tiny glowing spark hanging in midair, and then that, too, went out.

F'fej whooped. "Come on," he shouted, undoing his scarf and flying helmet. "Fall's over!"

Path turned on her right wing and followed the blue dragon down. To Mirrim's surprise, she saw that it was nearly dark. The sun always set with amazing speed over the sea.

*Turn to section 107.*

## * **104** *

When they came out of *between*, Mirrim stared at the fingertip-wide score in the palm of her glove. The hide was simply not there anymore, as if it had been melted away. To her horror, the palm of her hand, too, had been threaded. Her palm shook as she examined the raw flesh, the tendons exposed. Carefully, she closed her fingers. Yes, they were still intact, but how it hurt!

"Path?" Mirrim croaked, her throat dry with pain.

"Take me down." She was shaking so much she hardly felt the bump as Path landed on the rock ridge on the other side of the Hold.

The second blue dragon was on the ridge already being treated for a badly laced tail. Brekke left his rider to smear numbweed and tie bandages on his dragon, and then ran to help Mirrim down. She saw the extent of her arm injury, and made her sit down against Path's leg while she fetched salve and fellis juice.

"Drink this," Brekke ordered, handing her a cup of strong-smelling potion. "My heavens, that's a nasty one. You'll be all right though, dear. You'll need to rest for a few days, and keep from using the arm, but you'll be all right."

"A few days?" Mirrim said, her eyes already swimming hugely in her face from the fellis juice. "But what about the wedding at Southern?"

Brekke shrugged sadly. "I'm sorry, Mirrim. I don't see how you'll be well enough to go."

Mirrim felt tears run down her cheeks, and she didn't have the strength to stop them.

*Turn to section 29.*

## * **105** *

When they came out of *between,* Mirrim stared at the fingertip-wide score in the palm of her glove. The hide was simply not there anymore, as if it had been melted away. To her horror, her palm, too, had been threaded. Her hand shook as she examined the raw red score, a hair's-breadth thick. The burned nerve endings screamed at her.

## Section 106

*Mirrim?* Path asked softly. *Fall is ending. F'nor says we may go down now.*

Mirrim recovered herself and laid her hand on her knee, palm up. Brekke had plenty of numbweed, and she might need some help fixing up the others who had been injured.

Path turned on her right wing and followed the blue dragon down. To her surprise, Mirrim realized that it was twilight. The sun always set with amazing speed over the sea.

*Turn to section 107.*

*   **106**   *

Before their astonished eyes, the skein of Thread crisped to blackened twists and fell into dust. Path hadn't so much as touched its end.

"Hey," Mirrim shouted as Camuth swooped toward them, following the Thread's destruction and narrowly missing being scorched by Path's flame.

"Sorry!" F'fej called, undoing his scarf and helmet as Camuth descended toward the beach. "I had the angle just perfect! Come on, Fall's over!" He whooped, grinning all over his handsome face. Mirrim smiled back in spite of herself. She knew what F'nor would say to such hazardous showing off. Path turned on her right wing and followed the blue dragon down. To her surprise, she saw that it was nearly dark. The sun always set with amazing speed over the sea.

*Turn to section 107.*

# * **107** *

After taking care of Path and herself, Mirrim helped Brekke with the other riders and dragons who had been Threaded. Under the light of the two moons, everyone took a refreshing swim in the still-warm tidal waters; everyone but Mirrim. Mirrim didn't join in at first. She felt a little shy about joining in the frolic, and stayed in the crook of Path's foreleg, rubbing the green dragon's hide with oil. She wore a loose white tunic that had been stained many times with salves and other preparations for her dragon's care. The smell of supper cooking tempted Mirrim, but reminded her she had duties to perform for Brekke, too. Path's eyes glowed with the green of contentment under her half-drawn lids. She wondered why they were not sporting in the water, but had allowed herself to be distracted by the promise of a sanding and oiling.

"Hey, wingmate!" F'fej shouted, crawling halfway out of the waves before he was recaptured and dunked by F'lessan and R'yon, the junior blue rider. The waves washed over the three of them. He reappeared in a moment, spitting out salty water, his sandy curls plastered to his head. "Come on in!"

Mirrim shook her head. "I must care for Path," she called back.

The younger dragonriders didn't accept that as enough of an excuse. As one they rose from the sea, rushed over to Mirrim, and dragged her screaming and struggling into the water with them. Path didn't stir a claw to save her.

"Path! Stop them!"

*It looks like fun,* she said placidly, rising from her coil. *I shall come in, too.*

"No!" Mirrim yelled, but her protest turned into a gurgle as she was pulled under the waves. The white tunic swirled around her legs like a creature with many arms. She fought free of her weyrmates, then stripped the tunic off over her head and threw it onto the beach. "That's better," she said, turning back to the weyrlings. "Now, where're the ones who dunked me?"

Shouting in mock terror, the young men shot away from the shoreline with Mirrim in pursuit. Path chose that moment to splash into the waves with them, causing a tidal surge that shoved everyone off in any which direction. Laughing, Mirrim crawled up on her dragon's back and took a swipe down at F'fej, who was floating near Path's forelegs.

"So you can smile," he said, tossing his head. "I sort of wondered. You're pretty when you smile."

Mirrim stopped her grab for his hair to mull over the compliment. Over the past sevendays, which were among the worst in her life, she'd had more admiring and approving comments made than she could remember before. Simply friendly observations, by friends, people who wanted nothing from her, merely to show her they liked her.

This must be the self-realization that Menolly told her about when they'd had heart-to-heart talks. Wait until the next time I see Menolly, Mirrim thought. Surely she'd be at the wedding, as the wife of the Master of Harper Hall. Mirrim's heart sank. If she didn't get moving to dispel her false guilt, *she* would be the one to miss the wedding.

That was the furthest she got at thinking about it. F'fej took advantage of her inattention to push her off the dragon's neck and into the water. Her pensive mood dissolved into a humor for play, and she dove and splashed with the rest of them until Brekke called them up for the meal.

Swimming helped unlock muscles knotted by the hard

work of fighting Thread, and served also to give the riders, and Master Robinton and Lord Lytol as ground-crew, tremendous appetites. There was very little left-over food, and the plates had been all but polished clean by assiduous eaters. Mirrim could hardly remember what she'd eaten, only that it was good. She was thinking about Dannen. It was too bad he had decided not to come with her. She was still pleased and bemused by his good-bye kiss. Her contemplation accompanied her the rest of the evening, and stayed with her until she fell asleep.

*Roll 1 D6 and return the number rolled to Mirrim's hit points.*

"Oh, yes, you must want Mirrim." She heard Brekke's voice through the wide-flung shutters. She looked out-side, and realized the sun was well up. "Mirrim! There's a message here for you from Dannen!" Mirrim groaned as she wrenched herself out of the soft mattress. Her muscles were sore, especially those in her thighs. She had held on firmly to Path's neck with her legs, as if worried that her gear might disintegrate in midflight. It would be a while before she was over that fear, or the discomfort. As accustomed as she was to riding, she still had to force her muscles to work hard.

She pulled on loose trousers and a tunic, forbearing to worry about underclothes until after she'd had a swim. Eschewing sandals, she brushed at her hair with a self-conscious hand and padded out on bare feet to Brekke.

There was a beast-drawn gather-wagon waiting near the wherry pen, and Brekke was chatting with the driver. She noticed Mirrim and beckoned her over. "This man is a trader, with whom Dannen has entrusted a message for you."

"It's private," the man grunted. He was stocky, not much taller than Mirrim herself, but he had long black hair and liquid black eyes like a tunnel snake.

"How did Dannen get a message to you? Is he back in Southern?" Mirrim asked, not entirely liking the man's looks.

"I deal with the north. We have fire lizards," the man jerked his head over his shoulder at a green lizard perched on the top of his gaudily painted wagon. "She brought word to me."

"Oh." Mirrim extended a hand. "May I see it?"

The man held his hands out, palm up. "It's in a code we traders use. I can't read, but I know what those signs mean."

"I see. So, what is the message?"

"It's private," the man said again, glancing sidelong at Brekke.

*If Mirrim decides she wants to hear the message in private, turn to section 109.*

*If she decides to let Brekke hear it, too, turn to section 111.*

* **108** *

After Path had taken a short rest on the ridge, she and Mirrim took their positions again, ready to wipe more Thread from the sky. A wild yell above her from F'lessan told her that Golanth had missed some of the clump he was crisping, and it was falling toward the Hold. She was close enough to burn it away before it fell another half length, beating one of the other greens to it by half a breath. The other rider threw her the high sign and turned toward his next target. Each of the smaller dragons had taken rest periods while the others closed ranks to cover their territories and so were relatively

# Section 108

fresh, while the larger dragons were only now beginning to tire.

Golanth had disappeared *between,* and Path reported that the bronze dragon had been laced on the back near the base of his tail. Mirrim cringed, knowing how F'lessan must feel—how *she* always felt any time Path got hurt. There were a lot of injuries this Fall. It was a good thing there was plenty of numbweed on hand.

Following edge was in sight, but Mirrim had more Thread coming her way. She could see that particular clump almost aiming for the Hold. The way it twisted and re-formed, looking like a handspan down a watchwher's throat—it was dangerous and unpredictable. The Threads in it were nearly all unwound to their full length. She hoped F'nor would get it, but it had swept by him, skipping weightlessly on the minuscule thermal created by Canth's flame. If she'd been thinking of herself and not of her job, she would have been terrified, but she ignored her feelings and reached for more firestone for Path.

"Mirrim!" F'nor shouted.

"I see it," she called back. "F'fej, with me!"

Together, Camuth and Path flew up to meet the clump, each angling to flame one end of its menacing expanse. Path breathed out, angling so that her flame would ignite one end of the Thread. Camuth, at his end, was doing the same.

*Roll 1 D6.*

*If the roll is 1, 2, or 3, turn to section 106.*

*If the roll is 4, 5, or 6, turn to section 110.*

# * **109** *

"All right," Mirrim said, nodding to Brekke. "Well, I was going to see to Dannen's runnerbeast. You can come with me, so when you send the reply, you can say it's doing well."

Brekke looked concerned, but didn't move to follow them. "I'm going back inside. Nice to meet you . . . ?"

"Dunnel," the trader said.

"Dunnel," Brekke echoed. She watched the two of them walk into the beasthold.

Dunnel followed Mirrim to the stable, where Dannen's beast was tethered. "He'd probably like to get out in the air," Mirrim said, turning to untie the beast's lead. It whickered, snuffing at her hand for a treat. It was a friendly creature. If only it wasn't so ugly! "As you see, he's alive and well. What is the message?"

"He says to stop chasing after those pieces. You don't know what you're getting into."

"This is from Dannen?" Mirrim asked incredulously.

"Uh-huh."

"It doesn't sound like him to me."

"Well, maybe I don't talk as pretty as he does. I don't speak to many people throughout a Turn. I travel all the time."

Mirrim narrowed an eye at him, trying to size him up. "Do you know what I think? I think you're from that trader, whoever he was. You can't scare me off."

"You figure things out, but you're dumb, girl," the man said, lunging at her.

Mirrim backed away from him. "F'nor! Lytol!" she

## Section 110

shouted, curling her hands and assuming fighting stance. She hoped she wasn't too far from the Hold to be heard.

**HOLDLESS MAN**
*To be hit: 10   To hit Mirrim: 9   Hit points: 10*
*Fists do 1 D6 damage.*

*If Mirrim loses, turn to section 113.*

*If she wins, turn to section 115.*

## * **110** *

Path flamed the twisting filaments, turning her head to destroy a silver tendril which snaked toward them like a whip as its other end was burned away by Camuth.
   "Look out!" Mirrim cried.

*Roll 3 D6.*

*If the total is less than or equal to Mirrim's value for Wisdom/Luck, turn to section 103.*

*If greater, turn to section 112.*

# * **111** *

"Just tell me what you want right here," she said, liking his looks less and less. She was reluctant to trust him, and was certainly not going to let herself be alone with him.

The man shuffled a little with a toe in the dirt. "I don't say things so good. He says he wants you to be private when you hear."

"I have no secrets from Brekke," Mirrim averred, putting her hands on her hips.

"Fine," the man gave in. "He says you should give up, stop chasing after those pieces from the plateau. You don't know what you're getting into."

"This is from Dannen?" Mirrim asked incredulously.

"Uh-huh."

"It doesn't sound like him to me."

"Well, maybe I don't talk as pretty as he does. I don't speak to many people throughout a Turn. My family and I travel all the time."

A Holdless man. Mirrim narrowed an eye at him, trying to size him up. "Do you know what I think? Dannen didn't send me a message. I think you're from that Telgar trader, whoever he was."

Brekke gave her a sharp glance, but her gaze turned inward, and Mirrim knew she was bespeaking a dragon. She was relieved, for it looked as if she had guessed right about the reason of this Holdless man's presence here. She knew better now than to trust a trader. He was supposed to scare her off, and was not very subtle in his persuasiveness.

Over the trader's shoulder, Mirrim could see F'nor

emerging from around the side of the Hold. He was still wiping oil from his hands. Canth had complained of scratchy hide the night before, and was probably up on the rock ridge, sunning himself. F'nor signed to her and Brekke to keep the man talking while he sneaked up on him from behind.

Mirrim hoped F'nor would hurry, for the trader was beginning to get impatient with these stupid women. Any moment, he might try to resort to the violence which was his next argument. Closer. Closer. Then F'nor pounced. Swiftly he wrapped one arm around the man's neck, and bent the other through the man's armpit. When his hands were locked together, F'nor had immobilized the man, who realized if he struggled, he'd break his own neck.

"What's going on here?" F'nor asked amiably.

"He brought me a false message from my friend Dannen, asking me to stop trying to find the artifact thief. Dannen would never tell me to give up."

"Who did the message come from?" F'nor asked. For a moment, the man didn't answer, so F'nor tightened his grip. "Who sent it?"

"A northern trader," the man gasped.

"What's his name?" demanded F'nor.

"I don't know," the ruffian whined. "I only know his mark." He struggled out of F'nor's grasp, and retreated to his wagon. When F'nor didn't pursue him, he turned the beasts and disappeared into the jungle.

"Well," F'nor was thoughtful. "That wretch isn't important. You were telling the truth, Mirrim, and now we have some corroborative proof to confront Lessa. We still do not have those pieces back, nor who is controlling the ring of thieves, but you are coming to the wedding. We'll investigate these traders after tomorrow. If you give me a description of this northern trader, I can have dragonriders from Telgar Weyr look for him. Casually, of course," F'nor added. "You are no disgrace to the Weyr. F'lar will back me up on it."

Mirrim didn't say anything aloud but "Thank you,"

but she was inwardly rejoicing. She skipped off to tell Path that they had better look their best on the morrow. They were going to the Lady Doriota's wedding, and escorting a very important guest!

*Turn to section 117.*

## * **112** *

Almost before the word was out of her mouth, the Thread flicked away from Path's flame and over her head. It hit Mirrim in the chest and writhed there on the front of her jacket, glowing with a malevolent silver light. Mirrim was too terrified to scream. She brushed at it with her glove. "Path! Go *between!*" But before they vanished into the cold blackness, the Thread had eaten a long, thin slice out of her glove.

*Roll 1 D6 for damage and remove from Mirrim's hit points.*

*If Mirrim is down to 0, turn to section 104.*

*If she still has hit points, turn to section 105.*

## * **113** *

Dunnel, or whatever his real name was, towered over the dragonrider. Grinning, he raised him arms and rushed forward. Mirrim dropped low and dived to the side at the last minute. As the large man stumbled past, she snapped out her leg to trip him.

It was a mistake.

Dunnel skipped over her outstretched leg. He moved surprisingly nimbly for such a big man. The swinging leg kept Mirrim off balance. She tried to dive away, but instead ended up sprawled on the stable floor. The dry straw stabbed through her shirt and against her cheek.

Then he kicked her. Hard. Against the ribs. Something inside went crack. The dragonrider screamed in pain as she tried to roll away.

"Path," she called frantically inside her mind. "I need help!"

Laughing, the big trader kicked her again. Mirrim rolled away from the blow, and it glanced off her leg. Still on her back, the girl kicked upward, aiming at her tormentor's knee. He skipped back and the kick swung wide.

Pain lanced along Mirrim's left side as she tried to pull herself up. She was still half bent when Dunnel rammed into her, sending her flying off balance once more. She slammed into the wall with a loud bang and found she could no longer breathe. All the air had been squeezed from her lungs.

Before she could recover, a thick, hairy fist appeared in the corner of the panting dragonrider's vision. Then it slammed into her left temple and sunbursts faded to total darkness.

Outside, the bellow of her dragon echoed off the stone walls.

*Turn to section 29.*

## \* **114** \*

It was tricky, figuring out the timing to send Path *between* precisely to the time she had been at the site before, when Lessa and Breide had taken her to task. As they emerged from the blackness, Mirrim felt her stomach spin with anxiety. She had never timed it to a point when she knew she would already have been there. Path settled down onto the lava flow above the dig, well out of sight of other dragons or any humans. It was a hot and sunny midmorning, just as she remembered it, and dust filled the air.

Scrambling down as best she could in her finery, Mirrim made her way casually into the place where excavation was going on. Her knees were wobbly, and she knew that just over another two hummocks were their earlier selves. Struggling against the feeling of disorientation, she made it to the side of the display hall.

Just in time, too, because Breide came hurrying out of the doorway. Mirrim had only enough time to flatten herself against the curving wall so as not to be seen by the steward. She knew where he was going. He was about to confront her other self.

Slipping around the corner into the cool darkness, Mirrim made her way over to the wooden chair frame that rested against the wall. She pulled it to where she'd have a good view of the table upon which the bottle sat, and crawled underneath. It made a concealing lean-to, and she could watch anyone who came into the hall through its pierced carvings. The white bottle was still on the table, in exactly the spot she remembered it.

She hadn't long to wait, either. A burly figure appeared at the doorway, looked around to make sure the room was empty, and made straight as the wherry flies to the table. Mirrim squinted to see his features. With one deft movement, he scooped up the bottle and stuffed it into his belt pouch. With his treasure safely hidden, he shot out of the room and into the sunlight.

Mirrim followed as soon as she could extricate a fold of her dress from under her lean-to. Running on her toes to the doorway, she looked around to find her quarry. He would be a bulky shadow with a belt pouch. That described roughly half of the workers on the site.

No, wait, there he was. Yes, she knew him, now that she could see his face. It was the apprentice from Telgar. Beterli, a failed candidate for Impression, who had started a nearly fatal brawl in Benden Weyr several Turns ago. He'd been expelled from the Weyr, and she never thought about him from that moment until now. Apprenticed himself to an unscrupulous trader.

She followed him around the corner of one of the largest buildings that had been fully excavated. As Mirrim rounded the third corner, she realized he had vanished. More to the point, she saw that she was too close to Path's original landing point. If she didn't move now, she might see herself, and that would change history. Well, never mind. Mirrim had her evidence now. She could swear with surety that he was the thief. She was an eyewitness.

"Path, I've seen him. That mean apprentice I told you about. I saw him take the bottle!"

*Good,* Path responded. *Are we going back now?*

"Yes," Mirrim said. "He got away from me, but I don't think he saw me following him." With a worried glance over her shoulder, she set out again for the edge of the lava flow.

Her dress hem was filthy from dragging through avenues of wet silt. With good fortune, she could scrub it quickly with sweetsand at Southern Hold, and dry it at the cookfires before anyone wondered what a dragon-rider was doing there. She caught up a fold of her gown and swirled it to dry the hems a little. They'd be frozen solid in *between*.

A noise ahead of her drew her attention, and she looked up. To her horror, Beterli stood there staring at her. Mirrim started violently, eliciting a venomous grin from the apprentice.

"I don't know how you got back here to the site so fast, or why you changed clothes, but it isn't going to help you. I still recognized you." He moved menacingly toward her. "And now you'll be sorry you spied on me."

Mirrim stared back in disgust. "If you don't let me go," she threatened, "I'll scream until everyone in the plateau comes running. I'll tell them all about you and the trader at Telgar Hold, and how you're selling Ancient Timers' artifacts for profit," Mirrim gazed coldly at him. Her only chance was to face him down. Beterli was a bully and a coward. "Lord Toric'll probably put you on hard labor for ten Turns."

Beterli stood back in shock. She guessed he might even have done hard labor at one time. "How on the Red Star did you . . . ?"

"That's not all. I know about the Holdless men that you employ here in Southern as thugs. It's a network of thieves, and when the Weyrleaders hear about it . . ."

She didn't finish her sentence, for at that moment Beterli leaped for her, his hands reaching for her throat. Backing away, she took a deep breath.

*Roll 3 D6.*

*If the roll is less than or equal to Mirrim's value for Intelligence, turn to section 120.*

*If the total is greater, turn to section 122.*

## * **115** *

Dunnel, or whatever his real name was, towered over the dragonrider. Grinning widely, he raised his arms and rushed forward. Mirrim dropped low and dived to the side at the last minute. As the large man stumbled past, she snapped out her leg to trip him.

The smile faded as the trip threw him against the shoulder-high stable wall. Both rose to their feet and stood facing each other across the straw-covered floor. Mirrim's leg hurt where it impacted against the thick muscles of the thug's leg.

"Path," she called frantically inside her mind. "I need help!"

The bellows of the enraged dragon rattled the stable partitions.

The sound jarred her attacker into action. Grabbing a shovel, he moved forward purposefully. Mirrim, looking frantically around, saw a set of runnerbeast reins. When Dunnel raised the shovel she swung the reins around in an arc and wrapped them around it.

For a few seconds the two stood facing each other. The woman's muscles knotted as they struggled for control of the weapons, then the man's greater strength prevailed. The gloating smile returned when Mirrim was forced to release the leather reins.

It was just as quickly erased when the dragonrider's foot snapped into his solar plexus. With an *oof,* the merchant's breath rushed out. Before he could recover, Mirrim kicked him again. Still, he didn't go down.

Stumbling awkwardly forward, Dunnel swung wildly. The first blow went high, but the second smashed into his smaller opponent's side. It hurt so badly that for a second her vision blurred.

The two combatants leaned only a few feet apart against the shoulder-high wall of a runnerbeast stall. The merchant thug's color was returning. Mirrim had bare seconds to act.

Grabbing the side of the stall the dragonrider used it to swing her legs over her head. The ball of her left foot drove the taller man into the stall. He was bouncing back out when the heel of her other foot thudded against his temple.

Once more he slammed into the partition. This time, though, he crumpled onto the straw and mud of the floor.

F'nor and Brekke rushed into the stable in time to see the thug fall. After he had assured himself Mirrim was all right, F'nor growled and used his foot to flip the fallen man over. He was already beginning to recover consciousness.

The areas around both of the man's eyes were darkening. Holding a fist before them, F'nor demanded to know who had ordered the attack.

"A trader," the defeated man mumbled.

"Who?" F'nor insisted, dragging the thug off the floor by his collar. Totally defeated, the hired thug cringed before the new threat.

"Who?" Mirrim echoed. Her side hurt as she talked.

"I don't know," the ruffian whined. "I can't read. I only know his mark." He struggled out of F'nor's grasp, and retreated to his wagon. When F'nor didn't pursue him, he turned the beasts and disappeared into the jungle.

"Well," F'nor was thoughtful. "He's not important. You were telling the truth, Mirrim, but now we have some corroborative proof to confront Lessa. I'm glad Brekke bespoke me when she did. It looks like Lord Lytol was right in not wanting traders on the plateau. From now on they'll have to get permission from the Lord Holders or the Weyrleaders. They won't like it, but they won't have a choice. We still do not have those missing items back, nor do we know who is controlling the ring of thieves, but you are coming to the wedding."

"What about the pitch pipe?" Mirrim asked anxiously. That had been the item which started all her problems.

"The what? Oh, Robinton's little toy. Well, that's all but forgotten already. You'll be at Southern tomorrow. You'll see." F'nor leveled a finger at her. "You are no disgrace to the Weyr. F'lar will back me up on it."

Mirrim didn't say anything aloud but a heartfelt "Thank you," but she was inwardly rejoicing. She skipped off to tell Path that they had better look their best on the morrow. They were going to the Lady Doriota's wedding, and escorting a very important guest!

*Turn to section 117.*

## * **116** *

To Mirrim, the strange man walking away was more curious than the minecrafter. After all, the crafter looked as though he was going about his business. This other fellow looked like he was well pleased with himself, and didn't have his mind on any job here. Mirrim knew well that working here on the plateau was slow going, with no quick or miraculous discoveries, only meticulous care and diligence to gather up all the pieces to the ancient puzzle. That's it: his attitude was wrong.

She followed him, stepping as casually as she could. Perhaps the others working here would think she was a visiting Lady Holder. Carefully she arranged her long plaits to conceal the Benden Weyr badge on her overtunic.

Her quarry walked purposefully down one of the

squares leading away from the display hall, and turned right past the end of the lava flow. She still hadn't seen his face. He skirted a couple of Smithcraft apprentices who were spraying water on the streets to keep the dust down. Mirrim had a brief moment of fear that he might make another right up the edge of the flow itself. She didn't want Path discovered. A green dragon in hiding beyond the dig would generate too many questions.

To her relief, the man kept going straight, heading for the edge of the plateau. Mirrim passed the two apprentices, who saluted her politely. She smiled absently at them, keeping the man in sight as he rounded a fold of frozen volcanic stone. Mirrim knew who he was now. He was the sullen trader's apprentice, the one who had left the hall before the fracas started in Telgar Hold, probably to slice her riding straps. Dannen would remember him, too.

Trying not to cough out loud in the dust-laden air, Mirrim crouched against the fold of lava and watched as the apprentice approached a man standing casually against the flow, as if passing a few pleasant moments before going back to work. The new man turned around when the apprentice hailed him. Mirrim bit her knuckles in excitement. It was the journeyman trader from Telgar! All the pieces were falling together now.

She strained her ears to distinguish their words. The journeyman was louder, seeming not to fear anyone overhearing them in this remote corner of the plateau.

"I arrived this morning," the journeyman announced. "G'lor carried me from Telgar with the Minecraft experts and the Smithcraft second. Out of kindness and deferring to my generosity—a mark here and there, some small goods at bargain prices—G'lor felt there would be no trouble to add a fourth passenger to his dragon's neck."

So that's how they were getting back and forth with their stolen goods. Innocent dragonriders were carrying them. In a way, Lord Toric had been correct about Northern dragons abetting thieves. The apprentice mumbled something and looked back over his shoulder. Mirrim ducked back behind the lava flow, and peered out again. They hadn't seen her.

"And it is a fine job you're doing, Beterli," the journeyman continued. "Of course we'll want more. If you've nothing for me now, I've wasted the trip."

And indeed he hadn't. Mirrim could see from her concealed vantage point that their hands were empty, and nothing was exchanged from one to the other. Mirrim wished she had caught them in the act. If Beterli had taken anything, he wasn't turning it over to his master just yet.

Yes, it was Beterli. Beterli had been dismissed from Benden Weyr for violence. After failure to Impress over many Turns, he'd attempted to kill, or at least seriously wound, Keevan, who Impressed bronze Heth and had his name shortened to the honorific K'van. Beterli seemed to have gone from assault to theft to attempted murder.

Mirrim had seen enough. She now had evidence to confront Beterli and his felonious master, at the wedding. She considered making one more jump in time, to ensure it was Beterli who took the little white bottle, or if the other apprentice was involved in the thefts as well. If she did that, she would be risking meeting herself. But now that she knew Beterli was involved, perhaps she could convince the Weyrleaders or Lord Holder Toric to question him, to prove her innocent.

Mirrim looked at the sun. It was nearly the time when her earlier self would be arriving. She and Path must hurry away, before Beterli and his master caught her overhearing them.

*If she wants to confront Beterli and his master at the wedding, turn to section 124.*

*If she chooses to time it again to get more evidence, turn to section 114.*

## * 117 *

In the sky above Southern Hold the next afternoon, there were dragons of every color delivering their loads of important guests to the wedding of Holder Sindain and Lady Doriota. Master Robinton, seated on Path behind Mirrim with his guitar case and harp case banging their legs on either side, was at his ease, as comfortable as if he had been on the biggest, most important bronze in all of Pern. Mirrim held herself positively erect with pride. She was determined not to make a single error, and enjoined Path to land precisely on the dot before the Hold door. Path's hide shone, and Mirrim had done much else to present their very best appearance. Her gear was spotless, her hair under the flying helmet freshly coiffed and scented, and in her own carry-sack was a fine dress of ochre, deep blue and burnt gold that becomingly softened the angles of her long frame. Several bronzes, with Lord Holders and Craftmasters, waited impatiently awing as Path circled with the rest of them above the Hold building.

"I think they're waiting for you to land first," Robinton whispered, leaning forward so his silvering hair tickled Mirrim's cheek.

"Oh!" Crimson, she directed Path down. In her enjoyment of the honor of flying Master Robinton to the event, she'd nearly forgotten that that included precedence for his escort's dragon. "I apologize, Master. I . . . I'm not used to . . . I'd forgotten. Path's only a green."

"It's quite all right," he assured her as she helped him get his bags down. While he waited, she stripped off

Path's flying straps. As soon as she had finished, the green dragon soared away to join the other dragons. "Have confidence, Mirrim," he urged her, his mellow baritone voice giving her strength, his blue eyes kind. "I'm fond of Path, green, purple, blue, or striped. I'll tell them I was enjoying the view. By the way, my dear, I admire your new reticence. It's very becoming."

Mirrim flushed, not knowing how to respond. Shouldering his instrument bags, Robinton took her free arm and escorted her into the Hold.

Zair squeezed onto his master's collar, hanging on for dear life above the case straps, but Mirrim firmly instructed her three fire lizards to stay outside. No matter if the Hold's fairs flew in and out through the windows; Mirrim wanted no situation to exist in which she could be reprimanded. Besides, she could see a fair of nine fire lizards already lying on the roof that sprang to the air to greet hers. Behind those, another pair, blue and gold, swooped out toward Reppa, Lok, and Tolly, creeling joyously. Somi and Kern! So Dannen was here somewhere. Mirrim prayed he wouldn't see her until she'd had a chance to change.

Breide greeted the guests at the door. He bowed graciously to Master Robinton and allowed himself a sedate "Good afternoon" and a nod of the head to Mirrim. She nodded back. When he turned away from them without saying anything else, Mirrim gulped in relief.

With a glad cry of "Menolly!" the Master Harper detached himself from her side and disappeared into the crowd. Mirrim was a little disappointed not to be asked along, but he had left her free to socialize on her own. She still needed to dress for the feast. There was sure to be a chamber for the use of visiting dragonriders.

Lessa and F'lar were already present and circulating through the hall when Mirrim emerged from the dressing room. She avoided the Weyrwoman carefully, catching F'lar's attention through the crowd. He nodded at her, glancing sidelong at his companion to make sure she hadn't noticed Mirrim. As F'nor had promised, the Weyrleader approved her presence, and would let Lessa know of it in his own time.

Southern had been much smaller when Mirrim lived in the Weyr. Obviously Lord Toric was adding dimension as his Hold grew richer. Mining concessions had already been worked out to the benefits of both Hold and Craft. Ore, black heavy-water, which was used by the Smithcraft in some compounds, iron, lead, and gold were found in plenty once Minecraftmasters had been allowed to explore the new territories.

As she mingled, Mirrim was curious to hear whispers going around concerning a find in a small Hold to the south in which interesting buildings had been found, architecture from the Ancient days. Mirrim could see that her Weyrleaders were listening for rumors with all their ears; Master Robinton, too. From the gossip among the guests, there was considerable suspicion that Lord Toric, after complaining bitterly that the Weyrleaders were seeking to conceal artifacts of the Ancient Timers from the rest of Pern, was indulging in a little of the behavior he condemned so heartily.

The wedding had given Lord Toric a chance to show off before the Northern Lords, and, in Mirrim's opinion, he was making the best of it. Traders, winecraftsmen, craftmasters, had been invited from all parts of the Southern Hold, giving the event a sort of gather atmosphere. The meadow was filled with booths, through which wandered the holders who had not been invited to the wedding. From what Mirrim could see and hear through the broad windows open to the warm summer evening, they seemed to be having as good a time as those inside. There was dancing, and tests of skill, and a brisk business going on in pastries and wine. Shouts of laughter sounded occasionally over the strains of the harpers playing for the dancers in the square. Under other circumstances, she would be down there with them. Toric had extended invitations to many senior dragonriders and craft seconds, besides the requisite guests. Mirrim herself barely squeaked by as a guest, asked only out of courtesy to the Master Harper. She didn't care; she was happy to be here at all.

The groom, clad in a warm red, stood now at the door greeting all those who came in with a sort of incredulous happiness on his face. That was Sindain, Dannen's friend. She wondered when she'd have a chance to introduce herself and ask after Dannen. On Sindain's shoulder coiled a very young bronze fire lizard, which another guest whispered had been a betrothal gift from the bride. Lady Doriota flitted here and there in her wedding dress of graduated shades of red, pausing occasionally to beam in the direction of her bridegroom. A tiny gold lizard rode her wrist. Mirrim sincerely hoped the couple was as well paired as their lizards. Even if it had been a marriage arranged by the ambitious Lord Toric, it appeared to have been a love match as well.

Mirrim craned her neck around, searching the throng for signs of Sharra, one of Toric's other sisters, and Jaxom, for of course they would occupy a place of honor at her sibling's wedding. Little Ruth was undoubtedly out with the other dragons, swimming, sunning, and napping in the sun. Since his confirmation, Jaxom had done much to continue the trend of prosperity Lytol had begun in Ruatha.

While she browsed, looking at everyone's finery and enjoying an occasional admiring glance directed at herself, Mirrim found herself studying a handsome red and gold gown worn by a tiny lady with a cloud of dark hair who was chatting with Robinton. To her dismay, it was Lessa, on F'lar's arm. Mirrim tried to backwing into the crowd before the Weyrwoman spotted her. Too late. She responded to Lessa's imperious beckoning, and timidly approached the Weyrleaders.

Lessa's brows drew down, and Mirrim quailed. "What are you doing here?" she demanded.

"F'nor gave me permission to come, Lessa." The dainty Weyrwoman always managed to make Mirrim eel like an overgrown clod. She stared down at the front of her overtunic, counting the stitches in the Benden Weyr badge until she felt the redness in her cheeks fading.

"For my sake," Robinton broke in, hastening to prevent an explosion. "Surely you wouldn't deny an old man a chance to spend time in the company of those ladies both young and beautiful?" He bowed and drew Lessa's hand to his lips. F'lar stood in the background, holding himself back unless his mate overreacted. There was really no need for his intercession. The Harper had the matter under control, and they all knew it.

Lessa made a face. "I don't know why no one ever learned to say no to you, Robinton. Very well, she can stay. But keep clear of Lord Toric, for the Egg's sake."

"Yes, Lessa," Mirrim promised, and fled, while F'lar and the Master Harper closed ranks behind her to placate the Weyrwoman.

"Well, well, well." A familiar voice interrupted Mirrim's thoughts. "How nice you look, green rider. I haven't seen you in sevendays." It was T'gellan, resplendent in a deep blue-green tunic decorated with copper scales, which set off his tanned skin.

"So do you, bronze rider," Mirrim said, her heart beating faster, but her voice determinedly casual. Her easy acceptance of his compliment seemed to set T'gellan slightly aback. Enjoying his discomfiture, Mirrim indulged herself and preened a little. Somewhere across the hall, gitars, drums, and a horn began to play a lively melody.

"Do you care to dance?" T'gellan asked, holding out a hand.

"I can't just now," Mirrim replied. "I've got to find a friend of mine. I've promised him six dances," she added wickedly. The young man's face was a study in bruised ego and curiosity. "Later, perhaps?" she offered.

"Yes, later. All right," the bronze rider assented, moving closer to her and staring down meltingly into her eyes. He took her hand. "Mirrim, this friend of yours . . ."

Mirrim instantly lost her carefully husbanded confidence. She had to escape from him before she made a fool of herself.

"Oh, your pardon, T'gellan," Mirrim said, peering over his shoulder and pretending to see someone. She waved a hand to her imaginary friend. "I must go. See you later?" Without waiting for an answer, she lost herself in the crowd, congratulating herself on a narrow squeak.

"Why didn't you warn me Monarth was here?" Mirrim asked Path irritatedly as she pushed her way between conversing groups and drudges bearing trays of delicacies.

*I did not think it was important,* Path told her. *Monarth is my friend, but I have many friends here.*

"Well, I just ran into T'gellan."

*You like T'gellan. I do, too.*

"Yes," Mirrim admitted uncomfortably, "but I wasn't ready to see him." She edged her way around the perimeter of the room. A small tray table full of snacks was set up at each pillar. Slices of firm cheese, fresh fruit sparkling with juice, and tiny spiced rolls tempted any passing guest. Mirrim helped herself to a handful of miniature pastries and meatrolls, and sauntered over to look at the wedding gifts. To her delight, Menolly was there, laying an exquisitely wrapped package on the table. The journeywoman Harper turned to see her, and she seized Mirrim in a warm embrace.

"Oh, Mirrim! How wonderful to see you!"

"Oh, I'm glad to see you, too! You look beautiful," Mirrim said, returning the hug and stepping back to admire her friend's gown.

Menolly did indeed look beautiful. She was dressed in shades of blue and blue-gray that picked up and emphasized the sea-blue of her eyes and offset the red highlights in her thick dark hair. Around her throat, she looked like she had on an ornate gold necklace. Mirrim grinned.

"Hello, Beauty," she cooed, coaxing the queen fire lizard out from under Menolly's wealth of hair. Beauty's head appeared between tresses, creeling imperiously, which turned to a pleased croon as Mirrim stroked her soft hide.

"We've left another of her clutches sitting on the hearth in warming sands." Menolly smiled, watching Beauty's eyes close lid by lid in bliss.

"My lot are outside with your fair," Mirrim sighed, "where they won't get into trouble. There must be two hundred fire lizards on the roof!"

A young man in a very smart new white tunic and red belt festooned with a journeyman harper's badge and that of Southern Hold swaggered up and put his head around their shoulders to peer up at Menolly. "Hello there, Menolly," he said mischievously.

"Piemur! How good to see you!"

"And who's this attractive friend of— My stars," he squawked, his smooth baritone strangling with surprise. "It's Mirrim!"

"Very funny," Mirrim fumed. "Nice to see you, too, Piemur."

"Thanks," he said unrepentantly. "I've got to mingle. See you later!" And he was off again into the crowd.

"He'll ask you to dance later," Menolly told her, the corners of her lips twitching with merriment.

"No, he won't. He remembers me too well from Turns back," Mirrim groaned.

"Piemur remembers me, too, he ought to; but he still loves to ask me to dance. He pretends Sebell would be jealous if he saw us, the scamp. We've all changed, and for the better."

She certainly was a different picture than the ragged, crop-haired waif that had been carried into Benden Weyr with the soles of her feet run off, those many Turns back. With a laugh, Mirrim realized that she, too, presented a different picture. She was more assured, gentler, more confident than she had been when she and Menolly first met, aged fifteen Turns. "How is Sebell?" she demanded. "And your daughter?"

"My daughter?" Menolly asked, her eyes already dreamy. She had probably been thinking exactly the same thoughts as Mirrim. "Oh, she's fine. She's gorgeous, and growing so fast! Silvina has her in charge. I wish you could have been in Fort Hold when I had the baby. I'd've been glad of your company, though of course Master Oldive had everything under control. Beauty creeled for joy when the child was born at last," Menolly said fondly. "Didn't you, my pretty?"

Beauty answered with a sentimental cheep that made both girls laugh. Mirrim fondled her until she laid her head down against Mirrim's slim shoulder.

"Sebell's here, of course," Menolly added, looking over the heads of the crowd for her husband. "He and Master Robinton are talking, catching up on Harper business, as usual. If either of them plays a note tonight I'll be surprised. I've a song for Lady Doriota, that goes with the gift we've given her. I'll play it myself if Sebell doesn't emerge. By the way, I've just seen T'gellan. What did you say to him?" Menolly inquired impishly. "He was suffering an attack of Threaded feelings."

"I made him see that he wasn't the only egg in the sand," Mirrim said with spirit.

"And there's a tall crafter asking around for you, Danten, or Drammon, or something like that. Very good-looking. Is he the other egg?" Menolly asked curiously.

"Dannen. He's only . . . a friend," Mirrim confessed.

Menolly tactfully changed the topic. "Doriota has a fondness for music. The Harper Hall is giving her a journeyman-made lyre," she indicated her package with a proud hand, "or should I say journeywoman-made?"

"You're so talented. I'd love to see it," Mirrim said, stroking the delicate sisal cloth covering, and hearing the strings call softly through the wrapper. "I wonder what's in this one?" she said, pointing to a handsome package next to Menolly's.

Most of the presents were bundled up in fine cloth with ribbons, or enclosed in ornate carved boxes. Mirrim and Menolly followed the queue of curious men and women wandering sunwise around the table. Not daring to lift the box lids, they took to guessing what each might be, depending on where it came from, and what its shape suggested. There was no way to be sure until Doriota opened them during the feast, so Mirrim made bets with her friend until that time should come when they could confirm or reject their guesses. Many gifts had no wrapping at all, and had a card or streamer attached, naming the donor.

In the second row of presents, the color white caught Mirrim's eye, an unusual concentration of white. She bent to investigate. It turned out to be a curiously opaque white bottle.

It reminded her of the bottle she saw in the long building in Southern, just before Breide accused her of thieving. Not that she hadn't actually taken something, but she didn't know what became of the other thing. He still didn't believe her, and with his reputation for recall and trustworthiness, Mirrim knew that the Weyrleaders believed him and not her. She picked the bottle up, frowning. The material was right out of her field of experience. If she closed her hand, the bottle would collapse in on itself, like a wineskin, but when she let it go, it opened out again. What was it made of? She turned it over to find the maker's name.

The painted dot with its black numbers stared up at her. It *was* the bottle from the dig. Someone had just left it here! Whom had she seen standing at the table just now?

"Mirrim? What's wrong?" Menolly asked, laying a hand on her arm.

"Nothing. Nothing, I'm looking for someone," Mirrim answered distractedly, searching the crowd.

There was a Minecraftmaster walking away. With a

start, she realized that he was the same man who had collided with her that terrible day in the display hall, when the bottle had been stolen. She stared at him, trying to reconstruct in her memory what she had just seen him do. Was he looking at the presents just like she was, or had he left that bottle as a gift to the Lady Holder, to placate her toward the Minecraft in her new Hold? Or had it been the big Holder, the burly fellow? He was familiar, too. She had seen him at the dig, certainly, but he was more familiar than that. Hold on, she had seen him with the trader at Telgar Hold. He may have been working for him.

All at once, she realized that the key to uncovering the culprits behind the thefts was in her hand.

"Path?" she inquired, and felt the dragon's loving thoughts respond to her. "Would you fly back and meet me at the main Hold entrance?"

*Of course, but why?*

"To clear up this problem of the missing artifacts. Menolly," she called to the puzzled Harper girl. "I'll be back later."

She decided not to change into all her riding clothes, instead taking just her gloves, helmet, jacket, and belt. Her gown had wide pants legs that seemed to form a skirt under her surcoat, so there was no need for the wherhide trousers. She didn't need full gear for the jump that she had in mind.

"We're going back *between* times, Path. That bottle's turned up again. That means that the person who took it is probably here. If I can just find out who it is, I can tell the Weyrleaders, and they can put a stop to the thefts."

*I will do whatever you want. When do you want to go?*

"Well, we can go before we were actually there, and see who was snooping around, or we can go after, when we were there but before the bottle was stolen. On the one hand, we might not see anyone, but on the other, I hate being somewhen twice. It makes me sick to my stomach."

If Mirrim decides to try the site before the time she arrived before, turn to section 119.

If she tries the time after she had been there, turn to section 114.

## * 118 *

Mirrim glanced around through the crowd. Menolly said that Dannen was here, looking for her. She needed him now! He'd been with her at Telgar, and without him, it was her word against Beterli's. With a sigh, she began to describe her adventures.

"At Telgar Hold, his master, the journeyman trader, had an item in his possession and said it was his property." She described it for Breide, who nodded as Mirrim enumerated each characteristic of the little stylus. "I asked him where he'd gotten it, but he refused to tell me, but I'd seen the identifying mark on it, and so I knew it was from the site."

"Is that all?" Breide asked. Beterli regarded them both with a stony expression, not that much different from that of the steward.

"No," Mirrim said reluctantly, since she hadn't actually seen Beterli do it, and the consequences for such a crime were serious. "I believe Beterli cut my riding straps. They split apart under my hands. I might have been killed, using unsafe straps to fight Thread."

"It's a serious crime, threatening the life of a dragonrider and dragon," Breide frowned. "It's a death offense to cause a dragon to die."

"She's crazy," the apprentice protested. "I'd never risk a dragon's life. She just didn't take care of her stuff. She's just trying to blame me."

"He's been on the site dozens of times," Mirrim turned to the steward. "You must have seen him on the days things went missing."

"I have seen him, but I can't testify that he took them if I didn't seem him do it. Do you have any more tangible proof?" Breide asked.

Mirrim looked around again for Dannen, and finally had to confess, "No. But I give you my word."

"Under the circumstances, I can hardly accept that as evidence."

Crushed, Mirrim stared down at the floor, trying not to cry with frustration. She couldn't think of any way to justify herself to the steward. Beterli grinned toothily at her.

"What is going on here?" Lessa asked, pushing through the crowd to the gift table, where a red-faced Mirrim stood before the Lord Steward with her head hanging.

"I'm afraid, Lady Lessa," Breide replied in a very low voice so as not to make an issue of it before the assembled guests, "that what we have here is the green rider possibly having borne false witness against Beterli, a trader apprentice. She has no evidence, and the man claims he is innocent. I have no reason to assume otherwise."

Lessa rounded on Mirrim, her eyes flashing. "You have done what?"

"Beterli took something from the display hall. I'm sure of it."

"When?" Lessa demanded.

Mirrim realized that she had now put both her feet in it. "I . . . went back *between* times, to see who had stolen the bottle I was accused of taking. I saw him in the hall." All at once she burst out, "He took it, Lessa, I know he did!"

"She has a grudge against me, just because I failed to Impress!" Beterli muttered, looking down on the diminutive Weyrwoman.

"It's the other way around," Mirrim protested, appealing to Lessa. "I didn't even know who he was until today."

"Go back to Benden. Now." Lessa's voice cut through her explanation.

"But my things are at Cove Hold," Mirrim babbled. "And Master Robinton . . ."

"Now." Lessa's voice was quiet, but cold as a glacier. "From this point on, you will be assigned to duties suitable to your judgment and abilities, for which at this moment I have little regard. Once again, you have disgraced the Weyr. Report at once to the Weyrlingmaster."

Miserably, Mirrim moved toward the door. She had made yet another mistake. Her spanking new gown looked like a drudge's uniform from the dust of the plateau site, and she felt that she was incapable of ever regaining her honor.

*Turn to section 29.*

## * **119** *

The cold of *between* seemed to last nearly forever before Mirrim and Path emerged on the west side of the Two-Faced Mountain. On Mirrim's instructions, the dragon set down between the ridges of the lava flow that went on to cover up part of the Ancient Timers' Hold. It had taken some careful thought to place them on the plateau at the right moment, but Mirrim used the position of the sun to make sure.

"Stay out of sight, Path," Mirrim cautioned her as she scrambled down the huge forearm. "If any dragons bespeak you, please ask them not to tell their riders you're here. We're not supposed to be here yet, nor to travel *between* times."

*I will be careful.*

As casually as she could, she removed her helmet and sauntered into the excavation. It was just the way she remembered it; everyone was racing around doing tasks. Master Nicat and Lord Lytol stood in the street chatting with Master Fandarel over a spread floorplan. Breide was beside them, waiting attentively for Lytol to notice him. Mirrim was relieved to see him there. It meant she could sneak into the display hall without being observed.

It was dark and cool in the big chamber. To her surprise, she found that there was no one else there at all. The white bottle stood on the table, just where she had seen it before. She ran a finger across its pliant surface, wondering how it had been made, with the strange nozzle on top, like the beak of a bird. It looked to have been extruded all in one piece, the way glass was.

She heard the hiss-swish of footsteps coming toward the doorway, and slipped behind the back of a wooden chair frame just as a shadow fell across the threshold. From her concealed vantage point, she saw a man come in. With the sun behind him, his features weren't distinguishable, but he was brawny, broad-chested, and thick-legged. Mirrim felt a tingle go up her spine. She could be watching the thief.

The man came closer, and disappeared from her limited field of view. She heard the bottle brush the tabletop as the man picked it up. Trying to see around the edge of the frame, Mirrim craned her neck and leaned her weight forward onto her hands. Just as the man touched the artifact, Mirrim felt the frame sliding away from her. She grabbed for it, but not before it shifted outward, making a scratching sound.

Just as she thought she was going to be discovered, Breide appeared in the doorway. He walked over to the man and spoke to him. Mirrim heard the bottle touch the tabletop again with a *pok!* Mirrim couldn't hear what the steward was saying, but she recognized the authoritarian tone Breide used. Obviously the man wasn't a Lord Holder, a Weyrleader, or a Craftmaster. Breide was always deferential to men and women of rank. Guided by the steward, the strange man was shown to the door and on out. Mirrim cursed. If only Breide didn't come back right away, she might be able to catch up with her quarry, and find out who he was. She was certain that he had been about to steal the bottle.

Cautiously Mirrim slipped out from behind the chair, brushing dirt off her best gown, and made her way out into the sun.

To her chagrin, Breide was coming back toward the hall, and there were two men walking the other way, both burly, both somewhat familiar. That one had to be that nearsighted minecrafter. He was peering closely at something small in his hands. Surely Breide wouldn't have let him take anything from the hall. What did he have there? The other walked with greater assurance, but his hands were empty. One of them was the thief. She needed to figure out which.

*If Mirrim chooses to follow the minecrafter, turn to section 125.*

*If she chooses to follow the other man, turn to section 116.*

## * **120** *

Mirrim summoned Path. With a rush of air under her wings, the green dragon appeared over the rise of the lava flow, bellowing. Beterli stopped in midspring, and gazed in horror at an angry dragon closing in on him at speed.

He turned on his heel and scampered for the dig. Mirrim didn't pursue him. She realized with the retrospect time had given her that Beterli would only attack her at a distance or by using agents, never face to face. He'd known exactly who she was at Telgar, though she hadn't recognized him yet. That had given him an advantage. He was the one who had cut her harness.

Returning to Southern Hold, she cleaned her gown and set out to find Lessa. Her fire lizards, disobeying her previous command, flew into the hall with her, creeling how worried they'd been that she'd gone off without them. After calming their hysteria, Mirrim sent them away again lest they anger Lessa, who still thought fire lizards were useless toys. The Weyrwoman was not happy to hear that Mirrim had taken her dragon *between* times, but at F'lar's urging listened to the rest of Mirrim's story.

"And if you don't believe me," Mirrim blurted out, "ask Path. She heard it all as it happened. And saved me when Beterli started to attack me."

Lessa was silent for a moment, bespeaking Path. Mirrim could hear only her dragon's side of the conversation, but she knew she was being backed up. "Yes, I see. The dragon never lies, and she did understand what was going on. Breide will be very happy to have the thefts end, and you have supplied us with real evidence as to how they were accomplished. Tighter security is already being drawn around the site. Oh, by the way, there's been a young man looking for you, Mirrim," Lessa added, not unkindly. "And he has already told me the whole tale of what happened at Telgar Hold. While I don't normally approve of dragonriders ferrying passengers about, Dannen is a charming and most persuasive young man. Beterli has been taken in hand by the Lord Warder, and Journeyman Sotessi will not long escape us. You have been cleared entirely of guilt."

F'lar took Lessa's hand and smiled at Mirrim. "Don't just stand here and gape, girl. Go and have a good time. This is a wedding! It's a celebration! There's the young man. Dannen is his name?"

"Yes, it's Dannen." Mirrim spun around as someone tapped her on the shoulder.

"There, I told you you'd get here in the end," Dannen declared, bowing to the Weyrleaders. "Thank you for delivering my message, Lady Lessa."

"Thank you for coming forward with your evidence, Journeyman Dannen," Lessa said graciously, and F'lar escorted her away through the crowd.

Mirrim watched them go, feeling vindicated. She had had her honor restored. If it hadn't been for Path and Dannen, she'd be back in Benden Weyr peeling roots until she was just another old auntie. Instead, she was restored to her full status as the dragonrider of green Path, free again to range Pern as she always should have been. Path rejoiced with her when Mirrim bespoke her to share the good news.

"Well," Dannen said, breaking the silence. He extended his hands to Mirrim, and she placed hers in his. "That's over. Now that you're not busy, what about my six dances?"

Mirrim smiled, and followed Dannen out onto the dance floor.

The End

* **121** *

Mirrim hurried back to Path, brushing at her best frock and trying to make herself presentable. She'd better stay out of Lessa's way now. She looked a slattern with all the dust from the display hall on her.

Path was fretting impatiently when Mirrim reached her. *We are here already,* Path said.

Mirrim knew that she was right, that her earlier self

had just landed on the plateau only a few dragonlengths behind them. Path's color was off, and Mirrim herself felt weak. She strapped herself in and called to Path to take them back. "Back to Southern Hold!"

First, Mirrim thought, she must make sure that the bottle was still there. The thief might return and take back his present, and then where would her evidence come from.

With a last pat at her hair, she hustled through the throng, even larger now, to the gift table. Her fire lizards, disobeying her previous command, flew into the hall with her, creeling how worried they'd been that she'd gone off without them. Sending them away again with a flick of her hand, she reached the table at the same moment as Breide. Their hands touched as Mirrim bent to take the bottle. "So," Breide said coldly. "You've decided to return this, have you?"

"I didn't take it," Mirrim announced, fed up with Breide's accusations. "He did." She pointed to the miner, who had returned to peer shortsightedly at another gift.

The crafter stepped over to the steward. "What does this mean, Breide?"

"Is it you, Dougal?" Breide asked. "This young lady accuses you of stealing artifacts from the plateau site."

"Nonsense," the miner scoffed, squinting into her face, trying to place her. "Lady, you must be mistaken."

"But I saw," Mirrim said firmly. "I followed you. He's got a whole box of small items hidden away. They're in a small hold on another row at the site. I can take you to it."

"Oh," the miner said, still attempting to keep his good humor in the face of a very serious matter. "It's all a mistake, my dear. I am permitted by Lord Toric and Lord Lytol to keep certain items temporarily. I examine and compare their metal content, which is why I have so many. And then I give them back. If you would care to come to my workshop one day, young woman, I'd be happy to . . ."

"What is going on here?" Lessa asked, pushing through the crowd when she heard Mirrim's voice raised over the hubbub.

"I'm afraid, Lady Lessa," Breide replied in a very low voice so as not to make an issue of it before the assembled guests, "that what we have here is the green rider bearing false witness against Masterminer Dougal."

Lessa rounded on Mirrim, her eyes flashing. "You have done *what?*"

"He took something from the display hall. I watched him."

"When?" Lessa demanded.

Mirrim realized that she had now put both her feet in it. "I . . . went back *between* times, to see who had stolen the bottle I was accused of taking. There were two men leaving the hall. I guess he was the wrong one."

"He most certainly was," Breide asserted.

"Go back to Benden. Now."

"But my things are at Cove Hold," Mirrim babbled. "And Master Robinton . . ."

"Now." Lessa's voice was quiet, but cold as a glacier. "From this point on, you will be assigned to duties suitable to your judgment and abilities, for which at this moment I have little regard."

Hanging her head, Mirrim moved toward the door. As she reached the threshold, she heard Dannen call out to her, but she ignored him. She had made yet another mistake. Her spanking new gown looked like a drudge's uniform, and she felt incapable of ever regaining her honor.

*Turn to section 29.*

## * 122 *

Mirrim started to scream but before any sound could come out, Beterli's fist slammed into her temple. Already weak and dizzy from being in the same time with her other self, Mirrim was quickly knocked unconscious. She came to to find Path peering anxiously over her.

Returning to Southern Hold, Mirrim discovered that the wedding was almost over. The white bottle had been found among the wedding gifts and in her absence Mirrim had been accused of leaving it there. Now there was no way she'd ever be able to clear her name.

*Turn to section 29.*

## * 123 *

"Mirrim?" Hearing her name, the girl spun around, and gave a sigh of relief.
    Dannen pushed through the crowd toward her. He was dressed in a fine light tunic dyed red, showing himself to be a member of the wedding party, and red-heeled hide boots that made him even taller. His lint-fine blond hair had been brushed down and wetted to keep it from floating around his head. When he saw Beterli standing

so close to Mirrim, he was immediately on his guard. "What's this ruffian doing here?"

"This is my witness, Lord Breide," Mirrim said, reaching out for Dannen's arm and drawing him closer. "This is Journeyman Farmcrafter Dannen. He will tell you what occurred at Telgar Hold when I confronted Beterli and his master."

"That's right, sir," Dannen asserted, collecting a murderous glare from the apprentice. He had caught on instantly to what was going on, and was more than willing to help. "The journeyman trader had an item in his possession and said it was his property." He described it for Breide, who nodded as Dannen enumerated each characteristic of the little stylus. "Mirrim here asked him where he'd gotten it, but he refused to tell her. She'd seen the identifying mark on it."

"Is that all?"

"No," Mirrim said, with some urging from Dannen. She was reluctant to say more, for fear of being accused of bearing false witness, since she hadn't actually seen Beterli do it, and the consequences for such a crime were serious. "I believe Beterli cut my riding straps. They split apart under my hands. I might have been killed, using unsafe straps to fight Thread."

"It's a serious crime, threatening the life of a dragonrider and dragon," Dannen put in. "It's a death offense to cause a dragon to die."

"I was told to do it," Beterli yelled in panic, drawing the attention of all the guests nearby. "Sotessi told me to! It wasn't my idea!" Responding to Breide's nod, two large wardsmen came out of the crowd and took hold of the apprentice's arms. Beterli realized he was trapped, and that he'd confessed. "It was only supposed to scare you off," he snarled, pushing his face close to Mirrim's. "You must be too dumb to scare."

Mirrim felt her palm itch to slap Beterli, but Dannen took her arm and held it firmly.

But Breide was already satisfied with what he had been told. "That is a matter for the Weyrleaders, dragonrider.

For now, I will take this villain to Lord Toric. I will explain the matter to him and to Lady Lessa. You are cleared of taint, as far as I am concerned. You will be welcome back to the site if you choose to visit." He bowed to her, almost smiling.

"Thank you, Breide," Mirrim said, returning the courtesy.

With a signal to his warders, Breide marched Beterli away. Mirrim watched them go, feeling vindicated. She had had her honor restored. If it hadn't been for Path and Dannen, she'd be back in Benden Weyr peeling roots until she was just another old auntie. Instead, she was restored to her full status as the dragonrider of green Path, free again to range Pern as she should always have been. And Mirrim didn't have to face Lessa, either. Path rejoiced with her when Mirrim bespoke her to share the good news.

"Well," Dannen said, breaking the silence. The excitement over, the crowd of guests went back to its revelry, ignoring the couple standing by the gift table. He extended his hands to Mirrim, and she placed hers in his. "Now that you're not busy, what about my six dances?"

Mirrim smiled, and followed Dannen out onto the dance floor.

The End

## * 124 *

Mirrim hurried back to Path, brushing at her best frock and trying to make herself presentable. She'd better stay out of Lessa's way now. She looked a slattern with all the dust from the display hall on her.

Path was fretting impatiently when Mirrim reached

her. *We are here already,* Path said. Mirrim knew that she was right, that her earlier self had just landed on the plateau only a few dragonlengths behind them. Path's color was off, and Mirrim herself felt weak. She strapped herself in and called to Path to take them back. "Back to Southern Hold!"

First, Mirrim thought, she must make sure that the bottle was still there. The thief might return and take back his present, and then where would her evidence come from.

With a last pat at her hair, she hustled through the throng, even larger now, to the gift table. Her firelizards, disobeying her previous command, flew into the hall with her, creeling how worried they'd been that she'd gone off without them. She ignored them, and reached the table at the same moment as Breide, and their hands touched as Mirrim bent to take the bottle. "So," Breide said coldly. "You've decided to return this, have you?"

"I didn't take it," Mirrim announced, fed up with Breide's accusations. "He did." She pointed. Beterli was near the table, waiting respectfully for his master, who was dancing with a pretty girl.

Breide's eyebrows rose. "I expect you can back up your accusations, and are not merely pointing out another to cover your own guilt."

"Certainly not," Mirrim protested, insulted. "I can prove it, too."

The steward shrugged and beckoned to Beterli. "Come here, young man," Breide called.

Beterli looked up to see who was addressing him, and flinched when he saw Mirrim. Mirrim observed that Breide didn't miss the reaction—he never missed anything—but he said no more until the ex-Candidate was with them. "Present your statement," he told Mirrim.

"This man and his master, a journeyman trader, have been trafficking in stolen artifacts from the site. He's the one who has been taking them from the display hall. I went back *between* times to the day when this bottle was stolen." At that, Breide's eyebrows soared upward again, and Mirrim continued. "I saw him speaking to the journeyman. Beterli brings them to his master, who sells them in Telgar Hold. I saw him with one only a few days ago. It had the white dot which marks every piece excavated on the plateau."

"Crackdust," Beterli said scornfully. "You can't prove that. She's bearing false witness, Lord Steward."

"We'll see. Mirrim, can you prove your charge?"

*Roll 3 D6.*

*If the total is less than or equal to Mirrim's value for Wisdom/Luck, turn to section 123.*

*If the total is greater, turn to section 118.*

## * 125 *

She elected to follow the minecrafter. Whatever he had had in his hands was probably one of the missing artifacts. He was so nearsighted he might not think that anyone could see him take things.

Keeping about thirty paces behind him, she followed the miner to a small hold, scarcely as wide as her outstretched arms. He muttered to himself as he stalked inside, leaving the sliding door open. Mirrim crept up to the hut and brought one eye around the door. The miner had a small tool in his hands, made of a bright red metal. When he rang it with a small hammer, Mirrim realized that the little tool was metal. What sort of metal was of that brilliant a red? Evidently the miner wanted to know that, too. With a smithcraft handglass, he went over the surface of the little object. When he had finished his scrutiny, he opened a small press to put the tool away. To Mirrim's amazement, the whole press was full of little bits and pieces from the dig. Several of them were turned upward so she could see the white identification dots.

Mirrim realized that she had made a discovery of importance, one which would dispel the shadow of guilt from over her. She was afraid even then of being accused of bearing false witness. Maybe she should try and get more evidence. And yet, she was anxious to time it back to the wedding. It was tiring being in a time twice. She would reveal her discovery before Lady Doriota accepted a stolen treasure as a wedding present.

*If she chooses to go back to the present and accuse the miner, turn to section 121.*

*If she chooses to time it again to get more evidence, turn to section 114.*